DARK PASSAGE

DARK PASSAGE

A Hannah Ives mystery

Marcia Talley

Severn
House

This first world edition published 2013
in Great Britain and the USA by
SEVERN HOUSE PUBLISHERS LTD of
19 Cedar Road, Sutton, Surrey, England, SM2 5DA.
Trade paperback edition first published
in Great Britain and the USA 2013 by
SEVERN HOUSE PUBLISHERS LTD

British Library Cataloguing in Publication Data

Talley, Marcia Dutton, 1943-
  Dark passage. – (The Hannah Ives mysteries series ; 12)
  1. Ives, Hannah (Fictitious character)–Fiction.
  2. Detective and mystery stories.
  I. Title II. Series
  813.6-dc23

ISBN-13: 978-0-7278-8278-3 (cased)
ISBN-13: 978-1-84751-486-8 (trade paper)

All Severn House titles are printed on acid-free paper.

Severn House Publishers support The Forest Stewardship Council [FSC],
the leading international forest certification organisation. All our titles that
are printed on Greenpeace-approved FSC-certified paper carry the FSC logo.

Typeset by Palimpsest Book Production Ltd.,
Falkirk, Stirlingshire, Scotland.
Printed and bound in Great Britain by
MPG Books Ltd., Bodmin, Cornwall.

For Susan, Alison and Deborah . . . and for our sister, Katie,
alive forever in our hearts and memory.
What happens with sisters, stays with sisters.

ACKNOWLEDGEMENTS

Writing is a solitary business, yet it takes a team to put a novel into the hands of readers. With thanks to my incredible team:

My husband, Barry Talley, who agrees that going on luxury cruises is a fine way to conduct research. And it's tax deductible, too.

My editor, Sara Porter, my can-do publicist, Michelle Duff, publisher Edwin Buckhalter and everyone else at Severn House who makes it such an incredibly supportive place for a mystery writer to be.

Daniel Stashower, who, before he became an award-winning author helping his friends invent ingenious devices like the Turbine of Terror, used to thrill young Cleveland audiences with his act, 'Dan and Mike, Magician and Clown Extraordinaire.'

Glenn Cairns, Security Officer for ships in the Carnival Line, who taught me how to run a safe, secure ship. If Glenn had been in charge of security on my fictional liner, *Phoenix Islander*, there would have been no story.

Cliff and Liz Rowe, whose generous bid at a charity auction sponsored by the United Church of Christ in Lovell, Maine, bought them the right to play starring roles in this novel.

My friend, Marie Cherry, for the 'ah-ha' moment. When Hannah grows up, she wants to be just like you.

Jim Steinmeyer, internationally-acclaimed designer of magical illusions and theatrical special effects, for permission to quote from his fascinating book, *Hiding the Elephant: How Magicians Invented the Impossible and Learned to Disappear,* Da Capo Press, 2004.

Once again, my fellow travelers at various stations on the road to publication, the Annapolis Writers Group: Ray Flynt, Mary Ellen Hughes, Debbi Mack, Sherriel Mattingley, and Bonnie Settle for tough love.

To Kate Charles and Deborah Crombie, dearest friends, confidantes and advisors; surely the reason why Skype had to be invented.

And, of course, to Vicky Bijur.

'The end result becomes a little work of theatre, a play with a simple plot that exists on a fairy tale level. The fantasies of a magic show can often be appreciated in everyday life: causing someone to disappear, becoming someone else, acquiring the ability to escape or walk through a wall. The play might be seconds long or be elaborately written to include a full story.'

Jim Steinmeyer, *Hiding the Elephant*,
Da Capo, 2004, p. 94

ONE

Philadelphia. The Birthplace of America. The Cradle of Liberty. The City of Brotherly Love.

Philly's only two hours away from my home in Annapolis, but I hadn't been there since the winter of 2008 when Navy trounced Army 34–0. I probably wouldn't have visited Philly on that mild day in May, either, or found myself sitting on an overstuffed chair in a restored brownstone near Rittenhouse Square, flanked by my two sisters, except for a bit of Fatherly Love.

And Aunt Evelyn, of course.

Evelyn was the widow of our father's older brother, Fred, who had died at the Battle of Inchon in 1950. She'd never remarried.

Ruth leaned into me. 'Look, Hannah. She's wearing the same outfit she wore to my wedding.'

I'd recognized it, too. A sequinned, ice-gray, gold-fringed tweed jacket and matching sheath that complemented her perfectly-coifed helmet of platinum hair. Her makeup, too, was perfect. Dark lashes, pale blue shadow, a touch of peach blush on her alabaster cheeks. Revlon's 'Love That Pink' – Aunt Evelyn never wore anything else – colored her lips and nails.

'I helped her pick out that suit,' Ruth continued brightly. 'At Nordstrom. Eleven hundred dollars, give or take.'

'She looks amazingly good, doesn't she?' I said.

Georgina, on my left, stiffened. 'No, she doesn't. She looks dead.'

We stared at the open casket – solid walnut polished to a high gloss and decorated with antique bronze hardware – where our late aunt lay on a bed of soft, almond-colored tufted velvet.

'Good for eighty-eight,' I amended, nudging Georgina lightly with my elbow. 'And under the circumstances.'

'Daddy owes us,' Georgina whispered. 'I'm here, but to tell the truth, I never liked Aunt Evelyn all that much.'

I shushed her. A shuttle bus from Riverview on the Schuylkill, the retirement complex where Aunt Evelyn had spent her final years, had just disgorged a stream of residents – on the high side of fifty-five and over – onto the plush, round Tabriz that decorated the marble floor of the funeral home lobby. As his sister-in-law's only surviving relative, Daddy stood at the door, greeting the mourners as they filed by ones and twos into the parlor where his daughters sat on straight-backed upholstered chairs opposite the coffin like a trio of obedient see-no-evil, hear-no-evil, speak-no-evil monkeys.

I had to admit that spending extended lengths of time with Aunt Evelyn had always been an act of charity, at least for me. In the early fifties – when the use of tamoxifen and targeted drug therapies for breast cancer lay well into the future – she'd undergone a radical mastectomy. Following my own bout with breast cancer – I'm totally fine, now, thank you very much – Aunt Evelyn sensed in me a kindred spirit, one who would surely never – as had her ever-dwindling circle of friends and bridge partners – tire of hearing lengthy tales about her debilitating surgery, her lymphedema, her phantom breast pain – in exhausting, clinical detail. Even Mother Theresa would have been driven to drink.

'I have no patience with hypochondriacs,' Georgina continued, keeping her voice low. 'If anybody ever deserved the epitaph, "See, I told you I was sick," it's our own dear Aunt Evelyn.'

I bowed my head and stifled a giggle.

'She kept her kidney stones in a glass jar, for heaven's sake!' Georgina added, upping the volume.

'I didn't know that!' Ruth chirped.

A woman leaning on a walker swiveled her head in our direction, an artfully drawn ebony eyebrow raised.

'Shhhh.' I laid a hand on Ruth's arm. 'You were away at college during the kidney stone ordeal,' I told her. 'It was pretty spectacular. The pain was excruciating – for all of us.'

'The doctor let her keep the stones?' Ruth asked. 'Gross.'

'Not exactly,' Georgina explained. 'Every day Aunt Evelyn peed into a sieve until they passed. "I nearly died!" she quoted, pressing the back of her hand melodramatically against her fore-head. "They were enormous! Big as marbles!"'

With a gentle hand on the man's arm, Daddy nudged a blue-suited octogenarian in the direction of his sister-in-law's coffin, captured the hand of a younger woman next in line in both of his while sending a scowl aimed at us over her red plaid shoulder. If we didn't clean up our act, there'd be hell to pay at the dinner we planned to have at Parc, a nearby brasserie, following the viewing.

Feeling chastened, I mused, 'You know, it's a shame that we only get together for occasions like this – weddings and funerals. I don't know about you, but it seems to me that there's always so much else going on that we really don't have time to visit each other properly. How long has it been since you've been to Annapolis, Georgina?'

Georgina bristled. 'I have four children, remember.'

As if I could forget. When Georgina's family came down from Baltimore for a visit – a short thirty-five-mile drive – it was like a military operation, requiring a movement order – ten typewritten pages, with appendices. Before I could think up a snarky reply, Ruth leaned across my lap and said, 'I think there's enough guilt to go around. I haven't been the best of aunts myself, but now that I have a full-time shop assistant at Mother Earth, there's no reason I can't pop up to Baltimore to visit with you and the kids more often, Georgina.'

I'd been about to elaborate on the amount of time I spend helping to care for my grandchildren – Chloe, Jake, and Tim – while my daughter Emily and her husband Dante are busy managing Paradiso, their luxury health spa, but I wisely kept my mouth shut. 'I think we should do something special,' I said after a moment. 'Just sisters. Just us girls.'

Georgina's sea green eyes sparkled with interest. 'Like what?'

I shrugged. 'I don't know. The idea just popped into my head.'

'Sisterly bonding,' Ruth mused. 'We could use a bit of that.'

Georgina squinted at a wall sconce, looking thoughtful. 'I know! We could go for a mani-pedi!'

Ruth, our superannuated flower child who had never, to my knowledge, even set foot inside a beauty parlor, let alone dipped her toes into a pedi-spa, grunted.

'With tea afterwards, and little sandwiches, or . . .' Georgina bounced in her seat, looking directly at me. 'If we asked nicely, do you think Scott would spring for a weekend getaway package at Spa Paradiso?'

Although scenically (and expensively!) situated at the far end of Bay Ridge Drive on a bank overlooking the Chesapeake Bay, Spa Paradiso was only three short miles from my home on Prince George Street. 'I mean *away* away,' I said.

'The Inn at Perry Cabin?' Ruth suggested, naming a popular luxury hotel in St Michael's on Maryland's eastern shore.

I shook my head. 'Further away than that.'

'The Mirbeau Inn and Spa in upstate New York? How about the Golden Door in Colorado?' Ruth's encyclopedic knowledge of luxury spas didn't astonish me, since she had copies of *Feng Shui World*, *Aromatherapy Today* and *Tathaastu* scattered all over her coffee table at home. 'Ten Thousand Waves in Santa Fe?' she continued.

Before she could whip out her iPhone and sign us up for some exotic hideaway in the Maldives where rooms start at $1400 per night, I raised a hand. 'Just so you know, I draw the line at treatments for the extremely rich and insane, like being massaged by snakes or elephants. Or soaking in hot tubs full of red wine.'

Georgina giggled. 'You're making that up!'

'Am not. There's a spa in Alexandria where teeny, tiny carp nibble dead skin off your toes.'

'Clearly, I lead a sheltered life,' Georgina whispered.

Several of Aunt Evelyn's friends wandered over to extend their condolences, so we squeezed hands, smiled and nodded as the orchestral strains of 'Somewhere Over the Rainbow' drifted out of the in-ceiling speaker directly over our heads. By the time our aunt's friends had moved on, the orchestra had segued into a piano and cello duet of 'Red Sails in the Sunset.'

As if prompted by the tune, Ruth said, 'How 'bout this? We could take a cruise. Didn't you and Paul have a fabulous time crossing the Atlantic on the *Queen Mary Two*?'

'It was divine,' I agreed with a grin. 'So classy. I should have packed my furs and brought along a pair of Irish wolfhounds with diamond-studded collars. And a man servant to walk them, of course.'

'Must have been nice,' Georgina pouted. She leaned across my lap in order to catch Ruth's eye. 'Scott and I aren't made of money, you know. And the twins are starting college in the fall.'

Ruth flapped a hand. 'After that mess with the *Costa Concordia*, not to mention the economy, which is tanking big-time in case you hadn't noticed, cruise lines are practically *giving* cruises away.' She patted my knee. 'Besides, we wouldn't be staying in the presidential suite, or whatever, like Hannah and Paul did.'

'*Queen* Suite, you moron,' I teased, batting her hand away. 'Paul and I had a plain vanilla stateroom with a balcony on the *Queen Mary*. Period. Nothing fancy.'

Ruth rolled her eyes. 'So you say, but I saw the pictures.' She began rooting around in her handbag. When she thought none of the mourners was looking, she pulled her iPhone out and swiped it on. 'Last week, one of my customers thought I looked frazzled and needed a break. We got talking about the Caribbean, so she forwarded an email about cheap cruises.' She tapped a few keys, then used her index finger to scroll quickly through the entries. 'Ah, here it is. Cruise for cheap dot com.' She squinted at the tiny screen, used her thumb and index finger to enlarge the image. 'Where do you want to go?'

I shrugged. 'Who cares? If we're going to be bonding, the destination hardly matters. It's the voyage that counts.'

'My vote goes to any place that takes U.S. dollars and they speak our language,' Georgina said.

'Quite a few cruise liners are home-ported in Baltimore these days.' Ruth leaned forward, addressing Georgina. 'The cruises listed here are incredibly cheap. Can you afford six hundred dollars?'

Georgina raised an eyebrow. 'Probably, but I'll have to discuss it with Scott first.'

'We'll all have to do that,' Ruth said. 'Husbands!'

'What about husbands?' While we had been plotting our getaway, Daddy had crept up on us.

Ruth blushed and dropped her iPhone back into the cavernous depths of her quilted handbag. 'Nothing!'

'Good. I'm relieved. I thought you were going to give me another pep talk about Neelie.'

Cornelia – nicknamed Neelie – was my widowed father's

longtime companion. The Alexander girls – my sisters and I – thoroughly approved of Cornelia Gibbs and couldn't imagine why our father hadn't popped the question. It had been more than a decade since our mother died, but we knew from experience that there was little to be gained by pushing the man. There's not much you can tell a retired navy captain. They're accustomed to being in charge.

As if to prove my point, Daddy tapped his watch. 'Visiting hours are over, duty's done, and I'm starving. How about you?'

I glanced around the parlor, surprised to find it empty except for the four of us and the funeral home director, standing discreetly near the heavy oak door, hands folded, looking somber. And poor Aunt Evelyn, of course, whose last meal before her fatal heart attack had been a chicken cordon bleu served up on a white plate with gold trim in the Riverview's posh dining room, accompanied by a glass of fairly decent Chardonnay. In the shuffling off this mortal coil department, I figured that was a fine way to go.

There would be no funeral service for our aunt. She was to be cremated, as per her request, and eventually – when Arlington National Cemetery slotted it into their way-too-busy calendar – she would be buried there with her husband, Captain Frederick T. Alexander, U.S. Army, in Section 35.

'I feel almost guilty about going out for *moule frites* while she's . . .' I nodded toward the coffin. '. . . well, you know.' I stood up and kissed my father on a cheek – warm, slightly damp and rough with stubble. 'You look exhausted.'

'I am.' He scrubbed a hand over his steel-gray curls as if trying to wake himself up, starting by stimulating his scalp. 'I'm glad we booked into a hotel tonight, rather than trying to drive back.' He linked one arm through mine and the other through Georgina's, then cocked his head in Ruth's direction. 'C'mon, Ruth. There's a bouillabaisse at the Parc with my name on it.'

It took only ten minutes to stroll from the funeral home back to our hotel at the corner of Locust and Eighteenth, directly across from Rittenhouse Square where bicycles were chained by twos and threes at intervals along the iron fencing. The evening was balmy, and the sidewalk outside the Parc Brasserie was crowded with couples dining elbow-to-elbow with their neighbors, seated on cane chairs at small round tables under burgundy-colored awnings that were so relentlessly French that even the *numéro de téléphone* was printed French-style – 21 55 45 22 62 – on the awning.

As the hostess escorted us inside the restaurant to a table for four, not far from the enormous zinc-surfaced bar where a variety of Belgian beer seemed to be on tap, Daddy said, 'I can't tell you how much I appreciate your support.'

'Are you kidding?' From her chair, Ruth reached up and curiously fingered the white lace curtain that hung from a brass rail over her shoulder as if she were considering whether to buy it. 'It's no secret that Aunt Evelyn and I weren't particularly close, but she was family, after all. I owe her something for that.'

'Ruth's lying to you, Daddy. She came to Philadelphia because of the molten chocolate cake with raspberry sauce you promised her.' I picked up the oversized menu, encased in plastic, turned to the back and scanned the desserts. 'As for me, I work cheap. After the *moule frites*, it's *crème brûlée pour moi, s'il vous plaît.*'

Two hours later, after desserts, cappuccinos and deeply warming glasses of Monbazillac, Daddy picked up the check and we wandered up to our rooms on the tenth floor. Daddy called it an early night, gave us each a hug, then disappeared into his own room just down the hall.

Georgina had to scan the key card three times before the light blinked green and the door decided to open but, once inside, she immediately kicked off her shoes and sprawled, spreadeagle, on the gray-green velvet sofa of the two-room suite the three of us were sharing. 'So, what about that cruise we were talking about?'

'Am I not allowed to catch my breath?' I dropped my handbag on the floor and crossed to the mahogany desk where I'd left my laptop. I flipped it open and powered it on. A few minutes later I was hunched over the screen, clicking around the website Ruth's customer had recommended. 'Do we want to sail out of New York or Baltimore?'

'Baltimore,' Georgina said without hesitation. 'Getting ourselves up to New York and back would add a couple of hundred dollars to the cost.'

'Right,' I said as I clicked on 'Baltimore' and waited for the screen to refresh. 'And I understand that parking is dirt cheap at the Baltimore Cruise Terminal, not to mention convenient.'

'How many days do you think we can afford to be away?' I asked a few moments later while scrolling down through a long listing of ships and sailing dates. 'Here's a five-day cruise to Bermuda and back, seven days to the eastern Caribbean. Here's one for nine days, twelve . . .'

'Five hardly seems worth the effort.' Ruth extracted a Diet Coke from the minibar in the vestibule near the door and pulled up the tab. 'I'll have to check with my assistant, but if she can put in a few extra hours, I should be able to clear seven days, or even nine. Lord, I haven't had a proper vacation since Hutch and I went on our honeymoon. Georgina?'

Georgina shrugged. 'Depends on the dates.'

'There's a nine-day cruise that leaves in three weeks for the Eastern Caribbean,' I said. 'San Juan, St Thomas, Dominican Republic, Haiti . . .'

'Who on earth would want to go to Haiti?' Georgina grumped.

'Can we afford twelve days, maybe?' I asked. 'Here's another one to San Juan, setting off on the twelfth of June, calling at St Thomas, St Maarten, Antigua and Tortola, then back.'

'Sounds divine, but no way I could talk Scott into covering for me at home for twelve whole days,' Georgina said. 'Seven, maybe. Ten, max. He *hates* to cook.'

I turned around in my chair and grinned. 'That's why God invented McDonalds, Georgina.'

She laughed.

I turned back to the laptop and leaned close to the screen. 'Looks like June is the window of opportunity, then.' I swiveled in the chair to face my sisters. 'Are we all clear, date-wise, for sometime mid-June?'

I could hardly believe it when both women nodded.

'OK. Why don't we each go home, discuss the plan with our husbands and decide how much money we're willing to spend. For planning purposes, the fares they're quoting here work out to about a hundred dollars a day, but that includes food practically twenty-four/seven and everything except the booze, so to my way of thinking it's quite a bargain.'

'Gosh,' said Georgina. 'You can hardly stay at a Holiday Inn for a hundred dollars a day, and all you get for breakfast is a donut and a cup of weak coffee with powdered cream.'

'I'll talk to Paul, then tomorrow night I'll set up a conference call and we can finalize things.' I flapped a hand at the laptop where photos of cruise ships, quaint colonial ports, pink sand beaches and palm trees had begun to slide and fade across the screen. 'If we're going to do this, we should probably hurry, or the slots might be gone.'

Ruth drained her Coke and set the empty can down on the end table. 'You don't need to call me about dates, Hannah. Hutch has been working on a big libel case so I hardly see him anyway. Even if they settle, there's no way he'll wrap that up by June, so whatever dates you two decide on is fine with me.'

'Will we share a cabin, like we're doing here?' Georgina asked.

I thought about the cabin that Paul and I had booked on the *Queen Mary Two* – twin beds squished together made up as a queen, with a pull-out sofa. Three people sharing would have been a tight squeeze. I was all for sisterly bonding, but crawling over a sibling in the middle of the night in order to go to the bathroom was taking sisterhood a bit too far. 'We'll definitely need two cabins,' I said. 'The rates are based on double occupancy, but we could . . .'

'I'll take the single,' Ruth interrupted. 'No worries there.'

I could have hugged her. I'd shared sleeping arrangements with Ruth before and, not to put too fine a point on it, the woman *snored*. 'Well, it's decided, then!' I snapped my laptop shut and sprang to my feet. 'C'mon, Georgina,' I said from the door that led into the adjoining bedroom. 'If we're going to be roomies, we better start practicing. You and I get the king. Ruth, the sofa is all yours!'

TWO

There are approximately 200 overnight ocean-going cruise vessels worldwide. The average ocean-going cruise vessel carries 2,000 passengers with a crew of 950 people. In 2007 alone, approximately 12,000,000 passengers were projected to take a cruise worldwide.

Cruise Vessel Safety & Security
Act of 2010 (H.R. 3660)

Paul slotted a platter into the dishwasher. 'I think that's a terrific idea.'

'You do?' I hadn't expected Paul to *disapprove* of our plan, but I wasn't expecting him to stand up and cheer for it, either. The man was practically waving pompoms.

Paul reached out a soapy hand and tapped the tip of my nose. 'I'll miss you terribly, of course, but what a wonderful opportunity, especially for Georgina. That girl doesn't get out enough, in my humble opinion.'

'That's because, as Georgina is quick to remind me, she has four children.' I scraped the leftover spaghetti sauce into a plastic container, snapped on the lid, then passed the dirty cooking pot to Paul. 'I'm hoping that Scott doesn't throw a monkey wrench into our plans. Georgina didn't seem too worried, but you know and I know that Scott can sometimes be a spoiled brat.'

'Don't be too hard on the guy. He's stuck with your sister through some pretty tough times.' Paul attacked a patch of burnt-on tomato sauce with a scrubby sponge. 'How's the new therapist working out?'

'Very well, I think. Georgina was worried when Doctor Christopher retired, but she's settled into a routine with the new guy that seems to be working out for both of them. She hasn't had a depressive episode in over a year.' I gave him the thumbs up. 'Kudos to the shrink and to the new meds.'

'Anyone is better than that quack. What was her name?

Voorhis?' Paul rinsed the pot with hot water and upended it in the dish strainer. 'What a piece of work *she* was!'

Paul was right. Georgina's first therapist had been so twisted that someone had murdered her for it. Sadly, Georgina had discovered the woman's body. She was still recovering from the trauma.

'When will you be gone?' Paul asked. He pulled the plug and watched in apparent fascination as the dirty water swirled in a counter-clockwise direction down the drain.

'Around the second or third week of June, depending.'

'On what?'

I closed the refrigerator door on the leftovers. 'There must be a gabillion cruise lines out there, Paul. Cunard, of course. Holland America. Princess. Seaborne . . .

'They're all owned by Carnival, aren't they? Carnival owns Costa, too.'

'Right. But Carnival doesn't own the cruise line we're interested in.'

Paul wrung out the dishcloth and draped it over the edge of the sink where it could dry. 'Hannah, sweetheart?'

'What?'

'Promise me something. Pick a cruise line that doesn't run into solid objects. Like Italy.'

I had to laugh. 'Don't worry, I have. It's one I've never heard of, though.' I picked up my iPhone and powered it on. 'They're called Phoenix Cruise Lines. According to the Phoenix website, they're owned by some fellow named Gregorius Simonides. Wikipedia says that young Greg is the second son of a Greek national. Rather than helping to lead his native country out of its current debt crisis, he's living and spending his father's fortune in the UK. He buys up still serviceable, but slightly shopworn ships and rehabs them.'

'Hence the name,' Paul commented.

'Gregorius?' I asked, puzzled. Then, 'Oh, Phoenix, you mean. Right. New life rising from the ashes.' I turned the iPhone screen in Paul's direction. 'Judge for yourself. From the pictures, his ships are fairly posh. Not as posh as the *Queen Mary Two*, of course, but posh enough.'

As Paul scrolled through a slide show of ships of the line, I said, 'The vessels are all named Phoenix something – *Phoenix*

Sun, Phoenix Wanderer, Phoenix Adventurer – you get the picture.
The *Explorer* goes through the Panama Canal to the Galapagos,
and the *Odyssey* cruises exclusively in the Mediterranean – no
surprise. If I can get the dates to work, we'll be on the *Islander*.
Eight days to Bermuda and back.'

Paul was examining a schematic deck layout of the *Islander*
when the instrument began *whoop-whoop-whooping* in his hand,
the claxon-like ring tone I'd assigned to my sister, Georgina. He
passed the phone to me as if it were radioactive.

'Hey, Georgina. I was just about to call you. What's the good
word?'

'I have good news and bad news,' my sister replied. 'Which
do you want first?'

If there's one thing I hate, it's the good news/bad news game.
I braced myself, figuring that the worst that would happen would
be I'd be setting sail on the *Islander* with only one of my sisters:
Ruth. 'I've had a long day, Georgina. Don't torture me. Give me
the good news first.'

Georgina's voice was upbeat, bubbly. 'The good news is that
Scott is in favor of the cruise.'

'So what's the bad?'

'He says if I want to go, I'll have to take Julie.'

My niece, Julie Lynn Cardinale, is fourteen years old going
on twenty-three. With her red hair and green eyes, she is the
image of her mother at that age. I was very fond of my niece
and at times, particularly during the Voorhis murder investigation
around ten years ago, Julie and I had grown very close. 'I think
that's a great idea,' I told my sister, truthfully. 'The ship has a
teen club and all kinds of supervised activities for kids. She'll
have a ball. And it nicely settles the question of how many cabins
to book, and who gets to room with whom.'

Georgina let out a long breath. 'I'm *so* relieved! I thought
you'd be pissed off.'

'Don't be silly. I adore your daughter.'

'Yes, but you don't have to *live* with her,' Georgina said. 'The
hormones are raging.'

'Emily was a handful at that age, too,' I reminded her. 'Now
she's a respectable mother of three and president of the Hillsmere
Elementary P.T.A.' I dragged a chair out from under the kitchen

table and sat down on it. 'I'm sure we can handle Julie, but does Scott understand that will double the price?' My brother-in-law was a successful C.P.A., as cautious with his own money as he was with his clients'. Except for occasional stints as a substitute church organist, my sister had never needed to work outside the home.

'When Scott told me not to worry about the money,' Georgina babbled on, 'I thought that aliens had come and taken over his body! I explained about the prices, about the staterooms with windows – I *have* to have a window, Hannah! – but he'd already visited the Phoenix website. Typical Scott. He sat me down, accused me of being naive, and launched into a lecture about hidden costs. Had I considered alcoholic drinks, for example, excursions, spa treatments, tips for the staff, souvenirs, like I was a teetotal idiot. I just sat in his office with my hands folded, nodding, smiling my oh-Scott-you-are-so-smart-and-I-am-such-a-dingbat smile, and when it was all over, he said we could afford up to $3000, but not a penny more.'

'Wow,' I said. 'Just, wow.'

'So I told him, three thousand dollars would be fine.' Georgina snorted. She lowered her voice then, as if Scott had suddenly walked into the room. 'That should allow me to drink heavily.'

I laughed out loud. 'You can buy the first round when we hit the hot tub!' After a moment I asked, 'What's happening with the boys?'

'I can't believe I didn't tell you! Sean and Dillon have summer jobs that start the second week of June. Sean's shoveling manure and wood chips at a nursery out on York Road, and Dillon's going to be a counselor at a day camp for inner-city youth at Notre Dame.'

Two sons down and one to go, I thought. 'How about Colin?'

'Scott's driving Colin up to his mom's in West Virginia,' my sister said. 'It was sweet of her to offer, really. Hannah, I so need this vacation!'

I could believe it. The twins were off to the University of Maryland in the fall, Julie would be entering high school and Colin had just graduated from kindergarten into the first grade, beginning what would surely be the lad's meteoric rise straight from Boy's Latin to Harvard. 'You know what, Georgina?'

'Yeah?'

I couldn't keep the excitement out of my voice. 'I think we're going to do this!'

'I can hardly believe it myself, Hannah. All the stars must be aligned.'

But were they? I had a sudden chilling thought. 'Passports?'

I held my breath until I heard Georgina say, 'Check.'

'I'm so relieved!' I explained about the cruise, the dates and the itinerary, which was basically out to Bermuda and back. 'Are you comfortable with me making all the reservations?'

'Of course,' Georgina said. 'Just tell me how much we owe and I'll write you a check.'

'I'd better hang up and get to it, then. 'Bye, Georgina, and I'm so glad we're going to make this work.'

'A window,' she said. 'I need a window. Don't forget.'

'Check,' I said, and pressed End.

Fifteen minutes later, down in our basement office with Paul kibbitzing over my shoulder, I logged onto the Phoenix website, selected adjoining cabins on deck four and entered my credit card number, expiration date, and CCV code. My mouse hovered over the Buy Now button. 'Here goes!'

When the screen refreshed, a special offer gave us two hundred dollars in on-board credits as a thank you for the last-minute booking. I'd be able to buy my *own* tropical drink with an umbrella in it when we hit the hot tub.

I hit Print and as the receipt rolled out of the printer, I relaxed into my chair. The Alexander girls were a sister act again, and that act was going cruisin'.

THREE

'240,676 people sailed on 100 cruises from the Port of Baltimore in 2012. "Since beginning a year-round cruising schedule in 2009, the Port of Baltimore has continued to make waves as one of the hottest cruise ports in the U.S.," Governor O'Malley said. [It] handled the fifth-largest amount of cruise passengers among East Coast cruise ports, 11th largest in the U.S., and 20th most in the world. In 2011 the Port began using a state-of-the-art, climate-controlled enclosed passenger boarding bridge. The bridge is mobile and flexible to accommodate various sized cruise ships. Baltimore is within a six-hour drive of 40 million people.'

Maryland Port Administration, January 30, 2013

'I thought this cruise was sisters only,' Ruth grumped when I telephoned her the next morning. 'I'm not sure I want responsibility for a teenager running loose aboard.'

'Julie's not *your* responsibility,' I said reasonably. 'Nor mine. She's Georgina's.'

'Shit, Hannah. Have you looked at Julie lately, really *looked*? She's developed – and I do mean developed – into a beautiful young woman. No telling what kind of trouble she'll get into.'

'Don't be silly! What possible trouble could Julie get into on a cruise ship?'

'You'd be surprised,' Ruth said, using her firm, older sister, voice-of-experience tone.

'Other than getting hammered and falling overboard,' I added, just to show I wasn't completely out of touch with current events.

'I watched a CNN special on cruise ship safety a couple of months ago,' Ruth continued. 'Did you know that a person falls overboard approximately every two weeks?'

'I do. I saw the same show,' I replied. 'But most of those accidents are alcohol-related, or suicides, not foul play.'

'With some exceptions,' Ruth said.

'There are always exceptions,' I said, 'but if the *Phoenix Islander* is anything like the *Queen Mary Two*, there'll be a zillion activities for teens, and they're pretty closely supervised. Julie's not going to be standing on the bow like a hood ornament with her arms outstretched singing, "My Heart Will Go On."'

'Well, *I'm* not going to babysit,' Ruth said flatly.

'Me, neither. There's a hot tub on board – several, actually – and one of them has my name on it.'

'And I'll be right beside you, sister, holding a pink drink with an umbrella in it. But . . .' she added after a beat, 'a cruise ship is like a small city. I'm worried that some creep will try to take advantage of Julie. You have to admit she's a bit naive.'

'Julie may be naive, but criminals certainly aren't. It seems to me that a cruise ship is the worst possible place to commit a crime. First of all, where would the perpetrator go? Aside from overboard, there's no place to run, no place to hide.' I paused to take a breath. 'Besides, the ship has a database that includes photographs of everyone, both passengers and crew. If some perv were stupid enough to try something, he'd be a cinch to identify. And, good Lord, there are security cameras everywhere!'

'I hear what you're saying.' Ruth hesitated a bit before continuing. 'OK, you're right, it's Georgina's problem. I, for one, am planning to engage in adult pastimes. Lectures, shows . . .'

'Ballroom dancing?' I interrupted.

Ruth snorted.

'On second thought, you could probably *teach* ballroom dancing.' My sister and her husband were semi-professionals. A few years back, when Ruth was sidelined by an injury, Hutch and his partner, Melanie, had even made it all the way to the finals of *Shall We Dance*, a television talent show. Ruth and Hutch still danced regularly in local and regional competitions.

'No dancing, thanks,' Ruth said. 'That would be like going to work early!'

'If you taught, they'd let you sail for free,' I pointed out. 'File that away for future reference.'

'Nuh uh. I'd rather attend lectures on the history of Bermuda, or crop circles, or how to avoid back pain. The rest of the time

I plan to lie around like a slug while somebody else cooks my meals and picks up after me.'

'You need a wife.'

Ruth grunted. 'Back into your cage, Hannah.'

I laughed and hung up on her.

Our boarding pass instructed us to arrive at the port of Baltimore no later than one, so on the day we were to set sail I picked Ruth up at the home she shared with Hutch on lower Conduit Street. Parking at the Port of Baltimore cost fifteen dollars a day, so to save her some bucks we'd offered to pick Georgina and Julie up too, but Georgina had telephoned in a panic just as I was heading out the door. Julie was running late, so they'd have to drive to the port themselves.

As we made our way up I-97, Ruth kept in touch with our sister by cell phone. By some miracle, we covered the twenty-eight miles to Baltimore in less than forty minutes and managed to arrive at the port at approximately the same time as Georgina. Uniformed parking attendants using orange batons directed us to parking spaces that turned out to be only a row apart.

'Wow!' Ruth leaned over the dashboard and peered at the *Islander* through the windshield, eyes wide as a toddler's at Christmas. 'I had no idea the ship would be so enormous!'

'Twenty-five hundred passengers and eight hundred and forty crew,' I said, quoting statistics I remembered from the 'Welcome Aboard: Your Adventure is About to Begin' brochure I'd received in the mail. 'Bigger than Paul's home town, actually.' I climbed out of the driver's seat and paused for a moment to admire the enormous vessel, its bow towering over us, high as a fifteen-story apartment building.

Ruth and I had packed light – one medium-sized wheelie bag each – but I was astonished to see what came out of Georgina's trunk. While we watched, she slung a large, steel-gray suitcase to the ground, followed by a matching carry-on. 'Your bags, Julie. You handle them.' Georgina reached inside the trunk for the more modest-sized suitcase she had packed for herself. 'You'd think we were going away for a month, rather than just a week,' Georgina complained as she slammed the lid of the trunk shut, aimed her remote at the car and locked the doors.

'I've never been on a cruise before, Mother, so how am I supposed to know what to wear? I had to pack for every situation, didn't I?' she said with a sideways glance at me, as if pleading for my support.

Judging from what Julie was wearing that day – strappy, medium-heeled sandals, a blue jean miniskirt, lime-green camisole with spaghetti straps and a sheer, flowered shirt – it would have been easy to fit her entire wardrobe into a single backpack.

I smiled. 'The hardest thing for me was what to wear for the formal evenings. Since I quit working in Washington, D.C. I don't dress up much. I was forced, actually *forced*, to go shopping at Lord and Taylor.' Paul had been a professor of mathematics at the Naval Academy for more than twenty years, and in the old days there had been frequent formal events at the college, but recently – except for the Ring Dance in May – not so much.

'So, what did you buy, Aunt Hannah?' Julie seemed genuinely interested.

'A pair of swishy black crepe pants and a couple of glittery tops that I can mix and match.' I was secretly pleased with my selections, and with the fancy sandals I'd bought at Nordstrom that same day.

Ruth tugged on the handle on her suitcase and began dragging it toward the terminal. 'My formal wardrobe dates back to the mid-seventies,' she called over her shoulder. 'It's so old it's back in fashion.'

'Can't you wear one of your fancy dance costumes, Aunt Ruth?'

Ruth shook her head sadly. 'Oh, honey, what with all the sequins and glass beads, those things weigh a ton. Wagons ho, ladies! Let's get this show on the road.'

It took us less than five minutes to cross the parking lot, following the signs into the terminal building where we joined a cast of thousands waiting to pass through the security checkpoints. The last time I'd seen lines that long was at Baltimore-Washington Airport on the day before Thanksgiving. As we snaked our way along the barriers toward the X-ray machines, Julie kept busy with her iPhone, alternating between texting and snapping photos which she uploaded almost immediately to Facebook.

'For Julie's sake, I hope there'll be a reasonable number of young people on board.' Georgina's eyes swept the backs and the faces of the people in line around us. 'What do you think the average age is here? Fifty? Sixty?'

I shrugged. 'Maybe more. But school's already let out for the summer, so I imagine there will be plenty of families on the cruise.' As if to illustrate my remark, a child somewhere began to wail miserably. 'See?'

'And, look over there,' Ruth added, nodding her head toward the entrance.

A boisterous group of young people and adults began streaming into the terminal, wearing identical red T-shirts imprinted in white with a stylized family tree and the words, 'OMG, I Survived Another Crawford Family Reunion.'

'Eleven, twelve, thirteen . . .' Ruth counted. 'My God, there must be thirty or forty of them. Haven't the Crawfords heard about birth control?'

I punched Ruth's arm. 'Don't be mean.'

While we'd been fooling around, a gap had opened in the line in front of us. I eased my bag forward, but it snagged on something. I stooped for a closer look. A rainbow-colored luggage strap embroidered with the name 'Elizabeth Rowe' had wrapped itself tightly around two of my wheels. I extricated the strap, then looked around for its likely owner.

Just ahead of me in line was a woman with short-cropped white hair; a pair of sunglasses perched on top of her head. I tapped her on the shoulder. 'Are you Elizabeth Rowe?'

The woman started, then turned to look at me, her eyebrows raised.

I held out the luggage strap.

'Oh, thank you!' she said, taking it from me. 'Cliff, look. I told you that clasp wasn't secure.'

The man I took to be Elizabeth's husband wore a blue-striped short-sleeve shirt that matched the color of the eyes that peered at me through his aviator eyeglasses. 'What did you say, Liz?'

Liz waved the strap under his nose. 'The clasp. It's broken.'

Cliff relieved his wife of the strap, opened and closed the clasp a few times experimentally, then handed it back. 'Looks fine to me. Maybe you didn't fasten it securely.'

Liz took a deep breath, then let it out slowly. I could almost read her thoughts. Not wanting to dive headlong into the middle of a family squabble, I smiled and asked, 'Is this your first cruise?'

'Oh dear, no. Since we retired, Cliff and I have been fortunate enough to be able to travel fairly extensively.'

'Do you live in Baltimore?'

'We spend most of the winter in Florida,' Cliff chimed in. 'But, when we get back from this cruise, we'll be heading back to our home in Maine.'

'Where in Maine?' Ruth wanted to know. 'My husband's family is from Limington, near Lake Sebago.'

'We live in Lovell,' Cliff said. 'A tiny town near the New Hampshire border.'

'Kezar Lake's in Lovell! I know it well,' Ruth said, surprising me. 'Hutch and I have stayed at the Lodge.' She eased around me to ask, 'Have you ever met Stephen King?'

Stephen King? Had my sister lost her mind? 'Don't be silly, Ruth,' I said. 'Everybody knows that Stephen King lives in Bangor. In a big, spooky house with a spider web on the gate.'

'He has a house on the lake in Lovell, too,' Liz informed me kindly. 'In fact, Lovell is where King was struck by a van and nearly killed back in 1999.'

Julie's thumbs paused mid-text. 'I *love* Stephen King! He's so twisted. In a good way.'

Like well-behaved cattle, we'd reached a divide in the rope barrier where a uniformed security guard sent the Rowes in one direction and our party in another. 'Have a great voyage!' I called as Liz hoisted her carry-on – still missing its strap – onto the conveyor belt.

Liz waved. 'Maybe we'll run into each other again!'

'I hope so,' I said, meaning it. 'Are you early seating or late?'

'Early!'

Cliff had already disappeared behind the X-ray machine, heading toward the metal detector. Before Liz disappeared, too, I cupped my hands around my mouth and yelled, 'We are, too!'

Soon we were standing at a long counter in a much shorter line, checking in. We presented our boarding passes along with our passports, had our credit card number verified, then posed, smiling, staring at a little dot above the camera like you do at the Department of Motor Vehicles while our mugshots were being taken. 'Here's your sea pass,' the clerk said a few minutes later, handing me the plastic identification card that would serve as both my room key and a credit card while on board.

'Let me see your picture,' Georgina said, snatching the card playfully from between my fingers. Her eyes narrowed. 'This is supposed to be a vacation, Hannah. You look like you're going to jail!'

'If you think that's bad, you should see my driver's license,' I said as I watched our bags being spirited away. The next time we'd see them, they'd be in our staterooms.

Before heading up the gangway, we were accosted by the first of a well-organized team of photographers who would pop up everywhere during the week, like paparazzi, to create lasting (but expensive) memories of our cruise.

'Why do we always have to pose in birth order?' I complained as Ruth arranged us in front of a backdrop of the Parthenon: Julie on the end, next to her mother, then manhandled me into the spot between Georgina and herself.

'Shut up and turn sideways,' she ordered. 'It'll make us look thinner.'

'Don't be such a bossyboots,' I muttered through teeth clenched in the say-cheese position.

Still blinking away the flash, I followed my family as they trooped up the gangway to the entrance on deck two where a crew member ran our sea passes through a scanner. 'Welcome aboard the *Phoenix Islander*,' she chirped. 'Your staterooms are not quite ready, but you are welcome to tour the vessel, and the Firebird café is open if you'd like something to eat.'

'When *will* the cabins be ready?' Ruth asked.

'There'll be an announcement on the public address system,' the woman said pleasantly. 'The Firebird is all the way forward, on deck nine.'

'Well, I could use a cup of coffee,' I said. 'You guys coming?'

'Julie and I will catch up with you.' Georgina consulted a printout of the *Islander*'s deck plan. 'We want to check out the teen center first.'

'Tidal Wave,' Julie added. 'From the brochure, it looks cool, but everything in the brochure looks cool.'

'It's on deck ten, just above the café,' Georgina called over her shoulder as she herded Julie toward the elevators. 'We won't be long! Save us a table!'

After they'd disappeared, Ruth muttered, 'The pictures in that brochure were taken with a wide-angle lens. The real thing is bound to disappoint.'

'Don't be such a sourpuss, Ruth! Come along with me. *Laissez les bon temps rouler!*'

FOUR

'As with any vessel, adequate provisioning is crucial, especially on a cruise ship serving several thousand meals at each seating. For example, passengers and crew on the Royal Caribbean International ship Mariner of the Seas consume 20,000 pounds of beef, 28,000 eggs, 8,000 gallons of ice cream, and 18,000 slices of pizza in a week.'

Wikipedia, March 31, 2013

At the entrance to the Firebird café stood an attractive, dark-haired steward whose name tag read 'Sheila – Australia,' a machine dispensing freshly squeezed orange juice, and a hand sanitizer. 'Norovirus,' said Ruth, as she gave her hands a squirt and rubbed briskly.

'A shot of O.J. would probably work just as well,' I scoffed as we entered the café, an enormous, horseshoe-shaped room with a spectacular 180-degree view. We were ahead of the crowd, thank goodness, so while Ruth held down a table for four in a booth near the window, I grazed the buffet tables, assembling a lunch of pasta Bolognese, green salad and fresh, hot rolls with butter. When I sat down, Ruth took off, but not before a server had appeared out of nowhere to take our orders for drinks. I didn't usually drink wine with lunch, but what the hell, I thought, handing Pradeep from India – as I worked out from his name tag – my sea pass. 'A glass of merlot, please.'

Tidal Wave must have passed muster because Georgina joined us after about fifteen minutes carrying a plate heaped with fried chicken, wild rice and sauteed green beans in one hand, and a small dessert bowl in the other.

'Where's Julie?' I mumbled around a mouth full of ziti.

Georgina nodded in the direction of the buffet. 'Filling up at the salad bar. She claims to be on a diet.'

'What on earth for? She's as thin as a rail! When we turned sideways for that photograph I'll bet she disappeared.'

'It'll probably last all of ten minutes once she sees the dessert buffet,' her mother said, pointing to the bowl that held her brownie smothered in hot caramel sauce.

Ruth eased over so that Georgina could sit down, and a few minutes later I did the same to make room for Julie. 'What did you think of the teen club?' I asked my niece.

'It's awesome! There's a disco, and a lounge with a drinks bar where they serve mocktails and stuff. And a separate room with tons of video games.' She paused to take a breath. 'And a rock-climbing wall – I can't wait to try that – and a bungee-jumping trampoline.'

Georgina smiled across the table at her daughter. 'When Julie asked the youth counselor how many teenagers were on board, she said two hundred and fifty.' Georgina picked up a green bean between her thumb and forefinger and popped it into her mouth. 'I don't know how many counselors it takes to ride herd on that many kids, but I think there'll be plenty to keep them and our girl occupied.'

Ruth paused, a forkful of beef stroganoff half way to her mouth. 'Julie? Over there? Don't look now, but those guys are totally checking you out.'

'Where?' Julie's gaze flit curiously around our section of the dining room, but she was way too cool to turn her head.

'Up at the grill, in the hamburger line. Wearing the red T-shirts.'

Chin slightly dipped, Julie glanced sideways through her eyelashes. 'Oh, *them*.' Her cheeks flushed. 'That's Connor and his cousin, Josh.'

It certainly didn't take Julie long to make friends, I thought to myself. Aloud I said, 'They look too old for the teen club.'

'They are,' Julie said. 'Connor and Josh are part of that ginormous reunion group. They're, like, twenty-one. They showed up at Tidal Wave to check it out for Josh's little sister. She's fifteen, but I can't remember her name.'

Julie scooped up the last of her potato salad, then shot up from her seat. 'I'm going to check out the desserts.'

As she flounced away, Georgina raised a knowing eyebrow. 'See? What did I tell you about dessert?'

Julie was still away, presumably trying to decide between the mini cream puffs, chocolate-layer cake, key lime pie and fresh-berry trifle when the public address system crackled to life and the hotel director – in a charming, Continental accent – introduced himself and welcomed us aboard the *Phoenix Islander*. After summarizing the itinerary and giving us the weather report – sunny, 78°F, 25°C – he informed us that our staterooms were ready.

I volunteered to fetch Julie, only to discover that it wasn't the enormous selection of desserts that was holding her up; it was – according to the name printed on his Crawford Family T-shirt – blue-eyed, sandy-haired, beachbum-buff Connor. If I had been decades younger . . . well, never mind. Julie hovered over the sneeze hood separating her from the chocolate-layer cake, feigning indifference as Connor urged her to try it.

I swept in like the Wicked Witch of the West. 'Say goodbye to Connor, sweetie. It's time to go to our staterooms.'

Julie grabbed a handful of M&Ms, waggled the fingers of her free hand at Connor, said, 'See ya!' and trotted along beside me out of the café. Georgina and Ruth had gone on ahead, so we followed them down the elevators to deck four, amidships on the starboard side.

Ruth was waiting for me in the narrow corridor, leaning against a framed photograph of Santorini – whitewashed houses and churches at sunset, perched along volcanic cliffs. I delivered Julie to her mother, then watched while Ruth slotted her card into the keycard lock, turned the handle, pushed the door open and stepped inside. 'Wow!' she said.

Our room was tastefully decorated, spotless and smelled like freshly laundered sheets. Our bags were waiting for us, too, neatly laid out on protective leather pads at the foot of our beds. A sliding glass door led outside to a balcony furnished with a small, round table and pair of wooden deck chairs. I wandered over, opened the door and stepped out into the breezy, early summer afternoon. Today our view was the city of Baltimore. Tomorrow, I knew, we'd be looking out over the vast expanse of the Atlantic Ocean.

Near the door to the balcony were a two-cushion sofa and a coffee table on which sat a small bottle of champagne buried up to the neck in a bucket of ice. 'There's a card with it,' Ruth said, picking it up. 'It's an invitation. Seems Captain Halikias is inviting you and a guest to a cocktail reception tomorrow night.'

'Cool,' I said, unzipping my suitcase, looking for my toiletries. 'You wanna be my guest?'

'What's the Neptune Club?' Ruth wanted to know, glancing up from the invitation.

'It's a frequent flyer rewards program for cruising. Paul and I signed up ages ago. Remember that cruise we took to Alaska's Inner Passage?' I looked up. 'I think that Whats-his-name Simonides bought out that cruise line, so the points carried over.'

A polite *tap-tap-tap* interrupted my explanation. Thinking it'd be Julie or Georgina, I opened the door wide. 'Is there anything I can get for you, Mrs Ives?' inquired our steward, whose name was Rodolfo, from the Philippines.

'I think we're all set, Rodolfo, but thanks so much for checking.'

As Rudolfo backed out the doorway, smiling broadly, Ruth reached for the champagne. 'This is what I call a warm welcome!' She began to remove the foil from the cork. 'Shall I do the honors?'

'Absolutely! But wait, let's get Georgina.'

I thumped the ball of my fist on the door to the adjoining cabin. It swung open almost immediately, and Georgina stuck her head in. 'Is this a private party, or can anyone join?'

I laughed. 'Come in, come in. And bring a glass. Where's Julie?'

'Taking pictures of the cabin on her iPhone and posting them to Facebook. What else?'

Ruth untwisted the wire hood that held the champagne cork in place, aimed the bottle at the open balcony door. 'Look out below!' The cork shot from the bottle and disappeared over the balcony railing. 'Ooops!' Ruth giggled. She divided the champagne equally among the three glasses. 'Cheers!' she said, handing a glass to me.

I took it and tapped my glass against hers, then Georgina's. 'Cheers! To a wonderful cruise!'

'And remember,' Ruth said before taking a careful sip. 'What happens with sisters, stays with sisters.'

FIVE

The Chesapeake Bay Bridge is a major dual-span bridge in the U.S. state of Maryland. Spanning the Chesapeake Bay, it connects the state's rural Eastern Shore region with the more urban Western Shore. With shore-to-shore lengths of 4.33 and 4.35 miles, the two spans of the bridge form the longest fixed water crossing in Maryland and are also among the world's longest over-water structures. A 3,200-foot suspension span over the western channel with a maximum clearance of 186 feet is high enough to accommodate ocean-going vessels and tall ships.

Wikipedia, November, 2012

'Where R U?' Paul had texted.

I stared at the display on my iPhone in disbelief, then began typing. 'AT&T signal amazingly strong on Mars.' I wasn't as fluent in texting abbreviations as I ought to be in this day and age, and Tweeting was a total mystery. I should take lessons from Julie. LOL.

Rather than text me back, Paul telephoned. I put the phone on speaker and 'fessed up. 'We're on the top deck, sitting in lounge chairs, drinking adult beverages and waiting to pass under the Bay Bridge.' I'd passed under the bridge many times before, of course, but always on a small pleasure craft. This time, I'd be approximately one hundred and fifty feet closer to its massive, steel undercarriage.

Georgina raised her glass. 'It's awesome.'

'Connie and I decided to take *Sea Song* out,' Paul continued. 'We are going to try to rendezvous with you as you pass by Annapolis.'

Paul and his sister, Connie, share a lifelong love of sailing. *Sea Song* is Connie's aging Tartan thirty-seven sloop. 'Did you bring a camera?' I asked.

'Of course.'

'We will stand at the rail and pose for you, then.'

Paul laughed. 'We won't be able to get *that* close, Hannah!'

Paul explained about AIS, a gizmo on *Sea Song*'s chart plotter that allowed them to track the position and speed of commercial ships. I learned that *Islander* was exactly one point three miles north of the Bay Bridge, travelling south at approximately twenty-two knots. 'Good to know, Professor Ives,' I said, although I could have come to the same conclusion by simply heaving my lazy bones out of the lounger and peering over the rail.

'So, other than sampling the selection of adult beverages,' Paul asked, 'what have you been up to?'

'We got settled in, then had a pretty serious fire drill. *Whoop-whoop-whoop*, grab your life preservers, report to your assigned lifeboat stations, crew takes roll-call, the whole shebang.' When I paused to take a sip of my mojito, Ruth grabbed the hand that held my phone and moved it closer to her mouth. 'Exhausting.'

'Ha ha ha!' Paul said.

'It amazes me,' I continued in a more serious tone after reclaiming my hand, 'how on such a huge ship you keep running into the same people.' I explained about Cliff and Liz Rowe who I'd met again in the spectacular, sky-view, multi-story crystal and glass Atrium after the fire drill while buying a latte at Café Cino. 'There must be a hundred members of the Crawford clan on board, and I swear they're all assigned to cabins on our floor, uh, deck.'

'By their red shirts ye shall know them,' Georgina muttered.

'Amen,' added Ruth, 'although they'll have to wash their shirts sometime, I suppose. Then what will we do?'

As if they knew we were talking about them, a boisterous group of five young Crawfords sauntered by, each carrying a long-neck beer wrapped in a foam koozie. The young men didn't appear the least bit interested in the Chesapeake Bay Bridge, stopping instead to admire one of the uniformed youth counselors as she hooked herself into a bungee harness and began testing out the trampoline.

'Hold on a minute,' I said. Passengers were rising from their chairs and flocking to the rail. While keeping Paul on the line, I joined them, elbowing my way into a space between two couples on the bow. I felt my pulse quicken. 'We're about to pass under the bridge!' I told my husband as all around me, passengers began *oh-ing* and *ah-ing*. 'It's hard to believe we can actually fit under it! I'm hanging up now! I'm going to take a video. Love you! 'Bye!'

I tapped the video app just in time to pan the entire four-mile length of the bridge, then tipped my head way back to point the lens skyward as we passed under the elaborate superstructure of the westbound span. I captured the spectacular view between the two spans as they curved gently away like a giant Erector set toward the molten ball of late afternoon sun, then panned up again as we passed under the eastbound span where the rumble and whine of the cars and trucks as they passed overhead was almost deafening. Although I knew there had to be plenty of headroom between the smokestacks of the *Islander* and the undercarriage of the bridge, the illusion was so compelling that passengers raised their arms as if riding a roller coaster, straining to touch its girders.

'There's *Sea Song!*' Ruth cried, pointing in the direction of the three obsolete navy telecommunication towers that dominated Greenbury Point, towers so tall and well-lit that they served as navigational aides for local mariners.

I shaded my eyes and squinted. Staying prudently well out of the sea lanes, *Sea Song*'s sail was a tiny triangle of white, far out of range of my iPhone camera. In case Paul had binoculars and was looking our way, however, I waved. 'Paul's sweet to do that,' Ruth commented.

'He's a bit of a nut, but I love him,' I said.

Dressed neatly, but casually, we dined that night at a table for four near a huge oval window, a table that would be ours at dinner for the duration of the voyage. Leaving the Bay, our view was of Maryland's western shore. From sailing with Connie, I recognized landmarks as we passed – Annapolis, the South River, the wide mouth of the West River where it opens up and divides into the Rhode. We were finishing dessert – a stunning peach melba – when we sailed by the chalky banks of Maryland's towering Calvert Cliffs, site of the nuclear power plant that kept our lights on back at home in Annapolis.

After dinner, Georgina and I deposited Julie with a youth

counselor at Tidal Wave, the trendy, flashy, seagoing teen center they'd explored earlier. In the hours since we'd last seen it, the space had been transformed into a disco. While a burly photographer snapped pictures of the gyrating crowd of teens, a DJ wearing headphones the size of Princess Leia's buns called the shots from his perch on top of a tall stool. Awash in an undulating sea of multicolored lights, Phreakin' Phil – or so I assumed from the name stenciled on a woofer by his feet – presided over an assortment of turntables, MP3 players and mixers, flanked by a pair of tall, narrow speakers, looking for all the world as if he were at the helm of Mission Control in Houston.

'It's karaoke night, boys and girls,' he drawled into the microphone as he cued up the next number, a song I'd never heard before. The singer was ditching her boyfriend for good, and she didn't sound terribly broken up about it, either.

I asked Julie who the artist was. 'Taylor Swift,' Julie said, her body jiving in time to the catchy beat. 'She's my absolutely *fave*!'

'I thought you were in love with Justin Bieber, Julie.'

My niece screwed up her face. Even in the inadequate lighting it said, plain as day, *you-have-got-to-be-kidding-me*. 'I am *so* over Justin Bieber, Aunt Hannah. Besides, he's going with that Selena. She sucks!'

'Thank heaven's for small favors,' her mother commented, raising her voice so I could hear her over the chorus of 'we are never, ever, ever, evers' blasting out of Phreakin' Phil's speakers. 'But I don't like you using that word, Julie.'

'Whatever,' my niece grumped.

Floyd from Arizona, a twenty-something counselor who was ruggedly handsome in a Hugh Jackman sort of way, explained that Phreakin' Phil – Phreak to his friends – was a pro at beat-matching, phrasing and slip-cueing, but Floyd might as well have been speaking to me in Greek. Smiling broadly, his teeth whiter than white under the psychedelic lighting, and oozing boyish charm out of every pore, Floyd helped Julie overcome her reluctance to join the karaoke party. After Floyd worked his magic, Julie shyly agreed to sing 'Total Eclipse of the Heart' by Bonnie Tyler toward the end of the evening, but she made us promise we'd be nowhere in the vicinity.

Amused, we agreed. Georgina and I left Julie in Floyd's presumably capable hands and wandered off to find Ruth. She'd promised to save seats for us in the Trident Lounge, four decks down from Tidal Wave and at the other end of the ship. We found her there, holding down the fort at a small round table. 'The place was filling up, so I ordered drinks for you both. I hope they're all right.'

I sank gratefully into the upholstered chair, then reached for my drink. 'Ah, a mojito. You know me too well, sister.'

Ruth grinned.

From her frown, I gathered that Georgina wasn't quite so pleased with her drink – a gorgeous, peachy-pink mai tai, loaded with fruit, but she thanked Ruth for it anyway. 'When does the show start?' she asked, her lips pursed around the straw.

Ruth checked her watch. 'Eight o'clock. Any minute now.'

As if the producer had overheard, the lounge lights dimmed, the spotlights flared and four middle-aged musicians – two guitarists, a pianist and a drummer – charged onto the stage. They wore white, button-free tuxedos with Nehru-style collars over electric-blue vests. Matching blue-striped ties were knotted at the necks of ordinary, pointed collar white dress shirts.

Georgina choked on her drink, coughed and whispered, 'The *Da Doo Ron Rons* are Japanese?'

'Korean,' Ruth corrected. 'Or so says Wikipedia.'

I melted into my chair. 'This should be interesting.'

'They're a rock and roll band, so they cover tunes of the fifties, sixties and seventies,' Ruth continued while staring at the stage and absent-mindedly chasing olives around the bottom of her dry martini glass with a swizzle stick. 'A good choice for our demographic, I should think.'

Without preamble, the combo launched into their signature tune, 'Da Doo Ron Ron,' a faithful tribute to The Crystals rather than that young upstart, Shaun Cassidy, who covered and re-popularized the song in the late seventies. Then they segued into an equally authentic cover of the Monkees' 'Daydream Believer' with the lead guitar channeling Davy Jones.

The lead guitarist was equally well cast as Jim Morrison. 'Morrison could light my fire any day,' Ruth said as she flagged down a server and ordered another round. 'His father was a navy admiral, did you know that? When Dad was stationed in San Diego they overlapped.'

I raised my glass. 'Missed opportunity, Ruth, but then, had you actually snagged the guy, you'd have been a widow at twenty-something.'

She raised her glass. 'True, but a rich one.'

The bass guitarist sported a Beatles-style do and managed a credible Paul McCartney, but when the voice of Elvis Presley or Roy Orbison was required, the job fell to the pianist. Alternately gravelly or sweet, the Korean's amazing voice soared effortlessly into the higher octaves in his rendition of 'Oh, Pretty Woman' which he performed complete with Orbison's trademark dark glasses. By the time he lit into 'Blue Suede Shoes,' the whole audience was singing along. At the end of the set, we put our drinks down on the table and clapped until our palms stung.

I went to bed that night with an earworm. Long after Ruth had turned out her light, plunging our stateroom into darkness, I lay on my back with Orbison's 'Crying' looping through my brain.

The tune was still haunting me at breakfast the following morning – *cry-y-y-y-ing, over you, cry-y-y-y-ing, over you* – as hard to shake as 'It's a Small World After All,' until Cliff and Liz Rowe showed up at our table and drove the melody, and all other thoughts, clean out of my head.

SIX

'Invisibility was the ultimate concealment.'
Jim Steinmeyer, *Hiding the Elephant*,
Da Capo, 2004, p. 90

We'd agreed to meet for breakfast at 7.30 a.m. but that plan got shot out of the water when Julie, burrowed deep into the sheets under her duvet, had turned into a block of stone. Georgina stood in the connecting doorway, gazing back into the darkness of her own cabin. She excused her daughter with an indulgent smile. 'Julie's not used to staying up so late, even on weekends. If Scott knew she didn't get in until almost midnight last night he'd have a conniption.'

I checked my watch; it was nearly 8.00 a.m. I was working on a headache, and if I didn't pump some caffeine into my veins pretty soon, I'd be more than grumpy. 'Ruth and I will go on down, then. Shall we bring you something, or do you want to call room service?'

Georgina stepped all the way into our stateroom and closed the door quietly behind her. 'I'm coming, too. Let her sleep. If she wants breakfast later she can pick up something to eat in the Firebird.'

My sisters and I headed aft toward the Oceanus dining room, conveniently located – at least for us – on deck four. We emerged from the narrow passageway into a bright, spacious lobby that was also home to the Oracle, the *Islander*'s trendy wine bar. An attractive young barkeep was already at work dumping ice into large, shell-shaped basins – one at each end of the sprawling, horseshoe-shaped bar – where splits of sparkling wine would be kept properly chilled. I made a note to check out the wine bar later.

Breakfast and lunch aboard the *Islander* was open seating, but that didn't mean it was a free-for-all. We were met by the maître d', who greeted us like long-lost cousins, then handed us off to the first in a long line of servers – Paolo from Brazil, who escorted us to a table for eight near a window. Not that there was much to see. Overnight we'd sailed out of the Chesapeake Bay, past Norfolk, Virginia and into the Atlantic Ocean, well out of sight of land.

A squad of Paolo's fellow waiters materialized out of the woodwork to hold our chairs until we were seated, whip open our napkins and float them gently into our laps. Then, with a slight bow, we were each provided with a menu.

Ruth studied the menu through her reading glasses. 'Ah, just like home.'

Georgina giggled. 'I don't know about you guys, but I have Eggs Benedict *every* morning.'

I scanned the long list of choices – omelets, Belgian waffles, crepes, quiches, oatmeal with all the trimmings – until I came to the Eggs Benedict. 'Ah, but are yours prepared with Coho salmon rather than ham, Georgina?'

Georgina laid her menu down. 'The truth? In my house, it's Spam on toast.'

'"Eggs bacon sausage and spam; spam sausage and spam; spam spam spam baked beans and spam."' Ruth's heroic attempt to channel Monty Python.

I buried my head in the menu. 'I don't know who either of you two are.'

Christina from Greece was hovering over my left shoulder, prepared to take my order for Belgian waffles with fresh fruit when a voice called out, 'Oh, look, Cliff. It's Hannah Ives.'

Still clutching the menu, I turned my head. Liz Rowe was chugging in my direction, followed by her husband. 'Do you mind if we join you?' Liz asked, dismissing their server with a wave of her hand.

'Of course not,' I said. 'Georgina, Ruth, you remember the Rowes, from when we checked in?'

'It's a lovely ship, isn't it?' Liz said, settling into the chair next to Ruth. 'One of the loveliest we've sailed on, isn't it, Cliff? They actually have *standards* for formal night, for one thing. Pity the poor passenger who shows up at dinner wearing blue jeans!'

Cliff grunted, presumably in agreement, and sat down next to his wife. I pictured him dressed in a tuxedo, and decided it'd look good on him. But then, *all* men look good in tuxedos. When Paul wears his, I want to jump his bones.

Nobody spoke for a moment as Paolo poured coffee all around and Christina took our orders. After Christina headed back to the kitchen, I said, 'My husband and I sailed on the *Queen Mary Two*, so I have to confess that it takes a lot to impress us. I'm really enjoying myself so far.'

'We're in a good mood today because Cliff won a hundred dollars in the casino last night,' Liz confided.

Cliff smiled around his coffee cup. 'Blackjack.'

'My husband's a good blackjack player, too,' I said, picking up my glass of orange juice, 'but he's a mathematician and has studied all the odds. The casino holds no attraction for me at all, I'm afraid. I'm much more interested in the hot tub.' I took a sip of juice, then raised my glass. 'And the champagne bar.'

'Do you knit?' Liz asked.

I stared at her, puzzled by the non sequitur. 'I beg your pardon?'

'Do you knit?' she repeated. 'There's a knitting club that meets at three o'clock every afternoon in the Oracle. Knitting, crochet, needlepoint. I read about it in the daily programme.'

Although the daily programme had been slipped into the notice box mounted just outside our stateroom door the previous evening, I had assigned it to my post-breakfast agenda, so hadn't gotten around to reading it yet. 'That sounds dangerous,' I said. 'Knit one, purl two, take a sip of champagne, knit one – or was it three? – purl, perhaps another sip.' I faked a hiccup. 'Could be interesting.'

'I'm going to try it out today,' Liz said. 'I'm working on a hoodie for my grandson. Would you care to join me?'

Her question took in all three of us, but I was the only knitter in the group. Ruth raised a hand, palm out. 'Not me. I've already signed up for a session of Ashtanga yoga in the fitness center.'

Ruth had graduated from Hatha to Ashtanga, a kind of power yoga, all fast-paced lunges and push-ups. Way too intense for me. 'Why ever not?' I said. 'I brought along a hat I've been knitting for my granddaughter. I had visions of lying in a deck chair, knitting, while being served tea and crumpets, but knitting

with champagne sounds way more fun.' I winked. 'It'll cut into
my hot tub time, of course.'

Chin down, Liz murmured, *sotto voce*, 'Don't look now, but
here comes David. What's his last name, Cliff?'

'Warren.'

'He sits with us at dinner,' Liz continued. 'He's a bit odd.'

'Odd in what way?' I asked while looking casually over my
shoulder to see if I could spot some guy acting strangely.

'Doesn't talk much,' Cliff offered.

'No, it's more than that, Cliff. He's nervous, edgy. Almost like
he's being stalked. And always scribbling in a little notebook he
keeps in his breast pocket.'

On *Islander*, diners were pre-assigned to tables of two, four,
six, eight or ten. My sisters and I shared a table for four, so
breakfast and lunch were the only opportunities we had to dine
with strangers. 'How many are at your table, Liz?'

'Four. We also sit with a retired schoolteacher from Washington
State, but she and David *definitely* aren't travelling together. She's
a hoot, but frankly, we don't know quite what to make of David.'

Several groups had trooped by our table by then, but I hadn't
noticed anyone who looked particularly nervous or distracted. I
kept my voice low. 'Which one is David?'

Liz jerked her head, indicating a table for six several feet away.
'Over there. In the blue blazer. Just sitting down.'

David Warren was the only passenger within a hundred nautical
miles wearing a sports jacket rather than a polo shirt, so he was
easy to spot. Under the jacket, he wore a pale yellow button-down
Oxford shirt. When he picked up a menu, a signet ring flashed
on the pinky of his left hand. He had a full head of dark hair,
streaked with gray, which he combed straight back and kept
neatly trimmed around the ears. He looked like a banker, or
maybe a stockbroker.

'What does he do? Did he say?' I asked.

'Real estate.'

'That covers a lot of territory,' I said.

'Real estate! Territory!' Georgina snorted.

I shot her a dirty look. 'You know what I mean.'

'I think David deals in commercial properties,' Cliff said. 'He
mentioned a shopping center.'

'He's obviously on his own,' Liz said. 'I heard him ask Elda – Elda Homer, that's the schoolteacher – if she'd be attending the Solo Travelers Lunch today.'

'A widower, then, looking for love.' Georgina is an incurable romantic.

Ruth must have been standing behind the door when the Good Fairy handed out the gift of curiosity. 'None of our business, is it?' she said, stirring sugar into her coffee.

But soon, it would become very much our business.

We finished our breakfasts and excused ourselves, with me promising to meet Liz later that afternoon in the Oracle, yarn and knitting needles in hand. Back in our stateroom, I extracted the plastic bag that contained my knitting from the drawer where I'd stashed it, then settled down in the chair to read the ship's schedule, grandly titled The Daily Programme. From the programme I discovered that *Islander* was travelling in a north-easterly direction; the sun came up at 5.24 a.m.; clocks would be set back one hour overnight; and dinner that night was formal. At 11.00 a.m. there'd be a talk on skincare by a famous, plump-lipped, blemish-free actress I'd never heard of; bingo in the Trident Lounge at 2.00 p.m. and yoga in the fitness center at 3.00 p.m., if you weren't already taking ballroom dancing lessons from Ted and Lisa. And if I *still* didn't have anything to do, a crossword puzzle and a Sudoku had thoughtfully been printed on the back page.

I scanned forward to the evening's activities. The show that night was a comedian followed by a magic act.

'Ruth, do you want to go to the show after dinner?'

'Don't forget we have that Neptune Club reception,' Ruth mumbled around a mouth full of toothpaste.

'Right. It'll probably be a bit of a bore, but at least the drinks will be free.'

'Your dance card is getting full, Hannah.'

'So, what are you going to do today, Ruth, other than twist your body into strange and unnatural positions?'

'Well, I'm not going to waste my time *knitting,* that's for sure.' She dabbed her lips dry with a towel. 'Wonder what Georgina feels like doing?'

I tapped quietly on the connecting door in case Julie was still asleep. Georgina opened it almost immediately. 'What's up?'

'Is Julie awake?'

'Finally! She's in the shower.'

'What's she going to do today, Georgina?'

'Julie's signed up for a teen barbecue and some sort of organized scavenger hunt. I'll hardly ever see her.'

'Does that worry you?'

Georgina raised one pale, well-shaped eyebrow. 'Do I *look* worried? So, I'm up for just about anything. Except knitting,' she added, with an accusatory glance at me.

Clearly, in the knitting department, I was outnumbered. 'I never promised we'd be joined at the hip, Georgina.'

Thirty minutes later, after Julie was safely delivered to one of the Tidal Wave youth counselors, my sisters and I found ourselves marinating in one of three hot tubs in the adults-only solarium. When we were pink and medium-well boiled, we wrapped ourselves in oversized Turkish towels and arranged ourselves on adjoining deck chairs with our reading – a Kindle for Georgina and actual books for Ruth and me – while solicitous uniformed attendants made sure we had everything our hearts desired. After ordering a bloody Mary, I did.

Georgina powered on her Kindle, considered my well-worn paperback. 'Don't you have a Kindle, Hannah?'

'I do, back home, but I figured reading it in a hot tub would be a bad idea. And what if I lose the charger? I'd be up the creek if my battery ran out in the middle of the latest P.D. James.'

'I like my Kindle because you can't really lend books,' Georgina said, kicking off her flip flops. 'Saves me the social embarrassment of having to remember who I lent that hardback to that I hadn't gotten around to reading yet.'

As we considered the people sprawled in the deck chairs around us, we decided that you could tell a lot about a stranger by what he or she is reading. *Final Sail* by Elaine Viets? I think I might like that person, while – not being snobbish or anything – I'd be unlikely to initiate a conversation with someone engrossed in a Jackie Collins novel. 'See that guy over there?' I asked, nodding my head in the direction of the Surf's Up Café. 'The blond in the red bathing trunks, with the hardback propped up on his gut?'

'What about him?' Ruth muttered from behind her ancient copy of *Zen and the Art of Motorcycle Maintenance.*

'Well, he's reading Harlen Coben. If he were reading an iPad, Nook or Kindle we wouldn't be able to see the cover, so we wouldn't have the slightest clue what he's reading.'

'So?' Ruth wanted to know.

'Serious disadvantage, Ruth, if you're on the prowl for guys. Hot or not? With a Kindle, it'd be hard to tell. Dude could be reading Danielle Steele, for all you know. Or a self-help book on overcoming addiction. But, if you can see he's reading Robert Crais, you've got your opening. ' "Oh, hi," you say. "I like Crais, too. Is that as good as his last one?" '

'I'm *not* on the prowl for guys, Hannah.'

'Neither am I. I just think it's interesting.'

Georgina studied the guy reading Coben thoughtfully for a few seconds. 'You think *he's* hot, Hannah?'

I tended to be attracted to tall men – my husband, Paul, towered over me – and although Red Bathing Suit was certainly tall, he was a little too, how shall I say, *fleshy* for my taste. 'Not really. Besides, I think he's married. See that skinny blonde standing in the buffet line? In the teeny-weeny black bikini? They came in together.'

'Where?' Georgina asked.

'She's fixing a hot dog,' I said.

Ruth sniffed. 'Looks like a Stepford wife. Or married to a Republican candidate for President. I'm sure it's a character flaw on my part, but I simply can't tell those women apart.'

As I watched Black Bikini cross the solarium to rejoin her husband, I had to agree with Ruth. The woman looked as if she'd been stamped out of a template: five foot five or six, fit and trim, aggressively-styled bottle-blonde hair, makeup applied with the skill of an artist. She handed the hot dog to her husband, but apparently she had failed the hot dog fixings test because he said something, then shoved the plate back into her hands so suddenly that the potato chips she'd heaped on the side of it went flying. She yelled something in response, spun around and stomped out of the solarium as elegantly as one can while wearing flip flops, dumping the hot dog, plate and all, into the trash can nearest the door.

' "The course of true love never did run smooth," ' Ruth quoted, bard-like.

'If he wanted a damn hot dog, he should have gotten it his damn self,' Georgina sputtered, staring after the woman. After she'd disappeared into the main pool area, Georgina flipped over on her stomach, stretched out full-length on the deck chair and returned to whatever she had been reading on her Kindle. The sun blazed through the glass canopy of the solarium, its rays catching the damp tendrils of her hair, turning it to burnished copper.

The Belgian waffles with fresh fruit I'd had at breakfast were taking their toll. Bathed in the warmth of the sun, I slept easily, until a stranger's voice suddenly roused me from my nap.

'Excuse me?' The voice was deeply male and melodious, like a late-night host on the Oldies But Goodies station.

My eyes snapped open. I blinked.

A man carrying a big-ass camera stood like a pillar at the foot of Georgina's lounger. Tall and sturdy, dark hair speckled his head like new growth on a Chia Pet. He wore a white polo shirt tucked into a pair of navy chinos, and deck shoes with no socks.

'Can I help you?' I asked, thinking how extraordinary his eyes were. They had been bleached to a pale amber, like the 3.2 beer we used to drink in college.

The question seemed to fluster him. 'Sorry. I just wanted to ask your friend here . . .' His hands full of camera, he nodded toward Georgina. '. . . if she'd mind if I took her picture.'

My sister was clearly asleep, Kindle flung to one side, head turned, her cheek resting on her folded arms.

'She's asleep,' I said, stating the obvious. 'What's it for?'

The man shifted his camera to one side and dug into his breast pocket with a thumb and index finger like fat sausages. 'Buck Carney,' he said, handing me his business card. 'I'm a photographer.'

'I never would have guessed,' I said, indicating the fancy camera with a corner of his card which read, when I glanced at it a few seconds later, *LeRoy 'Buck' Carney, Freelance Photographer*, with an address and telephone number in Atlanta, Georgia. 'LeRoy,' I said. 'No wonder they call you "Buck." '

'Yeah, well . . .' he began.

I squinted up at him. 'Didn't I see you taking pictures last night in the disco?'

'Yeah, it's a dirty job, but somebody's gotta . . .'

'You were going to tell me what you wanted my sister's picture for,' I cut in. 'Do you work for the cruise line?'

'In a way. C.L.I.A? It's the cruise line association. They're doing a coffee table book to hand out to VIPs – senators, congressmen and the like. They hired me to take the pictures.' His eyes flicked toward Georgina, still blissfully unaware we were talking about her. 'The sun lighting her hair? The white bathing suit? Irresistible to an old shutterbug like me.'

Something in his gaze made me feel slightly uneasy, but where was the harm in a photograph? I nudged my sister gently on the shoulder. 'Wake up, Georgina. This guy wants to know if it's OK to take your picture. He wants to use it for a book he's doing for the cruise lines.'

Georgina opened an eye, gave the photographer a few seconds' worth of attention, then buried her head between her forearms again. 'Just as long as he doesn't block my sun.'

Buck raised his camera, aimed and took a rapid-fire series of shots. 'Thank you,' he drawled, stepping back toward the pool. ''Preciate that.'

'No problem,' Georgina muttered into her lounger.

After Buck wandered off, I returned to my novel, but had read only a paragraph when Ruth poked me with a finger. 'Look who just came in. Isn't that the David guy that Liz and Cliff were talking about at breakfast?'

David Warren, still dressed like the manager of a country club, had wandered into the solarium. He glanced around the room, as if looking for someone, shook his head slightly, then retreated to a table on the other side of the pool, not far from where we were lounging. Once seated, he reached into his pocket, pulled out a small notebook and began flipping through it until he came to a blank page. His eyes went on to scan mode: up to the solarium's crystal canopy and down; one end of the glass enclosure to the other.

'He's not looking for any *one*,' I suddenly realized. 'He's looking for some *thing*.'

Ruth agreed. 'I'll bet he's an undercover inspector.'

'A mystery passenger,' Georgina added. 'Like one of those mystery shoppers, you know? Reports back to management?'

Ruth swiped a rivulet of sweat from her brow. 'Wonder what he's looking for?'

I shrugged. 'Safety violations?'

An attendant balancing a tray of drinks on the flat of his hand stopped beside David's chair, but was waved off impatiently. The interruption must have broken the man's concentration, because he tucked the notebook back into his breast pocket, stood, and shuffled out of the solarium the way he had come.

'If he's an undercover inspector, he couldn't be more obvious,' I said. 'One doesn't usually wear a sports jacket, chinos and penny loafers when going to a swimming pool.'

'Funny how we keep running into the same people,' Ruth muttered before returning to her book.

'Yeah, isn't it?' I agreed, thinking about the Rowes.

Day one of an eight-day cruise. Somehow I suspected I hadn't seen the last of David Warren.

SEVEN

'She vanished as quickly as an electric light goes out when the switch is turned.'

David Devant, *Secrets of My Magic*,
Hutchinson, 1936

S itting for hours in a hot tub can suck the energy clean out of you. Add a gorgeous lunch of broiled lamb skewers, baby arugula and lemon vinaigrette, followed by a square of baklava, and all you can think about is a nap.

Ruth had already headed off for her yoga session when I hauled myself off my bunk, collected my knitting and made my way aft to the Oracle.

I was ten minutes early.

The attractive barkeep I'd noticed there earlier that morning was alone, moving busily behind the bar, arranging empty glasses on a tray, presumably preparing for the arrival of the knitters who, if the number of splits being chilled was any indication, were expected to be heavy drinkers.

I sidled up to the bar. 'Hello,' I said. 'How does this work exactly?'

The barkeep – Pia from Italy – looked up, smiled, and tucked an errant strand of her straight black bob behind an ear with her little finger. 'What would you like? Phoenix specializes in Greek wines, of course.' She indicated the iced basins. 'Our featured wine today is Ode Panos, a sparkling wine from Domaine Spiropoules. It's lovely.'

I dug the sea pass out of my pocket and slid it toward her across the bar. 'I'd like to try some, thanks.'

Pia ran my sea pass through her portable scanner and handed it back. 'Shall I start a tab?' When I nodded, she slid a bottle of Ode Panos out of its ice bath, quickly and expertly removed the cork – with a muted pop and a wisp of smoke – tipped the flute against the lip of the bottle and slowly poured.

Since nobody else had arrived, I asked, 'Have you been working on *Islander* long, Miss . . .?'

'It's Fanucci. Pia Fanucci.' She handed me the glass. 'Not on this particular ship, no, but Tom and I have been with Phoenix Cruise Lines for a while. We used to work on *Voyager.*'

I took a sip of the wine. Pleasantly bubbly, a touch of rose, a bit of green apple with a hint of banana. A little too perfumy for my taste, but as a mid-afternoon aperitif, not bad. 'Is Tom your husband?'

'No, he's my work partner.' She brightened. 'I guess I should explain. When I'm not tending bar, I'm Tom's assistant. He's Thomas Channing, the magician. He goes by Channing exclamation point,' she added, drawing a line in the air and dotting it with the tip of a well-manicured finger.

I knew all about One Name celebrities, like Elvis, Cher and Madonna. My son-in-law's real name was Daniel Shemansky, but ever since he and my daughter returned east from Colorado, he'd styled himself just plain Dante. Not that Dante was particularly famous, but their luxury bay-side spa, Dante's Paradiso – get it? – seemed to be thriving.

'You should come see the show,' Pia continued.

I set my glass down on a paper coaster, carefully centering the base over a black-and-white sketch of the ship. 'I read about it in the program and was thinking about going tonight.'

'You'll enjoy it,' Pia said. 'I'm a newbie, but Tom's been in show business a long time. Atlantic City, Las Vegas. He's been working the cruise ships now for about three years. He designs his own illusions, although there's a guy in Virginia who actually builds them for him. They're totally amazing.'

I grinned. 'What kind of magician would he be if they weren't?'

Pia beamed. 'Exactly!'

'So you get cut in half, float in mid-air . . .' I waved a hand vaguely. 'That sort of thing?'

'*Exactly* that sort of thing,' she chuckled. 'My favorite is the Zig-Zag Box, but the highlight of the show, really, is the Indian Sword Basket.'

'Eeeek!' I squeaked. 'I've always wondered about that. Are the swords fake?'

'Oh, no, they're very real. You'll see!'

'How's the comedian? I see he's on first.'

Pia shrugged. 'He's OK, I guess. But this is his first gig for Phoenix Cruise Lines, and I think he's a bit too blue for a family audience. Last night we had people walk out. Not good if he's opening for us.'

'Not at all,' I agreed. 'But I promise to tough it out, laugh at all his jokes – lame or not – and look forward to seeing you and the amazing Mister Channing Exclamation Point. And I'll bring my sisters.'

Pia smiled. 'You won't be sorry.'

I thanked Pia again and carried my wine over to a comfortable, white leather chair decorated with brass studs. I settled in, arranged my knitting on my lap, and took another sip, transporting myself to the whitewashed houses and brilliant blue sea of Santorini, a place I'd visited only in my imagination.

I was jolted out of my daydream when a group of teenagers erupted into the lobby from the elevator and breezed into the bar. Each girl carried a sheet of paper and a pencil. 'Hi, Aunt Hannah!'

'Julie! What are you doing here?'

'We're on a scavenger hunt.' Julie flapped her list in my direction. 'We're supposed to count the number of jeroboams in the Oracle bar. I don't even know what a jeroboam is!'

Pia Fanucci pointed behind her where four giant wine bottles were arranged, like pillars, supporting a glass shelf on which was displayed a sterling silver plate with an engraved inscription commemorating an international wine award. 'Those are jeroboams.' Pia explained, 'They hold about four litres of wine each.'

'Four!' shouted one of Julie's three companions. Heads down, they scribbled the answer onto their worksheets and disappeared as quickly as they had arrived.

'Your niece is a pretty girl,' Pia commented after they were out of sight.

'I know. She's going to break hearts some day.'

'How old is she?'

'Just turned fourteen.'

'She looks older.'

'I know. They grow up so quickly. Seems like just yesterday she was playing dress up with her Barbies.'

'Keep an eye on her,' Pia said as she swiped up a few drops of water from the polished surface of the bar with a damp rag.

I'd set my drink down on a circular end table and had reached for my knitting, but the cautionary tone in Pia's voice brought my hand up short. 'Should I be worried?'

Behind the bar, Pia appeared to be checking the rag for imperfections. After a moment, she dropped it into a sink. Her gray-green eyes met mine. 'Oh, I don't know. It's just that working as a bartender I see a lot of alcohol-related craziness. Sometimes I think they should raise the drinking age to thirty. After the hormones have stopped raging, anyway. But in some guys, the hormones never stop raging, you know? Had an eighty-something-year-old in here the other day . . .' she started to say when the elevator doors slid open and Liz Rowe stepped out into the lobby. Liz carried an oversized crewelwork bag; the business end of a pair of knitting needles protruded from the top. I waved at my new friend. 'Over here, Liz.'

Liz joined me, set her bag down in the chair next to me to reserve it, then hustled over to the bar to get herself a glass of sparkling wine, cutting my private chat with Pia short. If only I'd had five minutes – and maybe a glass of Ode Panos – more, I might have been able to cut through the rhetoric about alcohol and hormones and find out why Pia had neatly avoided answering my question. I drained my glass. By the time Liz rejoined me, I was ready for a refill, too.

More passengers trickled in, until the knitting group numbered around twenty. Projects ranged from small, like my hat, to highly ambitious, like a queen-sized lace-weave afghan. I had no idea how the woman had fit it into her luggage. One guy, who wielded his hook with the lightning speed of a gunslinger, was crocheting – I am not making this up – a Stetson hat. I was listening to him explain how he'd modified the handle of the crochet hook to accommodate rug yarn in order to make the tiny, tight stitches he needed for his project when I noticed that David Warren had showed up. He was leaning on the bar, talking to Pia.

'David knits? That's a surprise,' I commented.

'What?' Liz glanced up from her work.

'David Warren. He's over at the bar.'

As we watched, David reached across the bar, seized Pia's

hand and pulled her gently toward him. He was speaking too earnestly, too quietly for us to hear, but Pia didn't seem alarmed. She listened, then nodded, before slowly withdrawing her hand.

'I don't think they're discussing *le vin du jour,*' Liz said.

As I watched, Pia shrugged, turned and, keeping her head bowed, began filling the glasses on the tray with sparkling wine.

David had been dismissed. For several seconds he didn't move; then he shook his head, did a smart about-face and disappeared up the double staircase that led to the upper decks.

'I wonder what that was all about?' I whispered.

'We could ask Pia, I suppose, but that would be nosy.' Liz's blue eyes sparkled.

'Of course it would,' I grinned, 'but that's never stopped me before.'

By the time four p.m. rolled around, all but a few of the knitters had packed up and returned to their staterooms. When the coast was relatively clear, Liz and I approached the bar. I nudged Liz. 'You go first,' she whispered.

We perched ourselves on a pair of bar stools, comfortably upholstered in the same white leather as the chairs.

'What can I get for you, ladies?' Pia wanted to know.

'I think I'm in the mood for something crisp and dry,' I said.

'You got it.' Pia bent down, opened the sliding glass door on an under-counter refrigerator, selected a bottle, uncorked it and poured me a glass. 'Try this. It's called Assyrtiko. If you like Chablis, you'll like Assyrtiko.'

I took a sip and smiled appreciatively. 'Zesty,' I said. 'A bit lemony. I *do* like it.'

I set the glass down on the bar. 'What did David want?' I asked, hoping to catch her off guard.

Pia's eyebrows shot up into her bangs. 'David? Oh, you mean David Warren.' She caught her lower lip between her teeth and made a major production of twisting the cork back into the bottle. Only after she'd returned the Assyrtiko to the fridge did she return her attention to us. She rested her forearms on the bar, leaned forward and spoke softly. 'He wanted to ask me a question. I used to know his daughter.'

'We're assigned to the same table at dinner,' Liz confided

before I could pry any further. 'I've tried to draw David out, but he doesn't say much. He looks so sad!'

Pia considered us seriously, her green eyes solemn. Something in what Liz had said must have struck a sympathetic chord, because she managed a cheerless smile and started talking again. 'He has reason to be. His daughter, Charlotte, used to work for Phoenix. About eighteen months ago, we were serving together on the *Voyager*. Somewhere between Jamaica and the Cayman Islands, Char simply vanished. They combed the ship for her, of course, but she never turned up. The only possibility was that she went overboard.'

I took a deep breath, then let it out slowly. 'Did she jump?'

Pia shrugged. 'Nobody knows. When Security checked the cams, they saw Char out on deck around half past five in the morning, talking on her cell phone. She wandered around the corner, out of range of the camera and poof! Gone! All they ever found was one of her red heels lying on the deck not far from where she must have gone over.'

Something was wrong with that picture. With the exception of the cabaret dancers, none of the staff on board *Islander* wore high-heeled shoes. 'Was Charlotte a dancer?' I asked.

'No,' Pia said, 'but it was her night off, and we were in port, so she dressed up to the nines and went out clubbing with some of the staff. Sadly, Tom and I had a show that night so I couldn't go along.'

'How do you know the shoe belonged to Charlotte?' Liz inquired gently.

'These were Giulia Ricci's,' Pia explained. 'Red leather. Cost the earth. Char saved her pennies for months in order to buy them.'

'The brand with the famous red polka dots on the soles?' I asked.

Pia nodded, leaned across the bar and lowered her voice. 'David kept the shoe. He showed it to me and asked if I could identify it as Charlotte's. He's been carrying it around with him in his briefcase.' She shivered. 'Creepy, if you ask me.'

'My oh my,' tutted Liz. 'No wonder he looks sad.'

'*Nobody* who knew Char believes she committed suicide.' Pia pounded on the bar with the flat of her hand, emphasizing each word. 'She was upbeat, bubbly, engaged to this great guy back home. Her contract with the cruise line was almost over, and she was looking forward to flying back to Minnesota in a couple of weeks. No *way* she would have killed herself.'

Under the circumstances, suicide didn't sound very likely to me, either. 'Could she have had an accident?'

Pia puffed air out through her lips. 'Are you kidding? The railings on these ships are forty-two inches high, almost as high as this bar. Could you fall over *this*?' She slapped the bar again.

'Not even if I were blind drunk,' I said.

Pia's remarkable green eyes flashed. 'And at five-thirty in the morning Char certainly wasn't drunk.'

I leaned forward, spoke softly. 'Do you think Charlotte was murdered, Pia?'

'Eliminate suicide or accident and what are you left with?' Pia let out a long, slow breath. 'Her father certainly believes it was foul play.'

'Under the circumstances, you'd think David wouldn't want to have anything to do with Phoenix Cruise Lines,' I said. 'Why is he on board?'

'I think he's conducting his own investigation. The official one was crap.' Pia paused to hand a glass of wine to another passenger and scan his sea pass. Once the customer was settled into a chair, she turned back to us. 'When we got back to Fort Lauderdale, the F.B.I. came on board, but what was there to investigate? Charlotte had simply vanished. Might as well have been abducted by aliens. The F.B.I. dismissed the case for lack of evidence. Verdict? Accident, possible suicide. And don't get me started on the Bahamian police!'

My geography of the Caribbean was pretty good, having spent six months of Paul's recent sabbatical living on an island in the Bahamas. Jamaica and the Caymans, I knew, were nowhere near the Bahamas. 'How the heck did the Bahamian police get involved?'

'All the Phoenix ships are registered in Nassau,' Pia explained. She jabbed an index finger toward the ceiling. 'You probably noticed the flag.'

Liz screwed up her face. 'Let me get this straight. A Greek citizen, living in the British Isles, owns ships that sail in and out of ports in the United States of America, and those ships are registered in the *Bahamas*?'

'That's right. It keeps taxes low.'

Liz shook her head. 'Jeeze Laweeze.'

Pia took a deep breath, let it out. '*Anyway*, the detective they sent from Grand Bahama spent about an hour on the ship, interviewed a couple of people, pawed through Char's things, then flew home. End of story.'

Something wasn't right. 'But why is David Warren investigating *this* ship, so many months later?'

'How do you Americans say it? The usual suspects? *Voyager* is in dry dock until early next year. Some of her staff ended up here. Like Tom and me.'

Pia grabbed a napkin from the pile near her elbow and dabbed at the tears that had started to spill from her eyes.

'You and Charlotte must have been friends,' I said sympathetically.

'Friends? You could say that. She was my roommate.'

Ouch! No wonder the tears. 'What was Charlotte's job on the *Voyager*?' I asked gently. 'Did she work for Channing, too?'

Dry-eyed, Pia considered my question. 'She was one of the youth counselors.'

A cold ribbon of fear snaked up my back. Was *that* what was behind Pia's warning to me earlier about keeping an eye on Julie? 'Jesus,' I croaked.

'Exactly.'

EIGHT

' *"Fake" is a technical term used by magicians to indicate
something that the audience actually looks at but camouflaged or prepared to look like something else.'*
Jim Steinmeyer, *Hiding the Elephant*,
Da Capo, 2004, p. 234

'How do I look?' Ruth wanted to know.

The last time I'd seen the dress – a gold, gauzy, floor-length floral with leg-o-mutton sleeves – Ruth had been standing barefoot in a mountain meadow with daisy chains twined in her hair. 'I'm surprised you kept the dress,' I told her. 'Once you got rid of Eric, one would think you'd want to get rid of everything that reminded you of the jerk.'

'Well,' my sister said, twisting her body one way, then another in front of the mirror, then pausing to smooth the gown over her hips. 'I divorced Eric, not the dress. Besides, it still fits.'

'Waste not, want not,' I quoted.

Ruth performed a pirouette, then faced me. 'What are you going to wear to this reception thing?'

I was already wearing my 'uniform' – the black crepe pants – but was sitting around in my bra being wishy-washy about what to wear on top. I'd laid three choices out on the coverlet, and asked Ruth for her advice. 'Which one do *you* think?'

Ruth considered my question carefully. 'The red with the sequins. Definitely. And you have those crystal earrings to go with it.'

Ruth had talked me into the earrings when we'd been browsing at the jewelry boutique on deck six, one of a cluster of shops behind the photo gallery, just off the atrium. We'd gone up to check out the photograph that had been taken of us when we boarded, one of hundreds arranged in slots on the wall. When we finally found it, we were amazed: all our eyes were open, so Ruth bought it. I had to pay for the earrings, of course.

I slid the sequinned top on over my head and offered my back to Ruth so she could zip it up. I dug the earrings out of the bag in the top drawer and hung the beaded loops from my earlobes where they swung like chandeliers. 'There!' I said, presenting myself for inspection.

Ruth slid an arm around my waist and hugged me close. 'We're quite the glamorous pair. Too bad Hutch and Paul aren't here to enjoy the view.'

I laughed, but I'd been missing my husband, too. After hearing what Pia had to say earlier that afternoon, I had wanted to discuss it with him. Paul always listened to my ravings calmly, helped talk me through them sensibly and, above all, logically. My sister tended to be more laissez-faire. She'd ridden many a bus to never-ever land during the Summer of Love.

'Do you think Georgina's pissed off that I'm not taking her to the reception?' I asked.

'Hell, no. You know how she is about cocktail parties. Rather than dress up, she's decided to take Julie to dinner at the Firebird tonight. I think she's feeling a bit guilty, like she's neglecting Julie by letting her have the run of the ship.'

Since my usual sounding board was back in Annapolis, and Ruth had kind of brought it up, I made her sit down on the sofa while I filled her in on what I'd learned from Pia Fanucci about Charlotte Warren.

Ruth poo-poohed my concerns. 'This Charlotte person was an *employee* of the cruise line, right, not one of the kids. Nothing happened to any of the kids on her watch, did it?'

I shrugged. 'I don't know. It's possible, I suppose. I'll have to ask Pia about that.'

Ruth pressed her palms together. 'I wouldn't worry about Julie, then. Every time I've been up to Tidal Wave the kids seem well-supervised. And when they send them out, it's always in groups. Honestly, those counselors have the patience of Job. The noise alone . . .' Ruth's voice trailed off. 'Have you been in the video game room?' When I shook my head 'no' she added, 'Sheer torture! Ten minutes working in that place and I'd blow my brains out.'

While Ruth slipped into her dress sandals, I wondered what David Warren hoped to accomplish by wandering around the *Islander*, carrying a red shoe and asking questions like Detective

Columbo. According to Pia, his daughter had disappeared a year and a half ago and from another ship.

I decided to concentrate on touching up my makeup. I was on holiday, after all. 'Stairs or elevator?' I asked a few minutes later as we headed for the Trident Lounge.

'It's only two decks up,' Ruth said, heading for the staircase.

I followed, figuring the exercise would do me good.

The entrance to the Trident Lounge was through the piano bar where a pianist with the improbable name of John Darling was sitting at a white Steinway grand, tinkling the ivories. As we waited to go through the receiving line, he finished 'My Way' and segued neatly into 'The Candy Man,' then 'That's Amore,' crooning his way through songs that had been popularized by the Rat Pack in the sixties.

'Did you bring the invitation?' Ruth whispered as we got close to the head of the line.

I patted my evening bag. 'Right here, but I doubt they'll ask for it.'

And they didn't. We were glad-handed through a series of ship's officers, arranged in ascending order by rank and number of stripes on their sleeves. We shook the hand of the head chef – wearing his double-breasted jacket and traditional toque – the entertainment director, the head of security, the hotel director, the deputy captain, and finally, the captain, each resplendent in crisp white gold-buttoned uniforms, loaded with braid. As the captain released my hand and allowed me into the lounge, I said to Ruth – who had preceded me, 'I feel thoroughly welcomed aboard by now, don't you?'

Inside the lounge, a vocalist accompanied by a piano and bass combo sang, 'Besa Me Mucho' in a throaty alto. Servers worked the room carrying silver trays of canapés; others weaved through the guests carrying champagne aloft. As one passed, I snagged a glass of wine and took a sip. I recognized it by now: Ode Panos. The house wine.

'C'mon, Hannah, let's find a seat. The room is filling up fast.'

Based on what Liz and Cliff had told me, they'd ply us with food and drink, then welcome us to the Neptune Club, the frequent cruiser club, with discounts and other incentives. I hoped they wouldn't drone on too long, as dinner was just an hour away and I was already signed up. It didn't cost anything, as Liz had said, and a penny saved is a penny . . . well, you know.

Just thinking about Liz, I spotted her, sitting with Cliff at a table for six near a bank of windows that looked out over the stern. Even from where I stood, I could see the water foaming in the ship's wake, leaving a white trail to mark our passage across the sea. I thought about poor Charlotte pitching overboard, and if she survived the fall, floundering helplessly in that wake, calling out as the ship pulled away, growing smaller and smaller in her view until it was merely a dot on the horizon and she was totally alone. I shivered and grabbed Ruth's arm, 'There's Liz. Let's see if we can sit with them.'

I waved at Liz, who caught my eye, smiled and waved back, indicating we should join them, and we did.

I was just getting settled in my chair when Liz said, 'Golly, there's David Warren. I'm going to ask him over, too.'

Cliff rolled his eyeballs back until only the whites were showing, stuck out his tongue and mimed hanging himself with a rope.

Liz punched him in the arm. 'Behave yourself, Cliff. I feel sorry for the guy.'

Cliff straightened up. 'Well, if you *must*.' He grinned at me. 'Liz is always doing charity work. David must be her next project.'

David had turned away from us by then, so Liz got up and chased after him. She returned a few minutes later with David in tow, saying, 'David, I'd like you to meet Hannah Ives and her sister, Ruth . . . sorry, I don't know your last name.'

Ruth extended her hand and David shook it. 'It's Hutchinson.'

I'd learned so much about David from Liz and from Pia that I'd almost forgotten we'd never been introduced. The 'nice to see you again' on the tip of my tongue was quickly replaced with, 'so pleased to meet you,' as David joined our group, taking the chair next to me. He'd spent the afternoon on deck ten, he informed us, walking laps around the jogging track, working off the pounds he'd put on in the late-night buffet the evening before.

To his credit, Cliff tried to draw the man out by asking about the real-estate market in Minnesota. Homes moved quickly there, it seemed, and the Minneapolis suburbs were ranked among the top twenty-five places in the country to live by *Money* magazine.

As David droned on about 'median sale price' and 'average days on the market,' I zoned out, preferring to sip my wine, pop the occasional cashew into my mouth, chew thoughtfully and study the room.

Who were the 'usual suspects' among this group? I wondered. All the passengers had been on former Phoenix cruises, I knew, or they wouldn't be at this party, but how about the crew? The captain? Nuh-uh. I'd read in the program that Nicholas Halikias had been in charge of the *Islander* for more than three years. One of the others, then?

The receiving line had broken up and the officers were mingling. In their white uniforms they were ridiculously easy to spot. I kept one eye on David, hoping he'd shoot daggers at someone in particular, pull out his notebook and make a note, but if his notebook was with him it wasn't making an appearance.

After about fifteen minutes of serious schmoozing, Captain Halikias stepped onto the stage, accepted the microphone from the chanteuse, and welcomed us aboard. Again. Halikias passed the mike to the Cruise Director, Bradford Gould, who had been hovering by the captain's left elbow. Gould also welcomed us aboard with the practiced, oily charm of a lounge singer.

'I've never felt so welcomed in all my life,' I whispered to David.

'Of course,' he snorted. 'They want you to re-up.'

A flurry of activity to the left of the stage caught my eye. Led by a sequinned-bedecked woman enthroned in a motorized chair, folks were being gently, but firmly herded into a line that meandered lazily around the bar. In short order, we learned that Emily Rothenberg – the woman in the chair – would be receiving a Trident platinum medal. 'Seventy-five cruises with Phoenix Cruise Lines, ladies and gentleman! Think about it! We love you, sweetheart!'

We watched as Gould bent at the waist, straining his starched white pants, and hung the medal, attached to a blue and white-striped ribbon, around Rothenberg's neck. She kissed it, held it up for the audience's inspection, and grinned as the audience erupted in wild applause. You'd think she'd just medaled for Greece in the Olympic Games.

'How many cruises have you been on, David?' I asked as the applause for Emily Rothenberg died away.

'Compared to Ms Rothenberg over there, I'm small potatoes. Only four.'

'You have me beat,' I said. 'This is only my third. What kind of medal do you get for three? Paper? Cotton?' I turned to Cliff and Liz to ask, 'Why aren't *you* standing up in that line?'

Liz patted her husband's hand. 'Next year, if all goes well, we'll make the Silver Trident category. We were awarded the Crystal back in 2010.'

Next up were two aging jocks, diamond-award winners at sixty cruises apiece, who apparently knew one another because they were high-fiving all the way from the stage back to their seats.

As a group of Gold Trident awardees neared the stage, I poked Ruth and said, 'Do you recognize that guy? The tall one?'

'Help me out, Hannah. Which tall one?'

'Waiting in line. Blond hair, kinda thin on top.'

'Well, *that* certainly narrows it down. Most of the guys around here are follically challenged.' She flushed. 'Present company excepted, gentlemen.'

'Wearing the tuxedo,' I amended, 'next to the bottle blonde in the electric-blue dress.'

'Ah, I see who you mean now,' Ruth said. 'He's the guy we saw in the solarium who didn't like the way his wife fixed his hot dog.'

The two had apparently gotten over the Incident of the Hot Dog in the Solarium because they were now joined at the hip, smiling toothily and holding hands.

'Ladies and gentlemen, please welcome to the stage our next Gold Trident award winners, Jack and Nicole Westfall!' Gould bellowed into the microphone. 'Jack, Nicki, so good to have you with us again. Fifty cruises, ladies and gentlemen!'

'He certainly looks like a Jack,' Ruth commented as we watch Gould drape gold medals around the couple's necks. 'She looks more like a Tiffany or a Brandy to me, or maybe even a Brie.'

Liz burst out laughing. 'I *do* like you, Ruth. You can sit next to me anytime.'

I had a sudden brainstorm. Through most of the proceedings, David had been sitting silent, inscrutable, like a stone Buddha. Turning to him, I said, 'My sister and her daughter are eating in the Firebird tonight, so there's only two at our table. Would you like to join Ruth and me at dinner?'

Cliff shot me a grateful glance as Liz jumped in to say, 'We wouldn't mind at all, would we, Cliff? Mix it up a little bit, right?'

It was the first time I'd seen David smile. 'I'd like that very much.'

Dinner was a gorgeous surf and turf, and how they managed to serve all four hundred or so diners at approximately the same time and still deliver the lobster moist and sweet, and the steak medium rare as I'd asked for, simply amazed me. 'You work magic, Paolo,' I told our server as he removed my plate, as clean as if I had licked it.

I'd wanted to draw David out about his daughter, and about what he hoped to accomplish while on board the *Islander*, but I kept losing my nerve. The subject was bound to be a sensitive one, after all.

It was Ruth who finally broke the ice. 'I just *love* to cruise,' she drawled, 'but my husband's an attorney, and the only way I'd get him aboard would be bound, gagged and tied up in a sack!'

Which wasn't far from the truth, I thought to myself.

Paolo handed dessert menus around, and as I studied it, trying to decide whether to have the key lime pie or the crème brûlée, David said, 'I've always cruised alone.'

Ruth swooped in. 'Doesn't your wife enjoy cruising?'

'I'm a widower,' David mumbled into his menu.

'I am *so* sorry!' Ruth laid an apologetic hand gently on David's sleeve and looked mortified. 'I shouldn't have assumed . . .'

'No, no, it's all right.' The corners of his lips twitched up, the semblance of a smile. 'What I can't stand is the matchmakers. Can't a person go on a cruise without, uh, cruising, if you know what I mean?'

Ruth nodded vigorously. 'The solo travelers lunch, for example, and the guys who are paid to dance with you.'

Paolo was hovering over my shoulder. 'Key lime pie, please,' I said, handing him the menu. Paolo had already moved on to David when I added, 'And, Paolo, perhaps a shot of tsipouro?'

Ruth looked up from her menu. 'What's tsipouro?'

'A kind of Greek brandy,' I replied. 'From Mount Athos, I think. Thought I'd give it a try.'

The key lime pie came in due course, and I'd taken only a bite when Paolo reappeared, carrying the tsipouro in a small glass, poured over crushed ice. 'This is for madam, too,' he said, setting a dessert plate in front of me. Arranged artistically in the middle was a pale green square, studded with sliced pistachios. I leaned down for a closer look. 'What's this, Paolo?'

'Is halva. You try it. Delicious. With tsipouro, is very good.'

Paulo waited by my elbow as I took an experimental bite of what turned out to be an impossibly rich nut butter and sugar confection. 'Now, the tsipouro,' he coaxed. I was expecting it to taste like ouzo, but the tsipouro was smoother, much cleaner than ouzo, but as with ouzo, the fumes shot straight up my nose. 'Whoa!' I turned to Paolo, fanning my lips with my free hand. 'That's quite an experience.'

He beamed like a proud coach, and I made a mental note to be generous with his tip.

After Paola was out of earshot, I leaned forward conspiratorially. 'That stuff is like rocket fuel!'

David grinned, his amiable nature fully restored, and toasted me with his water glass.

'Paul and I enjoy cruising, David, but this trip was supposed to be all about the sisters.' I indicated the empty chair. 'Unfortunately, Georgina seems to be avoiding us lately.' I grinned across the table at Ruth. 'I hope it wasn't something I said.'

We sat in companionable silence for a while. I was sipping my tsipouro cautiously, waiting for the right moment to bring up the delicate subject of Charlotte when Ruth swooped in again, this time for the kill. 'Do you have any children, David?'

If her question upset him, there was no sign. 'I had a daughter, but she died,' he said simply.

'I have a daughter, too,' I told him, 'and just to *think* about losing her is a pain beyond bearing.' I wondered if I should press him, but his response had been so blunt, so matter-of-fact that I thought I'd risk it. 'Several years ago, my infant grandson was kidnapped, and the agony we went through before he was returned safely to our daughter's arms was indescribable.'

There was a short silence then, as if David were sizing us up. 'Charlotte worked on a cruise ship,' he confided at last. 'A sister ship to this one called the *Phoenix Voyager*. Somehow, she went overboard. But there's more to it than that, I know,' he declared, a steely edge creeping into his voice. 'Much, much more.'

I reached across the table and laid a hand on his sleeve. 'I'm so sorry, David. Did they ever find . . .?'

Anticipating my question, David cut me off. 'Charlotte's body? Yes. Many months later, on Little Cayman. When the phone call came, that was the day that my wife took her own life. Until then . . .' He let out a slow breath; his Adam's apple pumped up and down as he swallowed, hard. 'Well, until then Elise could talk herself into believing that Charlotte was still alive, that she'd somehow managed to swim ashore. Perhaps living a Robinson Crusoe existence somewhere on a remote island, surviving on breadfruit, coconut and bananas, weaving clothing out of palm fronds.'

David sank back in his chair, spread his arms wide. 'I can tell by the expressions on your faces that you're wondering what this crazy old man is up to. Well, I'm here because something very fishy was happening on that ship.' He sat up straight, fire in his eyes. 'I'm fed up to here with the cruise line,' he snapped. 'They've been stonewalling me since day one and I've run out of patience. I'm going to find out what *really* happened to my daughter. That phone call she was seen making?' he continued. 'It was to my wife and me.' The stony determination in his eyes turned to agony. 'Every day for the rest of my life, I'll have to live with the fact that when the phone rang at five in the morning, I simply turned over and let voicemail pick up. We'll never know what Charlotte was going to tell us, but whatever it was, I believe that she died for it.'

The sheer pain in David's eyes and his story was making it hard for me to keep my own emotions in check, but I managed to blurt out, 'When you didn't pick up, did Charlotte leave a message?'

'She did, and that's why I'm here. I can remember every word.' He screwed up his eyes and took a deep breath. ' "Something bad is going on, Dad, and I need your advice. Call me back, OK? I don't know what to do. Love you." '

Just like a character in a B movie, I thought, to leave a cryptic message rather than coming right out and saying whatever was on her mind. Why is it never, 'Charlie's robbing the company blind,' or 'Henry slipped cyanide into Sandra's drink?' It would certainly save the police a lot of time should the whistleblower end up dead, like poor Charlotte Warren.

'When we listened to the message, I called her back right away, of course, but the phone went to voicemail. I simply figured she was out of range – it happened all the time on the cruise ships – but when Charlotte never called us back, I worried. We didn't get the call from the captain until three days later. Basically he told us that he didn't know what had happened to our daughter.'

'Three days after she disappeared?' Ruth sat back in shock. 'What the heck were they waiting for?'

David slumped wearily against the cushions, the energy percolating out of him as he spoke to us now spent, leaving him looking drained. 'They suspected she was hiding somewhere on the ship, I suppose. Even the surveillance tapes weren't conclusive.'

I asked David the same question I had asked Pia earlier. 'If Charlotte disappeared from the *Voyager*, why are you sailing on *this* ship, David?'

David smiled cryptically. 'I'm following up on a hunch. It may be a complete waste of time, but I owe it to Charlotte – and to Elise – to pursue it.'

My antennae began to twitch, and before I or anyone else could stop me the words had already escaped from my mouth: 'If there's anything we can do to help . . .' David looked so unbearably sad, I wanted to get up out of my chair and hug him. 'Really, I mean it.'

'Take it from me,' Ruth chimed in. 'When Hannah's curiosity is piqued, there's no stopping her. It's easier to take a mouse away from a cat.'

David managed a weak smile and nodded, although his response was perfunctory. 'Thanks. I'll be sure to let you know.'

NINE

Our dinnertime conversation with David had depressed me more than I could say, reminding me, as it did, of our own family's journey through despair when our grandson, Timmy, disappeared.

When Ruth and I arrived at the Orpheus Theater, Georgina and Julie were already there. My heart did a little dance when I saw them. From where we stood, ranks of comfortable red plush velvet chairs were arranged in tiered semicircles facing an enormous stage, and Georgina had snagged premium seats in the second row.

'Good job!' I said as we eased into the row.

'They even have little tables for our drinks!' Julie chirped, setting her glass of something clear and bubbly – Sprite, I presumed – down on the small round table that separated her chair from mine.

A server appeared immediately, so we ordered drinks all around, and settled in.

In spite of what Pia had told me about the comedian, I was looking forward to the performance. I recognized his name from the Comedy Channel – Tony Malone – but with the exception of a short stint on *Comic Relief*, I'd never seen his act.

At the appointed hour, Malone exploded from the wings onto the stage, literally tackling the standing microphone as he passed.

'A funny thing happened on my way to the theater . . .' He paused, anticipating the groans of the audience, and we didn't disappoint.

When we quieted down, he continued, 'You're not going to believe it, but two vultures got on board my plane, and each was carrying two dead raccoons. The stewardess looks at them and says, "I'm sorry, gentlemen, only one carrion allowed per passenger."'

I had to laugh, but then, I'm a sucker for puns.

'Last night I was told that some passengers complained because of my material. Too adult, they said, a little too blue. Holy cow, I said, didn't they see my act on television? Who were they expecting, Mother Theresa?' Shading his eyes with a hand, Malone squinted beyond the spotlights and into the audience. 'So, any children out there tonight?'

Julie squirmed, making herself small in the chair as if hoping she'd not be singled out as a 'child.'

When I looked around, about a dozen small hands were raised.

'OK, OK,' the comedian continued, 'so this is for the kiddies. What do policemen eat for dessert?' He paused for a few beats, then shouted, 'Cop cakes!'

Encouraged by a smattering of pint-sized laughter, he forged on with additional 'clean' material. 'A couple of years ago, I heard this knock at my front door. I open it, right, but nobody there. So I start to close the door, when I spot a snail on the doorstep. I pick up the snail and throw in it the trash. Two years later I hear another knock at the door. Again, nobody there except this damn snail. You know what he says? "So what was that all about?"'

Beat. Beat. 'Ba-da-bing!'

A few people laughed, but I suspected most of them didn't get the joke.

Malone changed tactics. 'The captain tells me that we have an international group of passengers aboard this cruise, practically a United Nations. Any Americans out there?'

We raised our hands, as did about half the audience.

'Brits?' he continued.

Maybe twenty hands shot up.

'Canadians? Australians?' He shaded his eyes and peered into the audience. '*No* Australians? Good, so did you hear about the Olympic gold medal winner from Australia? He loved his medal so much he had it bronzed!'

Malone launched into a series of one-liners – 'How does Moses make his tea? Hebrews it!' – like an old-fashioned baggy-pants comic.

I was rapidly losing the will to live.

Julie slouched in her chair. Even in the darkened theater, I could see she was pouting. 'This is so lame,' she said at last.

'I quite agree,' I whispered, 'but I have it on good authority that the magician will be better.'

She jiggled the straw up and down in her Sprite, then drained the glass noisily. 'As if.'

By that time, Malone had lost most of the audience. The noise level in the theater gradually rose as people began talking, or making their way to the bar, and Malone had to shout to be heard over them.

'Did you hear about the dyslexic devil worshiper?' he yelled. 'He sold his soul to Santa!'

After ten excruciating minutes where I was wishing – no, praying – for a shepherd's crook to extend from the wings, hook this clown by the neck and drag him off stage, it was finally over. The curtain rang down, the lights came up, and servers materialized from every corner of the room to take our drink orders.

'I think I need a double,' Ruth groaned.

Julie perched on the edge of her chair and turned to her mom. 'Do I *have* to stay? They're showing part two of *Breaking Dawn* in the outdoor theater tonight.'

'Haven't you seen *Breaking Dawn* numerous times already, Julie?'

'Well, yeah, but I could look at Robert Pattinson all day . . . you know? Please, Mom!'

For some reason, Georgina looked at me. 'Do you think I should let her go up on her own?'

Before I could weigh in with my two cents, Julie quietly erupted. 'Mother,' she moaned, 'I am *not* a child!'

Georgina patted her daughter's bare knee. 'I know you aren't, sweetheart. Are you sure you know where you're going?'

Sensing victory, Julie was already on her feet. 'Of course I do. I've been all over this ship.'

Georgina checked her watch. 'OK, but be sure you're back in the room by eleven-thirty. And Julie?' She reached out and grabbed her daughter's hand, dragging the girl backward. 'Don't make me come looking for you.'

Julie bent down and brushed her mother's cheek lightly with her lips. 'Thanks, Mom.'

With a casual flip of her apricot hair, she turned and bounced up the aisle.

Georgina melted back into the upholstery. 'I think I'll take that refill now.'

I moved into the seat that Julie had vacated and set my empty wine glass down next to Georgina's. Waving my hand, I caught the attention of a server a couple of rows over. 'Help is on the way.'

I was in the middle of telling Georgina about our dinner with David Warren when an officer I recognized from the Neptune Club reception strolled out onto the stage – Bradford Gould, the entertainment director. 'And now, ladies and gentlemen, it is my extreme pleasure to present to you, all the way from Las Vegas, Nee-va-da, the ah-maze-zing Channing!'

From all corners of the theater, spotlights focused, blood red, on the curtain. The theme from *Star Wars* came blasting from the speakers; the curtain rose to reveal Thomas Channing, dressed in traditional tails, his lapels glittering with sequins.

Channing was older than I had expected – in his late forties or early fifties – and extraordinarily tall, perhaps six foot four. His abundant silver hair was swept straight back and glistened blue in the spotlights.

The music grew softer. On a nearby table sat a large silver ball. Channing draped the ball with a black silk cloth and we watched in amazement as it began to rise. When he held the cloth by the corners, the ball didn't drop. It began to dance, floating beneath the cloth. Slowly the ball crept up, until it was riding along the edge of the cloth, hypnotically, back and forth, back and forth. It dove under the cloth again, then up, then down as if the ball had a life of its own.

When the ball trick was over, the music changed. I recognized Zimmer's theme from *Batman the Dark Knight*. The rapid urgency of the strings, accented by the percussion and low brass, washed over us like an oncoming steam locomotive, indicating that something big was about to happen.

Pia Fanucci drifted out on the stage wearing a pink Chinese gown and carrying a parasol. While she danced with the parasol like a lover, Channing wheeled a tall upright cabinet onto the stage. He opened all the doors, Pia climbed in and, one by one, the little doors were shut over her body.

The Zig-Zag Box.

Pia's face, her hands and her left foot were clearly visible through openings in the cabinet's front, and she waggled them just in case anyone in the audience had failed to notice.

As the music surged, Channing inserted two large metallic blades horizontally through the cabinet's mid-section, presumably dividing Pia – ouch! – into thirds. He then slid the mid-section of the cabinet away from the top and bottom thirds, taking Pia's mid-section along with it, turning her into a human zig-zag.

I stared hard at the cabinet, trying to shatter the illusion. I was still puzzling over it, watching closely while Pia's parts were being reassembled, and the wicked-looking blades, one by one, were removed. Then Channing opened the cabinet and Pia stepped out gracefully, completely unscathed. She bowed prettily, then scampered off stage right.

The audience went wild. Spotlights roamed the theater, fog began to curl about the stage, smoky tendrils drifted into the front row of the audience as the familiar strains of Ravel's *Bolero* began to weave their spell.

Pia returned pushing a four-legged, wheeled table. On top of the table sat a woven basket about three feet in diameter. She'd done a lightning quick costume change, and was now dressed in a sunshine-yellow harem-girl outfit, complete with ankle bells and matching toque.

Channing tipped the basket toward the audience and ran his hand around the inside, demonstrating that it was completely empty. He took Pia's hand, holding it while she stepped up on the table and into the basket. Channing passed the lid to Pia, who balanced it on her head, then slowly sank until she was completely hidden inside.

From a nearby table, Channing selected a sabre with a long curved blade, held it overhead by its elaborately decorated handle and brandished the weapon – *snick-snick* – like a Saracen warrior during the Crusades.

Oooh went the audience as the highly polished blade flashed in the spotlights.

From his pocket, Channing produced an orange, tossed it into the air, and with a single *thwack*, split it neatly in two.

Aaah!

The music pulsed, throbbed, intensified. The magician inserted the tip of the sabre into one side of the basket, pushed hard on the hilt as if meeting some resistance, then with slightly more effort shoved it through. A second sabre was inserted in the opposite side of the basket, then a third, and a fourth. Only two sabres remained, and they went into the basket from the top as the audience *oohed* and *ahhed* over the urgent pounding of the soundtrack.

Placing both hands on the table, Channing spun the basket – one, two, three times around. Finally, with a flourish, he whisked off the lid.

For a moment, nobody moved or dared to breathe. Then, gradually, hands raised above her head, Pia emerged, unfolding slowly, sinuously, like a cobra.

We clapped like crazy, of course. Channing took Pia's hand and helped her down to the stage. As gracefully as a prima ballerina, Pia spread her arms and bowed, wobbled slightly, put her hands together prayerfully, bowed again, then backed away on tiptoe, like a good little harem girl, still smiling.

Channing returned to the basket and whirled it around again three times. We thought the trick was done, that he'd take the basket and push it off stage. But Channing had another surprise in store. The music made a crescendo, the magician reached inside the basket once again, and pulled out another young woman, this one dressed in a lime-green harem-girl outfit.

I gasped – along with everyone else in the audience. After a split second of stunned silence, the theater erupted into wild applause.

'Bravo!' I shouted. I cupped my hands around my mouth and

whooped-whooped like a mother at a Little League baseball game.

'Where the *hell* did she come from?' Ruth asked.

Georgina bounced in her seat she was clapping so hard. 'I didn't think there was room for *one* girl in there, let alone *two!*'

'They weren't actually *in* the basket, silly. There has to be a secret compartment under the basket, or a trap door.' Sister Ruth, the skeptic.

If there was a trap door, I couldn't detect it. The basket sat about two feet off the floor on a four-legged table that spun easily on casters. You could see completely under the table, all the way to the magician's polished shoes and as far as the curtains on the other side.

Channing took each woman by the hand, raised their hands high, and the trio bowed in unison. Smiling broadly, Channing released their hands, indicating with subtle flapping motions that they should return to the basket. When they were in position, one on each side, the two assistants spun the table three times – was a *third* girl going to materialize? But no, the show was over. Except for wheeling the basket off the stage, their work seemed to be done.

As I watched the girls go, I noticed a dark spot on the leg of Pia's harem pants. At first I took it for a trick of the stage lights, but then the spot began to grow, spreading quickly from the area of her thigh down to her knee. And was it my imagination, or had Pia begun to limp?

Channing apparently hadn't noticed anything out of the ordinary because he continued to bow right, left and center, basking in the limelight and the applause.

'Ruth, Georgina, look!' I whispered. 'I think Pia's been cut!'

Their attention had been focused on the magician, but they turned to look just as Pia and the basket disappeared into the wings. 'Maybe it's her period?' Georgina suggested. 'God, how embarrassing!'

'Not on the outside of her leg, it isn't!' Ruth pointed out sensibly.

I had visions of a wounded Pia smiling bravely in a show-must-go-on sort of way until she got backstage, then collapsing in a heap of bloody chiffon and gold trim. 'I hope she's OK,' I said.

The second assistant skipped out onto the stage just then, smiling stiffly. Clearly this was not part of the act, because even from where we sat, I noticed Channing's eyebrows shoot up in annoyance. The girl grabbed his hand and bent at the waist, forcing the magician into another bow. With her head close to his, she whispered in his ear.

Within seconds, the two had vanished. The stage was empty. As we watched, wondering and worrying, the emcee rushed into the whirl of multicolored lights and swirling fog, pressing a microphone to his lips. 'Ladies and gentleman, wasn't that spectacular!' His free hand windmilled. 'Please put your hands together for the Amazing Channing and his lovely and talented assistants, Pia and Lorelei!'

But Channing and his two lovely and talented assistants had already made their final bow.

Slowly the applause died out, the emcee bid us goodnight, the fog slowly dissipated, the house lights came up, and we were left to stare at a blank curtain. I wouldn't find out until late the following morning just how talented Channing's assistants actually were.

TEN

'Alcohol is involved in at least 62.5 percent of on-board assaults with serious bodily injury, 35 percent of simple assaults, and 36 percent of sexual assaults. While this data suggests greater concern with responsible serving of alcohol and curtailing alcohol misuse, some cruise lines now offer 'all you can drink' packages at flat rates for the duration of a cruise. Bar sales is one of the top sources of on-board revenue for cruise ships.'
Testimony of Ross A. Klein, PhD before the Senate Committee on Commerce, Science, and Transportation, March 1, 2012

I spent a restless night. When I wasn't stewing about David, I was fretting about Pia. When the first light of dawn finally came, I gave up on sleep. I padded to the bathroom, then stepped into a pair of jeans, wrestled a T-shirt on over my head, slid my feet into a pair of flip flops and slipped out of the room, leaving Ruth huddled under her duvet, gently snoring.

Breakfast wouldn't be served until 6.30 a.m., but I knew that coffee and donuts were available in a corner of the Firebird café for the early birds – joggers, displaced spouses, and insomniacs like me – so I made my way up to deck nine. I filled a mug from the urn, stirred in some half and half and carried it over to a seat by the window where I could watch the water boil white around the hull as the liner sleeked its way through the sea. The Zen of it was calmly reassuring.

From the program I knew we'd be sighting Bermuda by mid-morning and docking at the port of Kings Landing shortly after noon. I hadn't signed up for any excursions, and I was grateful for that now, as I didn't intend to step foot ashore until I found out what had happened to Pia.

'Hannah! I thought I might find you here.'

To my surprise, the speaker was Georgina, who rarely managed to make it out of bed before eight and never, to my knowledge, even ate breakfast. Her hair was twisted into an unruly knot at the crown of her head and held in place with a leopard-print claw clip. She carried a paper cup of coffee in one hand and a powdered donut in the other.

I grinned up at her. 'So, who are you, and what have you done with my sister?'

Georgina snorted, then plopped herself down opposite me. She took an experimental bite of the donut, frowned, set it down on a napkin, then brushed powdered sugar off her dark blue T-shirt. 'Julie's still asleep, and I didn't want to turn on the light, so I decided to wander up for some coffee.'

'How was the movie last night, did Julie say?'

'It was "fine," the popcorn was "gross," the girl she sat next to was "dumb," and the idea of playing Charades was "lame, totally." Believe it or not, Julie was back at the cabin by eleven. I was reading when she came in and I nearly fell out of my bunk.' Georgina tore open a packet of demerara sugar and dumped it into her cup, stirred. 'What gets you up so early? It's not even six.'

'Worried about Pia, I suppose. I'm sure that was blood I saw on her costume.'

'I think so, too. Who can we ask, Hannah?'

I shrugged. 'If she were injured, they must have taken her to the clinic. But I can't exactly go down there and ask. Patient confidentiality and all that. I'm hoping she'll show up as usual at the Oracle today.'

Georgina reached across the table and squeezed my hand. 'I'm sure she's fine, Hannah. She walked off the stage, after all.'

I managed a smile. 'Don't know why I'm being so mother-hennish. Pia reminds me a bit of Emily at that age, I suppose.'

'Attractive, bright, idealistic and strong-headed, right?'

I grinned. 'Get used to it, sweetie. It's genetic.'

'Speaking of Julie,' Georgina said after a moment, 'what are you planning to do today? She wants to hang out at the pool, but I've got an appointment at the day spa for a massage.'

'Nothing definite,' I replied. 'Thought I'd go out on deck and take pictures as we sail into Bermuda. Do you need me to watch Julie?'

'No, no. She'll be fine. Just curious, that's all. How about Ruth?'

'No clue. We decided to talk about it over lunch. Will you be done by then?'

She nodded. 'As relaxed and boneless as a rubber chicken. Let's meet at the Oracle, then. Eleven-thirty?'

I nodded. 'It's a date.'

The Oracle was on deck four, so it was easy to reconnoiter on the way to our stateroom. On my third ever-so-casual pass, a steward I'd never seen before was working behind the bar. My heart sank into my shoes.

I consulted the young man's name tag. 'Prakash, I was looking for Pia. Will she be working today?'

Prakash wiped his hands on a towel and studied me thoughtfully. 'I expect her to arrive sometime this morning, madam. Is there anything I can get for you in the meantime?'

I made a show of consulting my watch. 'I need to check on my niece in a few minutes,' I improvised. 'Do you know when she's scheduled to come on duty?'

'I am so sorry, madam, but I do not. Until Pia comes, I stay.' Prakash began scooping crushed ice into the wine coolers. I'd been dismissed.

I'd actually promised Georgina that I'd check in on Julie from time to time, so I decided to work off the Belgian waffle I'd splurged on at breakfast in the Firebird café by walking up the ten flights of stairs that would take me to the swimming pool area on deck nine. Julie was there, sitting on the edge of a hot tub, her legs dangling, enjoying the whirlpool with two girls about her age. I waved as I passed by, but didn't embarrass my niece by actually speaking to her.

I spent the next half hour at the guest relations desk signing up for an Internet account, and the fifteen minutes after that recovering from sticker shock – sixty-five cents per minute! – over a four-dollar latte at Café Cino.

In the library on deck seven, I spent three dollars and twenty-five cents – five minutes – checking my iPhone for email which consisted of a birthday reminder for my sister-in-law, Connie, and a brief message from Paul saying he loved me and hoped I was having a good time.

I made a pit stop at our stateroom, where I found Ruth taking a shower following a Pilates workout in the fitness center. 'Why you want to exercise on vacation is completely beyond me,' I said as my sister emerged from the bathroom wearing nothing but a towel wrapped around her head like a turban. 'I just stopped by to see what you were doing.'

'There's an acupuncture lecture at 11.00 a.m. I'll be about fifteen minutes late for lunch, if that's OK with you.'

I shrugged. 'Fine. Nobody's calling the roll.'

Ruth stared into the closet. 'What on earth should I wear?'

'To an acupuncture class? Something with teeny tiny holes in it, I imagine.' Promising to let Ruth know the minute I found out anything about Pia, I left her to sort out her wardrobe and dress in peace.

Prakash was still tending the Oracle bar. He looked up suspiciously when I approached, so I simply smiled and ordered a split of the day's special, something called *Cair Blanc*, and carried the glass over to a chair in the corner of the bar where I could keep an eye on the elevators.

Although billed as *demi sec*, the wine had too many apricot notes for my liking. From my chair, I surveyed the room, casting about for a potted palm to pour it into when the elevator doors opened and Pia stepped out.

Overcome with relief, I took a gulp of wine, grimaced then choked it down.

Pia limped across the lobby and slipped behind the bar. Prakash grinned, obviously relieved to see her. He made a production of handing over the towel he'd been using to wipe water rings off the bar, then left as if he had an important engagement elsewhere.

I left my glass on the table and approached the bar. 'Pia, you *were* hurt during the show last night, weren't you?'

She didn't answer my question right away. 'I saw you there, sitting in the second row.'

I nodded. 'I thought the show was terrific, by the way, but after the basket trick, when I saw the blood . . .'

Pia raised both hands. 'There was a little accident, a miscalculation. I'm fine, really.'

'Did you see a doctor?'

'Of course. Tom made me. He was terribly upset, of course.

It was just a scratch, I told him, nothing to worry about, but they stitched it up anyway.' She held up her hand, fingers splayed. 'Five stitches! Imagine.'

'I guess I thought they were trick swords. Clearly not.'

'Oh, the swords are real all right!'

'Or that you weren't really in the basket.'

Pia laughed out loud. 'No, I was actually in the basket. And Lorelei, too. There's more room inside there than you might think.'

'But how . . .' I started to ask, then paused. 'Sorry. I shouldn't be asking you to give away secrets. Wouldn't want you to break the magicians' code and get blackballed or something.'

'Magicians' code? Don't make me laugh. Nothing is secret anymore. You can read about how to do the illusions in any number of books, and a couple of years ago, there was even a Masked Magician on TV. "Magic's Biggest Secrets Revealed."' Pia drew quote marks in the air. 'He wore this God-awful mask like Hannibal Lecter for the early episodes, but eventually you found out he was a magician named Val Valentino. Val's not very popular among his fellow magicians these days, as you can well imagine.'

I decided to bring her back to the point. 'But how did you get hurt?'

'Most people assume that I'm just a bit of fluff, a helpless little tool for the magician, but really, I'm pretty much in charge of that trick. The swords are plunged into the basket in a particular order, so after each thrust, I have time to rearrange myself. Sometimes I even help the sword pass through.'

'So what went wrong last night?'

Pia shook her head and shrugged. 'We've done that trick hundreds of times before, but last night Tom had the swords in the wrong order.' She touched her leg gingerly. 'The second one nicked my thigh.'

'You could have been killed! Or, Lorelei.'

'Yeah, well . . . I probably shouldn't be telling you this, but I'm worried about Tom. He hasn't been himself lately. I even mentioned it to him. What's wrong? I said. You seem preoccupied, but he just shrugged it off.'

Pia raised a finger – *just a minute, I'll be right back* – and left me to serve a glass of wine to a customer. When she came back, she continued where she had left off. 'He claims it's because of this new illusion he's working on. Checking the apparatus, practicing, getting the timing just right. He plans to debut the trick in a couple of weeks, but that's not going to happen if he can't get his act together.' She paused and laughed sadly. 'So to speak.'

'Will you and Tom be working tonight?'

'We're off tonight, but we'll be on again day after tomorrow. I should be fine.' She shrugged. 'If not, Lorelei can fill in and there just won't be an extra girl in the basket.'

'What does Lorelei do when she's not scrunched down in a basket with you?'

'She's a blackjack dealer.'

I'd walked through the Vegas-style casino – almost impossible to miss as it occupied almost half of deck five – but I'd never seen a live blackjack player on duty. They seemed to have been replaced with 'virtual' dealers, video representations – sometimes guys, sometimes gals – that smiled creepily at you from large television screens, with no personality other than the one they'd been programmed with. Like avatars, they say hello and make comments, and their eyes follow you like haunted house characters as you walk by. 'Glad to hear the dealers aren't all robots,' I said.

'Do you play blackjack?' Pia inquired.

'No, but my husband does. He's pretty good at it, too, but he claims that studying the game only helps you to lose more slowly.'

That made Pia laugh.

It was after eleven and the bar was filling up. 'I should let you get back to work, Pia.' I touched her lightly on the arm. 'I'm glad you're OK.'

'Thanks. Can I get you something to drink?'

I waved the offer away. 'Thanks, but no. I've got to meet my sisters for lunch.'

After I left the Oracle, I rode the elevator up to the swimming pool deck, where I paused for a moment at the splash pool to watch in amusement as dozens of squealing, giggling children dashed crazily about, trying to avoid – or not – the water jets that erupted unpredictably around them. Buck Carney, the photographer we'd met earlier in the solarium, knelt on one knee at poolside, capturing their antics on film, seemingly oblivious to the spray that was soaking his shorts.

Julie was no longer in the hot tub, but I spotted her seated at a table near the Tiki Hut Beach Bar with a group of her friends. I thought I recognized some of the boys from the Crawford contingent, but as I drew nearer they beat a hasty retreat, leaving Julie alone with two of the girls I'd seen her with earlier.

Julie grinned when she saw me, set the glass she was drinking from down on the edge of the table where it teetered precariously for a moment, then crashed to the deck in a shower of crushed ice, orange slices and pineapple. She pressed a hand to her mouth. 'Oooops!'

Her companions stared, wide-eyed and innocent as fawns caught in the headlights.

It took a moment for the situation to sink in. 'Julie Lynn, what have you been drinking?'

Julie flushed. 'Dunno.'

Julie's girlfriends shot to their feet, no doubt planning a quick getaway before things turned ugly. I grabbed the freckled blonde by the arm, bringing her up short. 'What's Julie been drinking?'

The girl glanced nervously at Julie, then back at me before stammering, 'Sex on the Beach.'

'Sex on the Beach,' I repeated, just to make sure I'd heard it correctly. 'Sex. On. The. Beach.' Vodka, I recalled. Peach schnapps. A touch of cranberry juice. From the number of empty glasses on the table, quite a few Sex on the Beaches had been consumed at that table, and nobody sitting there now was anywhere near the age of twenty-one.

The blonde was rapidly shaking her head. 'But we didn't . . . I mean, it wasn't me!'

Although frightened, she seemed perfectly sober, which was more than I could say for Julie, who slouched in her chair, grinning crookedly. When I scowled at her, Julie began to giggle.

I released the girl's arm, said, 'You two, get out of here,' and aimed a cold stone glare at my niece. 'Julie Lynn Cardinale, what the *hell* were you thinking?'

Still smiling, Julie shrugged. 'Tasted really good, Aunt Hannah.'

'Get up!' I ordered.

Julie rose unsteadily to her feet, supporting herself by resting a hand on the table.

'How many of those did you drink?' I asked, indicating the debris remaining at the scene of the crime.

'Dunno.'

I seized Julie's face by the chin and forced her to look at me. 'How *many*?'

I'd frightened her now. A tear slid down her cheek. 'Two, maybe three?'

'Come with me!' Holding my niece firmly by the upper arm, I dragged Julie over to the Tiki Bar where Beshad and another bartender whose name tag was hidden by a towel draped over his shoulder were mixing drinks. Rage boiled up inside of me and exploded in the bartender's face. 'Beshad, how old does this girl look to you?'

Beshad started, stared, eyes wide. 'Excuse me?'

'Somebody has been serving this child alcoholic drinks, and for your sake, I hope it wasn't you.'

'I just came on at eleven,' he stammered. He shot a nervous glance at the other bartender. 'But, ma'am, there's no way we would allow someone your daughter's age to buy alcohol. She'd have to show her sea pass to pay for it, and then we'd *know* she was underage.'

I stood there, slack-mouthed, letting the truth of what he'd told me sink in. I confronted my niece. 'Julie, who bought those drinks for you?'

Another tear leaked out of her eye; she swiped it away with her free hand. I felt her shrug. 'Some boys.'

'Boys,' I repeated. 'You mean those boys who hightailed it out of here just before I showed up?'

She nodded.

I dragged Julie over to a chair and helped her sit down. 'If they were buying you drinks from the Tiki Hut, Julie, they were not boys. They were *men*.'

'I knoooow,' she sniffled miserably.

'Were they from that Crawford family, Julie? Jason and whatshisname, Colin?'

She shook her head, ponytail wagging. 'Nuh, no. Not Connor,' she sobbed, but she was staring out to sea when she said it, so I suspected she was lying. After a moment, she turned a tear-stained face to mine. 'Are you going to tell Mom?'

'Of *course* I'm going to tell your mother!'

'She's going to be *so* mad. She'll tell Dad and I'll be grounded for the rest of my life!'

'Everybody makes mistakes, Julie Lynn, but smart people learn by them.'

'Aunt Hannah?' Julie whimpered. 'I think I'm going to barf!' Her eyes were wide and frightened; she pressed a hand against her mouth.

With me holding on to her arm, we reached the rail with only seconds to spare. Julie leaned over it, spewing her breakfast and what remained of the drinks she had consumed all over one of the lifeboats that was tethered several decks below.

There is nothing quite so pathetic as a sick child. Until the dry heaves passed, I held Julie close, stroking her hair.

'Seasick?' someone asked, passing behind us.

'You could say that,' I replied.

Several minutes later I escorted Julie back to her cabin, sat with her until she drank an entire bottle of water, then tucked her into bed to sleep it off.

ELEVEN

'*In 1609, a fleet of nine ships owned by the Virginia Company of London set sail from Plymouth, England with fresh supplies and additional colonists for the new British settlement at Jamestown, Virginia. Admiral Sir George Somers commanded the flagship, the* Sea Venture, *but en route there was a terrible storm and the ship was dashed against Bermuda's treacherous reefs. The crew managed to get to land and so began Bermuda's settlement.*'

Theresa Airey, *www.bermuda.com/visitors*

Needless to say, Georgina was not amused when I tracked her down at the spa. Technicians were still applying a clear coat over the Chick Flick Cherry on her toenails when I ratted Julie out. 'That little . . .!' Georgina sputtered, waving away the technician and rising to her feet. Slightly hampered by neon-green toe separators, she shuffled toward the door, closely followed by the technician who kept repeating, 'Ma'am, ma'am,' as she tried to rescue my sister from the certain tragedy of ruining a forty-dollar pedicure.

I'd planned to spend the early afternoon on deck, sightseeing and taking photographs as the ship negotiated the intricate shipping channel between the coral reefs, making its way north around St George's Island, before heading south-west across the top of the main island and tucking into King's Wharf, the cruise ship harbor directly opposite Hamilton, the capital of Bermuda. Instead, with Julie passed out next door, I spent the time in my stateroom with Georgina, trying to talk her out of hunting down the whole Crawford clan with a double-barreled shotgun.

'Even if we could identify the actual lowlifes responsible for giving Julie those drinks, they didn't exactly *force* Julie to swallow them,' I pointed out reasonably. I thought about Julie leaning miserably over the rail, heaving. 'And I think she's learned her lesson.'

Georgina frowned. 'Ruined my day, I can tell you.'

'I can imagine.' I squeezed her hand. 'When the ship docks, Ruth and I are planning on going ashore. Do you want to come?'

Georgina rose wearily to her feet. 'No, I'd better stay here with Julie. You two go on ahead.'

'Tell you what, Georgina. Ruth and I will case the joint. Then tomorrow, we'll all go out and explore. Sound good?'

'Fine,' she said, without much conviction.

I walked my sister to the connecting door and waited while she checked on her daughter. 'Why don't you stay in our cabin for the time being?' I suggested. 'You can keep the door open; that way you won't disturb Julie.'

'Disturb?' Georgina snorted. 'I'd like to shake that girl until her eyes rattle in that empty skull of hers. But don't worry, I won't.'

Something outside the window caught my eye. The view was no longer the endless blue of the Atlantic Ocean. 'Look,' I said, pointing to the balcony window where the twin clock towers of the Royal Naval Dockyard were picturesquely framed. 'We seem to be in port.'

Georgina wrapped her arms around me and gave me a serious hug. 'I forgot to thank you for taking care of Julie. Not everyone would have stepped in like that.'

'We're family,' I said. 'That's what we do.' I retrieved my handbag from where it hung on the back of a chair. 'Ruth is waiting for me in the atrium. Are you sure you don't mind?'

Georgina made sweeping motions with her hands. 'Shoo, shoo! Don't worry about me. That's why God invented room service.'

Since we missed it, Ruth and I had a late lunch – a proper fish and chips – at the Frog and Onion Pub, a building reclaimed out of the cooperage of the old fort. The shopping arcade in the clock tower offered porcelain, fine china and crystal, silverware, Harris Tweed jackets, and the kinds of Scottish woolen goods typical of duty-free shops everywhere, and were of absolutely no interest to me. I was much more taken with the charming boutiques that featured local art and crafts, and I managed to pick up a few souvenirs for the grandkids at a shop called Bermuda Triangle. With a name like Bermuda Triangle, how could I resist?

At the Dockyard Glassworks I bought a rum cake for Paul,

then spent a good hour drooling over the pieces on sale at Bermuda Clayworks. My credit card would take a major hit, but I couldn't resist one of Joe Faulkner's contemporary salt glaze ceramics – a whimsical, tilted teapot with a teal-colored, orange-peel texture.

Carrying our shopping bags, Ruth and I visited the visitors' information center near the ferry landing, weaving our way to the ticket counter through untidy racks of overpriced souvenir hats and T-shirts. We bought four three-day bus and ferry passes that would allow us to explore the island at our leisure. By then we were exhausted, and a proper English tea was in order. Fortunately, there was a tea room nearby.

The next day, with Julie up and about, but still looking a little green around the gills, we all ventured ashore.

As punishment for her poor judgment at poolside the previous day, Georgina had banned Julie from participating in the teen excursions she'd previously signed up for. Missing the glass-bottom boat cruise wasn't a particular heartbreak, but when her mother yanked her out of the teen swim with the dolphins excursion, too, the lesson stung.

To her credit, though, Julie took the two days we'd set aside to explore Bermuda as an opportunity to rehabilitate herself in our eyes, tagging along with the adults and at least pretending that she wasn't embarrassed to be seen in our company. 'We promise not to bore you with talk about income taxes and the stock market,' I told my niece as we were passing through ship's security in order to disembark.

From King's Wharf, we took the ferry to historic St George, where we picked up a pocket map of the town at the King's Square Visitor's Center not far from a huge bronze sculpture of George Somers, who founded the place in 1609 when his ship, *Sea Venture*, wrecked on a nearby reef. We strolled along the narrow lanes, exploring Bridge House and the Old Carriage House before stumbling onto Somers Garden, named after old George himself.

We toured the quiet garden – sunk several feet below street level and thoughtfully planted with native specimens – pausing at a charming little moon gate to take pictures.

'"Somers intended to return to Bermuda to collect additional provisions for the Virginians in Jamestown,"' Ruth read from the brochure we'd picked up, '"however, he died on the return voyage.

In the event of his death he asked to be buried in Bermuda. His nephew partially honored the request by taking out Somers' heart and entrails and burying them . . ."' Ruth paused and caught Julie's eye. 'You'll like this, Julie. Says here that the nephew sent his uncle's body back to England in a barrel of rum but buried his innards here.'

Julie looked up from her iPhone and rolled her eyes. 'Gross.'

'The amount of time you spend on your iPhone, Julie, anyone would think you're bored,' Ruth teased.

Julie glanced up again from the tiny screen. 'Bored? Nuh uh. When I'm bored I send a text message to a random number saying, like, ' "Don't worry, I've hidden the body" ' or ' "I'm pregnant." ' ' But she tucked the phone into her pocket. 'Signal's not very strong here, anyway, Aunt Hannah. I was just playing Bejeweled.'

'She spends *hours* playing that game,' her mother complained.

As for me, I could have spent hours exploring perfect little St Peters Church on Duke of York Street, built in 1612 and the oldest Anglican Church in the western hemisphere. When we'd exhausted the possibilities at St Peters, the church warden on duty, a white-haired, grandmotherly type, directed us up the hill to the Unfinished Church, a massive Gothic revival ruin perched, cathedral-like, on a hill overlooking the sea. With its towering stone walls, brick columns, grassy floor, and only the sky for a roof, it was the sort of atmospheric ruin, like Tintern Abbey, that sends poets and painters into creative spasms. I had to confess that it warmed my unapologetically Anglophilian heart.

'Was it wrecked by a hurricane?' Julie wanted to know.

'Worse than that. The parishioners squabbled for years over the money it was costing. In the end, it was never finished. Just sat here, abandoned. Hurricanes since then have done the rest.'

Ignoring well-placed signs that warned visitors against venturing inside the crumbling ruin, Julie dashed down the grassy strip that had once been the nave, spinning like a ballerina.

'Julie Lynn, get back here!' Georgina called half-heartedly, but she was smiling when she said it.

Julie skipped back in our direction. 'This would be a cool place to have a wedding,' she said breathlessly, then stopped in her tracks. Something over my shoulder had apparently caught her attention. 'Say, aren't they those people from the ship?'

I turned to see where she was pointing. A group of around twenty was straggling up the steep grade of Government Hill Road. 'I think every tourist in town today is from the ship, Julie. Which people in particular?'

'The ones from Maine.'

I pushed my sunglasses up on my forehead and squinted into the crowd. Indeed, Cliff and Liz Rowe were chugging our way, leading the ragged pack. The photographer, Buck Carney, trailed along after them, like a caboose.

We hadn't seen Cliff or Liz for a couple of days, so when they reached the church a few minutes later, we invited them to join us for coffee after they finished touring the ruin. 'Or are you obliged to stick with the group?' I inquired.

'Not at all,' Liz laughed. 'And I'd welcome a little vacation from some of them, to tell the truth. See that woman in the yellow slicker over there? Honestly, I don't see why she even bothers to leave the ship. "Can't drink the water, can't eat the food, don't know what I'd do without my canned tuna and Tang,"' Liz quoted. 'She's impossible.'

I had to laugh. 'You've been to St George before?'

'Several times. Why?'

'We've invited you for coffee, but we don't have the vaguest idea where to go to get some!'

'Well, you're in luck,' Cliff said, waving his arm in a forward-ho kind of way. 'Follow me.'

Cliff led us back down Government Hill Road to an unpretentious luncheonette on York Street called Temptations Two. We placed our orders at the counter, then squeezed ourselves around a table normally reserved for four by the window, not far from the bottled drink coolers.

'I haven't seen much of David Warren, lately,' I said. 'Has he been to dinner?'

Liz nodded. 'Every night, but he still doesn't talk much.'

'Do you think he's been going on any of the excursions?'

'I very much doubt it,' Cliff huffed. 'The man's on a mission. Thinks he's Sherlock blinking Holmes, but frankly, he's not cut out for it.'

'I told him he should hire a private detective,' Liz chimed in. 'He said he already had. The P.I. took every penny he had, and came up with virtually nothing. So David hired another one, some hotshot P.I. from Miami. Even took out a second mortgage, and cashed in one of his IRAs to pay the guy.'

'And . . .?' I prodded.

Cliff shrugged. 'Don't know. He's still on David's payroll, as far as I know. Throwing good money after bad, if you ask me.'

'Sad,' Ruth said. 'The man's obsessed.'

'He is,' Liz agreed, 'but if it were my daughter who'd disappeared under similar circumstances, I'd be obsessed, too.'

Thinking about Emily, I had to agree. 'What does he hope to do on the ship while everyone else is ashore?' I wondered aloud.

Liz shrugged. 'He told me he was staying on board in order to pursue some line of inquiry. Whatever that means.'

'Means he watches too much *Law and Order*,' Cliff snorted.

I rested my elbows on the table and leaned forward so I could speak without the other customers overhearing. 'What I don't get is this: let's say it wasn't an accident – that, for whatever reason, his daughter *was* murdered and tossed overboard. Let's also assume, as David seems to do, that the person or persons responsible for Charlotte's murder got away with it and are now travelling aboard the *Islander*.'

Everyone nodded. They were with me so far.

'So, assuming I am the murderer, and I find out that my victim's father is on board the same ship and, furthermore, that he is on to me . . . what do I do?'

I didn't realize that Julie was paying any attention until she glanced up from the game on her iPhone and said, 'Bash him on the head and dump him overboard, too.'

I leaned back in my chair, gently patting Julie's ponytail as if she were a good little puppy. 'Exactly. That's precisely what I'd do.'

'Maybe that's why he's keeping such a low profile,' Ruth said.

'A low profile isn't going to cut it,' I said. 'What he needs to do is shake things up a little. And watch his back.' Using a spoon, I scooped the foam out of the bottom of my cup.

Ruth fixed me with a narrow-eyed stare. 'Hannah, you're not going to get involved, are you?'

I paused, took a breath, poised to protest in a no-of-course-not sort of way, but I was already lying awake at night worrying about David, wondering about Charlotte, reviewing scenarios, pondering who Pia's 'usual suspects' were and scribbling lists of possible suspects I'd seen at the Neptune Club reception on the pages of my mind. At lunch the other day, David had responded to my offer of help with a perfunctory don't-call-us-we'll-call-you, but he'd been smiling when he said it, and I took that as a sign of encouragement.

'I think I already am,' I answered truthfully. 'I can't get what happened to Charlotte out of my mind. If it had been Emily . . .' I couldn't go on. I took another breath and let it out slowly. 'If there *is* a murderer on board the *Islander*, Ruth, he's certainly not going to stand up, wave his hand and shout, "Look, it's me, over here!" That's all I'm saying.'

Ruth skewered me with her eyes. 'Unless someone rattles his cage.'

I smiled. 'You might well think that, but I couldn't possibly comment.'

The return ferry deposited us back at King's Wharf with an hour and a half to spare before departure time. Rather than head straight to the ship, we decided to visit the Clock Tower Mall since Georgina had missed it when she stayed in to nurse Julie through a lulu of a hangover the previous day.

I was fingering a gorgeous teal-colored silk pashmina when the first crack appeared in Julie's Dear Dutiful Daughter façade. 'I'm bored,' she whined.

'How about a Bob Marley T-shirt?' her mother suggested.

Julie heaved an exasperated sigh. 'I'd rather have that rainbow hat with the rasta braids. Not!'

Ruth returned the painted bowl she had been checking for a price tag back to the shelf. 'I'm bored, too, Julie. How about we go for Häagen Dazs, just you and me? Nannini's is just at the end of the hall.'

Julie took off in a cloud of dust, with Ruth trailing along behind. After they'd gone, Georgina and I gathered up our purchases – a pashmina for me and a pair of wooden candlesticks for her – and took them to the counter.

I was rooting around in my handbag for my credit card when Georgina whispered, 'Don't look now, Hannah, but there he is again.'

'Who?' I asked, handing my VISA card over to the cashier.

'That photographer,' Georgina said, indicating the next shop over with a jerk of her head.

I craned my neck in order to see over a rack of embroidered tablecloths.

Buck Carney stood framed by a display of ethnic masks. I wondered vaguely what 'ethnic' meant in the context of Bermuda; the masks all wore expressions that ranged from startled to horrified and, unless I was badly mistaken, had been carved out of trees by natives in the Congo.

As I watched, Carney snapped another picture, then lowered his camera. He grinned sheepishly and waggled his fingers in my direction – Hi-How-Are-Ya? – then trained his lens unconvincingly on an elderly couple trying on hats.

'So I see.'

'He looms, Hannah, like Snoopy on the doghouse. I wish I had never said it was OK to take my picture.'

'Why don't you tell him to go away?'

'I tried to. Yesterday he followed me and Julie, and I asked him to stop. Taking my photo is one thing, but I don't want him hanging round Julie. He took on such a sad-eyed, kicked puppy look that I didn't have the heart to say anything further when I saw him snapping away again. It's just a camera, after all, not a gun.'

I remembered thinking something along the same lines when I had originally encountered Buck at the pool, but that didn't stop me from feeling guilty for not acting on my unease at the time. We gathered up our bags and wandered out of the shop, heading in the direction of the ice-cream parlor. There was plenty to mull over and, lost in thought, we walked quietly until we reached a scented-candle shop, where Georgina paused outside for a moment. 'Just what the cruise lines want in their pictorial book, huh? Redhead Sunbathing. Redhead Strolling With Daughter. Redhead Exiting Restroom.'

'You're kidding.'

'I am,' Georgina said with a chuckle, 'but only just.'

It was hard to believe that five days had already flown by when the *Islander* pulled out of King's Wharf for the return trip to Baltimore. Julie had been on such good behavior during our

family outings that Georgina relaxed the rules and allowed her
to return to the teen club. On one condition. Not caring how
much embarrassment it might cause Julie, Georgina actually
escorted her up to Tidal Wave, subjected whatever youth counselor
was on duty at the time to a lengthy interrogation – what will
you be doing? where will you be going? who is going to be in
charge? – before actually letting Julie go.

In the meantime, I was determined to maximize the time we
spent together as sisters, which had been the whole point of the
cruise, after all. After lunch on Thursday, I insisted we all put on
our bathing suits, grab a good book and chill out in the solarium.

It didn't take much arm twisting.

We weren't saying much, luxuriating in the delicious depths
of the whirlpool. I was in a near meditative state with my eyes
closed, until some child – who shouldn't have been in the adults-
only solarium to begin with, I should point out – shrieked. I
opened my eyes, and had to blink twice.

'Georgina, isn't Julie supposed to be at some Nintendo Wii
bowling tournament?'

Georgina shook her head, setting tendrils of her butterscotch
hair trembling. 'What?'

I pointed a wet finger. 'Over there.'

Dressed in her bathing suit, flip flops and a gauzy cover-up,
Julie stood with her back against the etched glass wall of the
Surf's Up café. Supporting himself by one arm braced against
the panel behind Julie's head, Connor Crawford leaned toward
her, his face only inches from hers. We were too far away to
overhear their conversation, but Julie appeared to be amused
because she smiled into the young man's eyes, pushed a hand
flat against his chest and gave him a playful shove.

Georgina rose out of the hot tub as if she'd been shot from a
cannon. Without even stopping to grab a towel, she marched
straight toward the couple, determination in her step and fire in
her eyes. Julie saw her coming, but for Connor it was too late.

Georgina grabbed him by the upper arm and yanked him
upright. 'You! Stay away from my daughter!' she shouted. 'In
case you hadn't noticed, Julie is fourteen years old. Do you
know how to spell that, young man? That's fourteen, as in
J-A-I-L-B-A-I-T.'

Julie's lower lip quivered. 'Stop it, Mother, you're making a scene!'

'I'm s-s-sorry,' Connor stammered. 'We were just . . .'

'I have eyes! I could see what you were just!'

Julie blinked, fighting back tears. 'The Wii was over, and I thought I'd come join you in the pool! Connor was only getting a hamburger.'

I'd reached them by then, still dripping but carrying a towel for myself and for my sister. 'Georgina . . .' I held out the towel.

She ignored me, her attention still riveted on the hapless Connor. 'I'm warning you, young man. If you so much as *touch* my daughter . . .'

Connor raised both hands in front of his face. 'I get it, ma'am. I'm going.' He backed away, stumbled over a lounge chair, then fled through the double doors that led outside to the main swimming pool.

Julie burst into tears. 'This is so embarrassing,' she wailed. 'You've ruined everything! I'm going to my cabin and I'm never coming out. Never! Do you hear me? *Never!*' And she dashed off toward the elevators.

'Well, that went well,' I said, handing a towel to the still-smoldering Georgina.

Georgina used it to wipe the sweat off her brow, then draped it loosely over her shoulders. 'I can't prove it, but I'm convinced that kid is the one who bought Julie those Sex on the Beaches. He probably thought it was hysterical to get a child drunk.'

'We can't be sure if Connor was there or not, Georgina. When I first saw Julie with the boys they were too far away for me to recognize anyone.'

Georgina screwed up her lips, then relaxed. 'Well, now *I* need a drink.'

'Should I go down and check on Julie?'

Georgina shook her head. 'She'll be all right. She'll sulk in the cabin for a bit, until that gets boring, then she'll be out and about, acting as if nothing had happened. Trust me.'

TWELVE

'Passengers are lured to [cruise ship] auctions of suppos-edly investment-grade, collector art. Free champagne flows like water. Since the sales take place at sea, making claims under consumer protection laws is difficult. Buyers may have little recourse if the art is misrepresented. Cruise ship auctions sell the art on display, but the winning bidder actually receives a different (but supposedly equivalent) piece which is shipped from the auction company's ware-house. Many art buyers at cruise ship auctions have later found that their shipboard masterpieces were worth only a fraction of the purchase price.'

www.Wikitravel.org, March 12, 2013

Apparently, Mother knew best.

Bright and early the next morning Julie was up, dressed in a pink-flowered sundress and white sandals, ready to join us in the Oceanus dining room for breakfast. Julie must have been hungry, because she ordered the farmer's special – steak, pancakes, scrambled eggs and fried tomatoes – a breakfast so large and relentlessly American that it would even have pleased the lady toting the emergency tuna fish and Tang.

For several days, the cruise director had been touting an art auction. Over breakfast, we decided to check it out. Ruth and I waited in the atrium while Georgina escorted Julie up to Tidal Wave and supervised while Julie signed up to audition for a teens-only talent show followed by a pizza party.

'Free champagne. What's not to like?' Georgina pointed out when she rejoined us in the atrium about fifteen minutes later. We snagged glasses of bubbly from a passing server. Earlier in the voyage, I'd passed through the art gallery on our way to check out our cruise photos; they'd planned it that way, of course. For the auction, however, space in the photo gallery had been appropriated to accommodate additional paintings, and others were displayed on easels arranged cheek by jowl, encircling the balcony.

Ruth consulted her brochure. 'Tarkay, Fanch, Krasnyansky, Dali, Peter Max . . . I've heard of them, but who the hell's Eslaquit, Tamrat and Loomis?'

I gestured with my champagne flute. 'That's an Eslaquit.'

We stared at the painting, an over-the-sofa-sized representation of a yellow-faced child wearing an electric-blue dress, posing in a field dotted with poppies. 'My God,' Ruth said.

'And here's another one,' I said, moving on. 'You can have a pair, if jaundiced children appeal to you.'

'The brochure encourages us to bid on a piece of this valuable art to take home as a memento of our trip.' Ruth considered me over the top of her reading glasses. 'I didn't see any psychedelic unicorns leaping over rainbows while we were sightseeing, did you? I'd rather take a photograph of Bermuda and have it framed as a memento, thank you very much.'

Artist Mikal Tamrat turned out to be primarily inspired by sunsets – or rises, it was hard to tell – thickly spread with a palette knife in oils of vibrant neon, although Loomis wasn't too bad, if your taste ran to naked figures and disproportional body parts rendered in pastels.

Georgina considered a Loomis thoughtfully while sipping her champagne. 'It's a lot like a puzzle that has to be put back together,' she said, tilting her head to one side. 'Remove the arm from the tree, pick the breast up off the floor . . .'

'Be careful with the bubbly, Georgina, or you might end up owning a painting of dogs playing poker,' I teased, moving on.

Ruth poked me lightly on the arm. 'Say, isn't that what's her name, the woman married to the frequent cruiser guy?'

I had to think for a moment, then it came to me. Nicole Westfall. The wife of Phoenix Cruise Lines' most recent Gold Trident award-winner, Jack Westfall. Dressed in a black sheath, cinched in tightly with a wide gold belt, Nicole balanced on dangerously tall heels behind a French provincial credenza, talking earnestly with a passenger. As I watched, she bent over a notebook, her golden hair swinging loose, and tapped one of the laminated pages. 'She must work for the auction house,' I said as we drew closer. 'This will be a busy day.'

'. . . to be honest with you,' I overheard Nicole tell the man. Ha! Honest people don't feel the need to remind you of how honest they are, as my mother always used to say.

'One must keep one's head about one at an auction,' Ruth announced grandly, 'especially when the bidding is fueled by champagne. It's *my* policy never to pay more than ten dollars for sad-faced clowns or starving orphans. For kittens or Elvis, I'm willing to go a bit higher, but only if they're painted on black velvet.'

That made me laugh so hard that I sloshed champagne on the floor. When no one was looking, I rubbed it well into the carpet with the toe of my sandal.

'This Dali isn't too bad.' Georgina was standing in front of a lithograph of two fishes, one red and one blue, entitled 'Pisces.' 'I wonder how much it's worth?' She peered closer. 'And, look, it's even signed!'

'If we were on land, I could answer that question,' I said, thinking about how often I pull out my iPhone to Google something. 'Maybe that's why they charge so much for the Internet on board, and keep the speed so glacial. Makes it hard to do due diligence.'

None of us were the least bit interested in anything Nicole Westfall had on offer but we were curious, so when the auction began some ten minutes later, my sisters and I stood well back, casually observing what soon became a sort of well-orchestrated, inebriated sales hysteria. Works I wouldn't have paid twenty dollars for – even if I'd had a place to hang them – went for prices in the thousands. 'You may pay a thousand dollars for this painting today,' Nicole drawled into her clip-on microphone, working the audience like a television evangelist, 'but when you get it home, the price can only go up, up, up, and up! Ten, do I hear ten thousand?'

It was as bad as watching QVC.

When one of the Dalis went for twenty thousand, Ruth made quiet *whoop-whoop-whooping* sounds.

I sent an elbow into her ribs. 'Shhhh.'

'Just my bullshit detector going off,' Ruth said. 'And when that idiot gets his masterpiece home and reality sinks in . . . well, I don't think there are any consumer protection laws out in international waters.'

We stayed a few minutes longer, watching in disbelief as Nicole knocked down a Peter Max and a Miro for more than it cost Georgina to send Colin to private school for a year. 'These people are nuts,' Georgina said. 'Let's get out of here.'

We ditched our empty glasses on a tray on top of the piano and retreated to lounge chairs on one of the upper decks where we soaked up the sun, people-watched and read until lunchtime.

After lunch, while Ruth went to the library to return a book, Georgina and I rode the elevator up to Tidal Wave to pick up Julie. She wasn't in the club room proper, nor in the video arcade, so we went looking for one of the youth counselors.

'Maybe the pizza party isn't over yet,' I suggested.

Georgina consulted her watch. 'It's almost two. It has to be over by now.'

The youth counselor on duty behind the desk smiled as we approached.

Georgina squinted at the young man's name tag. 'Wesley, have you seen Julie Cardinale? I checked her in around ten.'

'Cardinale?' He bent his head, ran a finger down a list fastened to a clipboard.

'Right.'

'After the pizza party broke up, she went into the bar.' He hooked a thumb to the right, pointing us toward Breakers!, the teen center's juice bar.

The bar was crowded with young people, sitting on toadstools around small, round tables, enjoying sodas and fruit smoothies. A few were drinking coffee. Everyone was trying to talk over whatever racket passes for music these days. We stood in the doorway and scanned the crowd. 'I don't see her,' I said.

Georgina took a deep breath and marched over to the bar. By the light of a colossal, blue-neon wave mounted and undulating overhead, one of the bartenders, a young woman, was busily filling a blender with ice, bananas and pineapple. The other was running someone's sea pass through a scanner. 'Excuse me,' Georgina asked the guy manning the scanner, 'but I'm looking for my daughter, Julie Cardinale. Have you seen her?'

Rohan from South Africa stared at my sister as if she'd just asked him to calculate the square root of pi out to twenty decimal places. Then he smiled. 'We see a lot of girls here, ma'am. Can you be more precise?'

The blender began to whine and grind. 'She's fourteen, with red hair!' Georgina yelled over the noise.

'Looks just like her mother here,' I pointed out helpfully.

The second bartender switched off the blender and grabbed a tall glass. 'I mixed her a Virginia Colada about half an hour ago,' she said as she poured. 'She was sitting over by the window with a couple of other kids.'

Georgina glanced over her shoulder, turned her head back and said, 'Well, she's not there now.'

While Georgina continued to quiz the bartenders, I wandered over to the tables and asked if anyone had seen Julie. Several of the boys remembered seeing my niece sitting with a mixed group of teens, but hadn't noticed when she left.

Back at the check-in desk, Georgina was having a fit. 'I checked her in at ten-oh-five Wesley, and it was *your* job to keep an eye on her!'

To his credit, Wesley's face was lined with deep concern. 'I'm sorry ma'am, but the pizza party broke up about the same time as the movie was starting, and that coincided with lunch . . . I was totally slammed. You know, she's probably just gone to the restroom, or back to your cabin.'

'*No*, she wouldn't do that. I was taking her for a pedicure at two o'clock. She was supposed to meet me *here*,' she said, stabbing the desk with an index finger.

I laid a hand on my sister's shoulder. 'It's not yet two, so why don't you stay here in case Julie shows up, while I'll go check the cabin, OK?' When she nodded, I said, 'I'll be right back.'

But Julie wasn't in her cabin, or in ours.

Thinking she might have gone to the Firebird for a quick snack, I made a circuit of the buffet before returning, empty-handed, to the Tidal Wave on the deck above.

When I got back, Wesley had found a chair for Georgina and had whipped his hand-held telephone out of its holster, using it to summon his supervisor. Over my head, an annoying squeal designed to attract attention blared out of a speaker, followed by an announcement. 'Will Miss Julie Lynn Cardinale please report to Tidal Wave on deck ten immediately? Julie Lynn Cardinale, report to Tidal Wave on deck ten.'

'Have you checked with the day spa?' I asked hopefully.

Georgina nodded; her lower lip quivered. 'Wesley called them. She's not there.'

'She has got to be on board somewhere!' I insisted. 'I'm going to get Ruth and we'll comb the decks, beginning with the swimming pool.'

But I didn't have to find Ruth; while I was reassuring Georgina, she appeared. 'I was in the library when I heard them page Julie over the P.A. What the hell's going on?'

As I filled Ruth in, Georgina began to weep openly. 'What if she fell down and is lying hurt somewhere?' Georgina turned her tear-stained face to me. 'Oh, God, Hannah, what if Julie has fallen overboard!'

I knelt on the deck in front of my distraught sister. 'It is the middle of the day, Georgina, and there are hundreds of people on deck. If anyone had gone overboard, they would have been noticed. Besides, there are CCTV cameras everywhere, and crew to monitor them. Julie did *not* go overboard. We'll find her, I promise.'

The speaker squealed again with another call for Julie to report to the Tidal Wave. This time when she heard it, Georgina came unglued. 'What is the goddamn point of checking children in if you're just going to let them wander off whenever they damn well please?'

'Settle down, ma'am,' Wesley said.

Georgina's pale face flushed dangerously red. 'Settle down? I'll settle down when Julie's back with me safely, and not one minute before!'

Looking desperate, Wesley punched numbers into his phone and spoke urgently to someone.

'Is there somewhere we can go?' I asked him when he'd finished the call.

'Security is on the way,' Wesley explained. 'They'll know what to do.'

Wesley had called out the big guns: Benjamin Martin, Chief of Security, wearing a crisp white uniform with black epaulets, each bearing two broad and one narrow stripe. I had no idea what the stripes meant on a Phoenix vessel, but if Martin were in the navy, he'd be a lieutenant commander, the rough equivalent of an army major. Accompanying him was a female officer wearing two stripes on her epaulets – his lieutenant, I gathered – who made a beeline for Georgina and introduced herself. 'I'm Molly Fortune. Let's go someplace quiet where we can talk.'

Georgina looked up with red-rimmed eyes. 'But Julie is expecting to meet me here!'

Officer Fortune took Georgina by the upper arm and gently helped her to her feet. 'Wesley will stay here, don't worry. And the rest of the staff is out looking for your daughter as we speak.'

Molly Fortune didn't object when Ruth and I tagged along, following her into the elevator, and out onto deck eight. As we made our way along the corridors, we passed crew members wearing blue vests marked 'security' in yellow. They seemed to be in a hurry.

Fortune led us to an office tucked away between one of the higher end staterooms and the ship's bridge. A desk dominated the room; three computer screens were mounted above it. If this was the *Islander*'s security command center, it was unimpressive. Officer Fortune indicated that we should sit down, then reached into a drawer and pulled out a box of tissues, which she handed to Georgina.

I remained standing. 'Can Georgina stay here with you while I go help with the search?' I asked the officer.

'All passengers are being asked to return to their cabins, Mrs Ives, family included. That's SOP. Standard operating procedure. We've launched a deck-by-deck, room-by-room search for your daughter,' she added, speaking directly to Georgina. 'Please, don't worry. We'll find her.'

'But, even if Julie were in someone else's room, why didn't she answer when you paged her?'

I could figure out the answer to that, but Georgina was already so upset that I kept my mouth shut.

We were startled by a strident blast on the intercom, and a disembodied voice saying, 'Code Adam, Adam, Adam.'

Georgina, who had to recognize the universal code for a missing child, began to wail. Ruth, sitting closest, wrapped Georgina in her arms and began briskly rubbing her back.

'I'm doing nobody any good here,' I said. 'SOP or not, I'm going out to look for her.'

'No, ma'am, you aren't,' Fortune warned. 'We can't have anyone wandering around the ship right now. Please sit down. We'll keep you updated. Can I get you anything? Coffee? Tea? Water?'

We declined, sitting together as we had at Aunt Evelyn's funeral, three silent and very distressed little monkeys, holding hands.

After what seemed like hours, but was probably only twenty or thirty minutes, the intercom crackled to life again: 'Code Sierra, Sierra, Sierra!'

Georgina started. 'What was that? Code Sierra. What does that mean?'

Fortune stiffened, used her phone to made a call and said, 'What's the situation?' As she listened, her shoulders relaxed. 'Good job, thank you. I'll tell the family. They've found Julie,' she said.

THIRTEEN

*'Passengers on cruise vessels have an inadequate apprecia-
tion of their potential vulnerability to crime while on ocean
voyages, and those who may be victimized lack the information they need to understand their legal rights or to know
whom to contact for help in the immediate aftermath of the
crime.'*

Cruise Vessel Safety & Security Act of
2010 (H.R. 3660)

Georgina leapt to her feet. 'Is she all right? Please tell me
Julie's OK!'

Molly Fortune smiled kindly. 'Your daughter's unconscious, Mrs Cardinale, but breathing. They've got her on a stretcher,
and they're taking her up to the medical center right now.'

Georgina grabbed Fortune by the arm. 'I need to go to her!'

'Of course you do, ma'am, and we'll get you there as quickly
as possible. Please follow me.' Fortune held the door open until
we'd all passed into the hallway, then closed it behind her, jiggling
the handle to make sure it was secure.

'Where was she?' I asked Fortune as she hustled us down the
corridor.

'On one of the lower decks, in an area we call I-95. It's
restricted to staff and crew, so we're not sure how Julie managed
to find her way down there. She was overlooked at first because
she was lying behind a stack of cardboard boxes that had been
flattened and bound up for recycling. One of the cooks found
her when he shifted a tub of empty wine bottles.'

I wondered how long Julie would have lain there if the cook
hadn't found her, and promised myself never to complain about
shipboard food.

The medical center turned out to be a state-of-the-art facility
near the bow on deck three, as well-equipped as any of my
doctors' offices back home in Annapolis.

When we arrived, a blue-vested emergency team had just transferred Julie from a stretcher to a gurney in a small examination room. Her hair was disheveled, dirt streaked her cheek, and a lump on her forehead had started to bruise. One foot was bare. A man in a white lab coat, who I assumed was the doctor, stood beside her. With no apology, Georgina pushed the doctor aside and bent over her daughter. 'Baby!'

Julie's head lolled, her eyelids fluttered in a desperate, but unsuccessful attempt to open them. Her lips moved, and she began to mumble.

Georgina leaned closer. 'What is it, darling?'

'Mommy, Mommy . . . I don't feel so good, Mommy.' Her voice was softer than a whisper, her words slurred, but nobody could mistake their meaning.

A nurse elbowed her way into the room carrying a tray of instruments covered by a sterile cloth. As she passed by, Fortune asked, 'Is the girl drunk?'

Georgina's head shot up and schrapnel shot out of her eyes. 'My daughter is *not* drunk. It's perfectly obvious she's been drugged. Just *look* at her!' Georgina picked up one of Julie's hands, raised it a few inches then let it drop where it lay, limp, lifeless, on the sheet. 'Use your eyes, people!'

The doctor stepped forward. 'I'm Doctor Springer. Which one of you is Mrs Cardinale?'

'I am,' Georgina said, her voice laced with exasperation at the dim-wittedness of the question.

'Mrs Cardinale, I understand your concern, but I'll need to examine Julie, and the sooner I can do that, the sooner I can prescribe appropriate treatment. Now, will you kindly step aside? Please?'

Georgina stood her ground. 'Well, I'm not leaving, and neither are my sisters.'

Dr Springer eased a pair of rubber gloves, one glove at a time, out of a dispenser that sat on a glass-fronted steel cabinet. 'That's fine, but bear in mind that I'll need space in order to conduct a proper medical exam. Pick one of your sisters, Mrs Cardinale. I don't work with audiences.'

Officer Fortune took the hint and backed out of the examination room. 'You'll let me know what you find, won't you, Doctor?'

He nodded. 'Of course. Nurse? Where's my stethoscope?'

'I'll go,' Ruth said graciously, saving Georgina the embarrassment of having to choose one sister over another. 'Georgina, do you want me to try to contact Scott?'

'God, no! *Please* don't call Scott until we have something definite to tell him!' A fat tear rolled down Georgina's cheek. 'Scott is going to kill me, he's absolutely going to *kill* me!'

I wrapped an arm around my little sister and drew her close, trying to comfort her as she sobbed. 'This isn't about you, Georgina, it's about Julie. And if we're passing the blame around, sweetheart, it was *Scott* who insisted you take Julie along on the cruise in the first place. But, you know what? *Nobody* is responsible for what happened to Julie except the person who attacked her. Not you, not Scott, not even those overworked young counselors in the Tidal Wave. Now, let's give the doctor space. Let the man do his work.'

Georgina resisted my efforts to pull her away from Julie's side. She seemed stuck there, like glue. I tugged again on her arm, and she stepped away with me so suddenly that I stumbled. I recovered quickly, though, and dragged her aside until we were standing with our backs pressed against the wall, watching anxiously from the sidelines as Dr Springer moved a stethoscope around Julie's chest, listening carefully each time, then lifted each eyelid and shone a light into her eyes.

'Are you a *real* doctor?' Georgina wanted to know.

Dr Springer didn't bother to look up. 'Yes, ma'am, with a medical degree from Baylor and everything. It's hanging on the wall out there in the office if you want to see it.'

'So why are you working on a cruise ship?' she sneered.

Dr Springer snorted in amusement, but chose to ignore her. He picked up one of Julie's arms, resting her small hand on his beefy palm. 'Julie, can you move your fingers for me? Julie?' He laid a hand on her ankle. 'Can you move your toes, Julie? C'mon, wiggle those piggies.'

From where I stood it looked as if, from the neck down, Julie was about as capable of moving her extremities as a rag doll.

The nurse arrived and clipped a blood pressure monitor on Julie's index finger, then drew a sample of blood from her arm.

I'd taken Julie to the doctors before, when she was a child, and the fact that she wasn't cringing, whining pitifully and backing away from the needle now simply broke my heart.

Nonetheless, I was impressed with the thoroughness of Dr Springer's exam. In the bedside manner department, I gave him an 'A,' too. He talked soothingly to my niece throughout the whole process, just as if she were awake. 'Julie, I'm going to examine your abdomen, now – you might feel a little pressure. And I'll need to lift your dress.'

Springer lifted the hem of Julie's sundress and eased the dress up to her waist. Georgina gasped then, and I noticed it, too. Julie's underpants – white cotton with tiny rosebuds, childlike and innocent – were torn. 'My God, my God, somebody's raped my baby!'

'We don't know that yet, Mrs Cardinale.' Dr Springer turned to the nurse who had been hovering at his elbow. 'Jeannie, *please* escort these women into the waiting room, then bring me a rape kit.' His arm shot out, grabbed the track-mounted cubicle curtain and drew it around the gurney on which Julie lay, cutting off our view. His well of patience with my sister had clearly dried up.

Moving Georgina the ten feet from the examination room into the outer office was a feat of strength; her shoes must have been made of lead. Eventually I managed to haul her to a chair next to Ruth, and I plopped down gratefully in the chair on the other side.

'Where's Security now, that's what I want to know!' Georgina folded her arms across her chest and scowled.

'They're probably securing the crime scene,' I told her. 'That's what professionals do.'

'We need to call somebody,' Georgina said. 'The F.B.I. has jurisdiction. Isn't that what George Whatshisname said?'

'Warren, and it's David. Yes, I believe that's what he said.'

'Whoever did this is going to pay.'

I had to agree with that and, if he valued his genitals, he'd better hope the F.B.I. found him before we did.

After ten agonizing minutes, Dr Springer rejoined us. 'We won't know until the blood work comes back, but I'm almost certain your daughter was drugged. From her symptoms, I'm guessing Ketamine, possibly Rohypnol or GHB, commonly known as date rape drugs. Ketamine can cause paralysis, loss of time, memory problems, distortions of sight and sound, among other symptoms. I think you should be prepared for Julie not being able to remember much about what happened to her.' He paused to let this soak in. 'The good news is that there is no evidence that Julie was raped. She has bruises on her upper arms, and on her thighs, but there's no sign of vaginal trauma. Your daughter is still *virgo intacta*.'

Georgina began to weep again, more quietly this time. 'Thank God, oh, thank God.'

'Is there an antidote for Ketamine?' I asked.

The doctor shook his head. 'She'll have to sleep it off, I'm afraid. Wait for the drug to pass out of her system. We'll keep her under observation here for a while to make sure there are no problems with her respiration. This can be an issue when she wakes up, particularly if she begins to vomit. And once your daughter does come out of it, Mrs Cardinale, you'll need to see that she drinks plenty of water.'

Georgina nodded. She understood. 'Can I stay with her?'

'Of course.' He tucked his pen into his pocket. 'One more thing.'

'What's that?'

'She'll need a change of clothing. I asked the nurse to bag up the clothes that Julie was wearing in case they're needed as evidence.'

'Thank you,' I said, feeling grateful that the doctor seemed to know what he was doing. 'Can we see Julie now?'

'Certainly.'

Back in the examination room with Julie, with the privacy curtain pulled around us, I eased my iPhone out of my pocket and tapped the camera app.

'Hannah! What the hell are you doing?'

'I'm taking pictures, Georgina, for evidence.' I photographed Julie's face, smoothing her hair back to get a better view of the bruise on her forehead. I took pictures of the marks on her arms and on her thighs. I captured a close-up of the broken fingernail – our girl had put up a fight – and the torn underwear.

Better to be safe than sorry, I thought. If the ship's security was not our friend – if Dr Springer's test results mysteriously vanished . . . I tucked the iPhone into my pocket and patted it protectively. Julie's insurance policy.

'What do we do now?' Georgina asked, stroking her daughter's hair.

'We wait until Julie wakes up; hopefully she'll remember at least some of what happened.'

FOURTEEN

'A ship on the high seas is as good as lawless.'
60 Minutes, 'Ships of Shame,' April 8, 2012

When Julie finally awoke, it was nearly dinnertime. The first thing she asked for was a glass of water.

They had transferred her to a hospital bed, so I cranked up the headboard. She managed to take a couple of sips from a water bottle, while I busied myself adjusting the pillow more comfortably behind her head. Julie patted the sheets, lifted the blanket, then gazed around the room in apparent confusion. 'Where am I?'

'You're in the ship's clinic, Julie.'

'Why? What happened?'

'We were hoping you could tell us that.'

Julie closed her eyes, squeezed them tight and rocked her head from side to side against the pillow. 'I don't remember.' She took a deep, shuddering breath. 'What happened to my clothes?'

Georgina leaned a hip against the edge of the mattress and laid a hand on her daughter's arm. 'They found you down in the recycling area, near the ship's kitchens, Julie. Do you know how you got there?'

Julie rubbed her forehead and winced. 'No! I've never been to the kitchens.'

'We came to pick you up at the Tidal Wave after the pizza party, but you weren't there. What did you do after the pizza party, Julie? Please think!'

Julie screwed up her face until her eyes almost disappeared. 'It's kind of a blur. I remember that it was early, so Katie and I decided to go to the bar and get a smoothie or something.'

'Julie, you have to tell me the truth. You weren't drinking again, were you?'

Julie's eyes grew wide. 'Alcohol? No, mom, honest! I had a coconut smoothie, I swear! Katie had a Coke.'

I glared at my sister. Upsetting Julie wasn't going to get us anywhere. 'The doctor suspects that somebody put a drug in your drink,' I said, trying to defuse the situation. 'Something that made you pass out. Did you see anybody do that, Julie?'

Julie sucked in her lower lip and shook her head.

'Did you leave your drink unattended?'

'No, never.' In spite of the direction of the conversation, she brightened. 'Nobody could put something into the drink anyway, Aunt Hannah, because it was in a plastic glass with a cover on it, you know, with a little hole for the straw!'

'That leaves the bartender, I suppose, or one of the waiters,' I suggested.

Julie folded her arms and frowned. 'No way. Not Wes. Not Ally.'

Wes had to be Wesley, but who was Ally? The female bartender we talked to wore a name tag that said 'Kira.'

'His real name's Aloysius,' Julie explained when I asked. 'He's from the Philippines.' She turned to Georgina. 'He's really nice, Mom, and he sends all his tip money back home to his mom. She lives in Olongapo, near where the naval base used to be.'

Dad had been in the navy, so I knew all about 'Gapo,' a city on Subic Bay near the naval base that the U.S. had turned back to the Philippine government following the Vietnam War. From what I understood, it was now covered with volcanic ash from the eruption of nearby Mount Pinatubo in 1991. What surprised me was that Julie knew so much about Gapo. Clearly she'd spent time chatting with Ally.

'When you left the bar, did Katie go with you?' Georgina asked.

Julie looked blank. A single tear rolled sideways down her cheek. 'I don't know.'

'What I want to see is the security camera footage,' Ruth said. 'That should tell us who was sitting with who and when. I wonder when we can talk to Officer Martin? Surely he's had a chance to review the tapes by now.'

'He told me he'd be looking at the tapes and getting back to us as soon as he had anything to report, and I trust him to do that,' I said. I felt as if I'd lived a hundred years since that morning, and now that Julie was safe, all I could think about was sleep. 'Georgina, if it's OK with the doctor, I think we should get Julie back to her own bed. And I don't know about you all, but I'm not thinking too clearly just now. We could all do with a little sleep.'

In the middle of the night, Julie was shaking me awake. 'Aunt Hannah, I remember something.'

I sat up in bed, not sure for a moment exactly where I was. I squinted at my niece in the dim light. 'Where's your mother, Julie?'

'She must have taken a sleeping pill. I tried to wake her up, but she just groaned and rolled over. I have to tell somebody before I forget.'

'Sit up here next to me, then, sweetie. I'm listening.'

Julie crawled onto the narrow bed and snuggled up against me. We leaned against the bulkhead and, although it was comfortably warm in the room, I covered our legs with the duvet. 'It's all fuzzy, like a dream, you know? But, there was this man,' Julie began.

My heart did a somersault, so I took a deep breath and tried to remain calm. 'Tell me about him.'

'He was wearing this black shirt with a little squiggle on it.' She pointed to her left breast. 'Right here, like on the pocket? I've tried and tried to remember his face, but it goes all weird on me. But I know the man had a ball cap on.'

Well, that narrows it down, I thought. Every man on board the ship must have a polo shirt and a ball cap in his suitcase, and half the women, too.

'Did the ball cap have any writing on it?'

Julie looked puzzled, then her face brightened. 'I was going to see the dolphins!'

That brought me up short. 'Dolphins?'

'Well, I missed the dolphin trip, Aunt Hannah, so when he said there was a place on the ship where I could see dolphins . . .' Her voice trailed off. 'That was pretty dumb, wasn't it?'

I put my arm around Julie and drew her close. 'You're the bravest girl I know, Julie. And what you've just told me is important. I think we need to wake your mother up now, and talk to Officer Martin. You probably don't remember him, but he's the head of security on this ship.'

Julie's lower lip quivered. 'Do I have to, Aunt Hannah?'

I nodded. 'We don't want the man who attacked you to get away with it, do we? What if he tries to do something to another girl? You were very lucky to get away.'

Julie's hand flew to her mouth. 'I think I'm going to be sick!'

The room stewards liked to surprise passengers by folding towels into whimsical animal shapes. On our first night at sea we had giggled over an orangutan clipped to a pants hanger. That night, Pradeep had transformed my towel into a floppy-eared puppy and had propped my sunglasses up on its nose. I'd set the 'dog' on my bedside table and I grabbed it now, sending the sunglasses flying. I pressed the towel into Julie's hands, and she held it to her mouth as she raced to the bathroom.

All the time I was dialing the telephone I could hear Julie retching miserably. There's nothing worse than being sick to one's stomach; any chemo survivor will tell you that. As I listened to Julie moan, I fantasized about going after whoever had done this to my niece with a pair of rusty garden shears, then dumping him – and his parts – overboard.

When I got through to Officer Martin, he agreed to meet us in our cabin right away, even though it was nearly one-thirty in the morning. While I waited, I shook Ruth awake and explained about Julie, then I went to the cabin next door to try to rouse my younger sister.

The four of us were sitting on the beds in the stateroom I shared with Ruth when Officer Martin arrived along with Molly Fortune who, judging from the notebook she was carrying, was there to listen and take notes.

We asked Julie to repeat what she'd told me earlier.

Hands folded on her lap, Julie obliged; then she bowed her head and studied her thumbs. 'He said he was taking me to see the dolphins.' She looked up. 'You don't have dolphin tanks on the *Islander*, do you?'

Martin smiled sympathetically. 'No. The owner has deep pockets, but not that deep.' After a moment, he asked gently, 'When you went to see the dolphins, Julie, where did this man take you?'

'There was this room, like a living room, with chairs and a coffee table and a sofa and things.' She rubbed her eyes with her fingertips as if trying to clarify the vision.

'Was there a window?' he pressed.

'I don't remember. I suppose there was a window.'

'Was it a room like this one?'

Julie's head wagged from side to side. 'No, I said like a living room. It didn't look like a normal cabin. And, wait! There was candy on the table! The kind that comes in the gold box!' She inspected her thumbs again, put one to her mouth and chewed on the nail. 'I can't believe I was so stupid!'

'Gold box?' Martin asked. Apparently he'd never bought the women in his life posh chocolates.

'Godiva,' Ruth and I answered simultaneously.

Impatient with waiting for Martin to get around to telling us about it, I asked, 'Have you been able to review the security tapes, Officer Martin?'

'We have. They captured Julie and her friend going into Breakers! and placing their orders at the bar. We see the two girls sitting at a table near the window, then three boys come up and join them . . .'

Georgina exploded. 'Crawfords, I'd bet my life on it! I am going to kill . . .'

Martin raised a hand to silence her. 'None of the other teens touched Julie's drink. We're sure of that. We've located Julie's friend, Katie, and interviewed her. She confirms everything that we can see on the tapes. The boys join them at the table, the waiter delivers the drinks, everyone is laughing and having a good time, the boys leave, then, according to Katie, Julie says she feels funny and has to go to the bathroom.'

'I don't remember that,' Julie said.

'On the way to the restroom, Julie goes around the corner and moves out of camera range. We have security cameras in all the lobbies, Mrs Cardinale, and Julie never got to the restroom, not on deck ten nor on any other deck. But what we did notice before she vanishes is that Julie is already weaving and staggering, holding on to the handrails for support. Ketamine is fast-acting, so we know that the drug had to be introduced into her drink by someone – either crew or another passenger – while Julie was at Breakers!'

'How about the glass she used?' I wanted to know. 'Do you know what happened to it?'

Martin frowned. 'It went out in the trash, along with literally thousands of others exactly like it.'

Georgina jumped to her feet. 'Call the F.B.I.,' she demanded. 'We're U.S. citizens – they are obliged to investigate.'

'I've already done that,' Martin said. 'Federal agents will be meeting the ship when it docks in Baltimore the day after tomorrow.'

'You're going to let everybody off the ship?' Georgina stopped pacing. 'The *pervert* who attacked my little girl, and who knows how many other little girls just like her, is simply going to *walk . . . off . . . this . . . ship*?'

'We will be turning all the evidence we've collected so far over to the F.B.I., Mrs Cardinale. They'll have a complete manifest – the name, address and photograph of everyone on board *Islander* right now – and that includes passengers, staff and crew. We've made copies of all relevant security tapes. They'll have the rape kit and the results of the tests we ran on Julie when she was brought in to our clinic, along with her clothing. And I can assure you that the place where Julie was found has been photographed and secured so that nobody can disturb it until the F.B.I. has completed their investigation.'

'The place where Julie was found has been secured, not the place Julie was attacked,' I pointed out. 'Because we don't know where she was attacked, do we?'

'No,' Martin said simply. 'Nor can we simply assume that because she was found in a crew area of the ship that a crew member was responsible. The room she described might belong to a passenger, or to one of the staff. There are any number of ways your niece could have ended up down on I-95. Our key card system is reliable, but not infallible.'

'I have a question about the security tapes,' Ruth chimed in after a respectful silence to let what Martin had just said soak in. 'This didn't happen to Julie in broad daylight. She had to have been taken somewhere private, where nobody could see. And Julie said the cabin had a living room, so it had to be bigger than this cabin, surely. Wouldn't that narrow it down?'

'*Islander* has over one hundred cabins larger than this one,' Martin explained gently. 'Doubles, and some smaller singles, too, some with living room configurations.'

I picked up from where Ruth left off. 'But all the cabins are directly off corridors, right? So at least *one* of the security cameras must have picked up on a guy in a black polo shirt wearing a ball cap and leading a young girl down the hall!'

Martin flushed. 'We don't have cameras in the stateroom corridors, I'm afraid. Surveys have told us that passengers consider it an invasion of privacy.'

I blew a raspberry. 'Why? Because they're bed hopping in the middle of the night?'

'Something like that. Or fighting, or throwing up on the carpet, or pouring beer over someone's head.' Martin sighed. 'Alcohol is too readily available. It doesn't make my job easy.'

Georgina wasn't impressed. 'As far as I can tell, this had nothing to do with alcohol, did it? What I want is for you to find this pervert and lock him up. You have a brig on board for this purpose, I presume?'

'No, ma'am, we don't, but until we get into port, this guy – whoever he is – isn't going anywhere.' He heaved himself to his feet. 'Is there anything else I can help you with tonight?'

'Thanks, no,' I said after a moment of silence had passed. 'Georgina?'

My sister, straight-lipped, shook her head.

Officer Martin opened the cabin door and stepped into the hall. Molly Fortune started to follow then paused, seized my hand and spoke to me, fast and low. 'You might want to contact an attorney,' she said.

'OK, but why?' I whispered back. 'Didn't you call the F.B.I.?'

'Oh, yes, he called the Feds. But that *first* call? It was to Boca Raton.'

Now I was thorough confused. 'What's in Boca Raton?'

'Phoenix Cruise Lines' headquarters,' she said ominously, then slipped out the door.

After Martin and Fortune left, the four of us sat in silence for a while, thinking. There were calls to make, to be sure, but until the *Islander* reached land we were pretty much on our own.

'Well, ladies,' I said at last. 'The way I figure it, we have little more than twenty-four hours to track this bastard down. And I think I know just where to begin.'

FIFTEEN

*'Unlike police in a community setting, who are objective
and are a disinterested party in their investigation, shipboard
security personnel are compromised by the fact that they
must investigate crimes on board a ship where their own
employer may be complicit in, or party to the crime. Can
these security personnel truly act in a disinterested, objective manner that places the interests of the victim above
those of the organization from which they receive their
paycheck and continued employment?'*

Testimony of Ross A. Klein, PhD before the Senate
Committee on Commerce, Science, and
Transportation, March 1, 2012

'It didn't happen,' Pia said. 'You know that's the answer I have
to give.'

'But young girls *have* been attacked before Julie!' I
pounded the flat of my hand on polished surface of the Oracle
bar. 'And it will happen again, and again, and again. Who knows
how many others will be assaulted if we don't unmask this
pervert. We've got to stop him, now.'

'I don't understand what you want *me* to do.'

'You're a smart woman, Pia, and I think you're starting to put
it together, just like Charlotte did. Julie's drink was spiked with
drugs and she disappeared from the Tidal Wave's bar. But she
wasn't the first girl that happened to in the Tidal Wave, was she?
You haven't told me the whole story, Pia. What are you hiding?'

Pia pasted on a smile. Her eyes darted nervously from one
corner of the lobby to the other. 'We can't talk about that here.'

'I completely understand, but where *can* we talk about it?'

Pia checked her watch. 'I'm supposed to be meeting Tom at
ten to practice with the new apparatus. He's setting it up backstage at the Orpheus, and I know there are no surveillance cameras
back there. Why don't you meet me there?'

So, Pia didn't want to be spotted talking to me on the surveillance cameras. I wondered why. 'You're frightened, aren't you?'

'Let's just say that there are some people who don't want to upset the status quo. Sometimes the safest thing is not to get involved.' Her hand shot under the bar and came back holding a Coke. 'Here, pretend you ordered it.'

I could understand Pia's reticence. Charlotte had been her roommate, and when Charlotte decided to get involved, it had cost her her life. 'I promise we'll be careful.'

When I saw Pia again a few minutes later, she was backstage helping Tom secure the clamps on four Plexiglas cylinders, approximately the diameter of a human body, joining them to make one longer cylinder. 'They have O-rings,' Tom explained, 'just like the sections of a rocket. Completely waterproof.'

I perched on one of the wooden crates that I assumed the cylinders had been shipped in. 'I've read about Houdini's water torture chamber. Is it like that?'

Tom swept a lock of silver hair out of his eyes and grinned. 'Nothing like that. There's going to be a ship's propeller spinning around in the middle of it.' He drew circles in the air with an index finger. 'Pass a watermelon through there . . . *wissshh, womp-womp-womp!*'

I was getting the picture. 'Then you send a person through? Ouch!'

Tom winked and his ice-blue eyes twinkled. 'That would be telling.'

For the first time in several days, I saw Pia smile. 'Note the nautical theme. Tom's very pleased with himself.'

'What will you call the illusion?' I asked.

Tom grinned. 'Haven't decided yet. If you have any ideas, let me know.'

'Have you ever performed the water torture trick?' I asked the magician.

'Back in the day,' Channing replied, without looking up.

'Tom started out as an escape artist,' Pia chirped. 'Handcuffs, locks, straitjackets, the whole nine yards.'

All of the props for Channing's magic act were stored neatly around us, fitted together like a jigsaw puzzle, taking up as little space as possible in the otherwise spacious backstage area. I saw the Indian Sword Basket and the Zig-Zag Box, and another box painted in yellow, red and green like a circus wagon. 'What's that?' I asked. 'I didn't see it in the show.'

Pia answered, 'A Vanishing Cabinet. We alternate between that and the Zig-Zag Box. Can't have the same show every night or the audience will get bored.'

Tom appeared to be completely absorbed with the adjustments he was making to one of the clamps on his illusion. I didn't waste any time getting to the point. 'Where were we, Pia?'

'There have been a number of sexual assaults during the time I've been working for Phoenix Cruise Lines, Mrs Ives, but the girls weren't as lucky as your niece. Most of them were raped.'

'How many victims?'

'I don't know exactly, but there were rumors. Four or five, at least.'

I sucked air in through my teeth. 'And they never caught who did it.'

'No.'

'What I don't understand is why the parents of the victims didn't come forward, make a fuss. How come it's not all over Fox, CNN and the local six o'clock news?'

'Security staff have been instructed to make the problem go away,' Pia confided. 'Sometimes they intimidate the parents – your daughter was drinking, she was acting flirtatious, dressing like a slut. They'd guilt-trip the parents, too, who were more than likely whooping it up in the casino while their daughter was being raped by some lowlife.'

'Blame the victim.'

'Exactly. I've heard of cases where Security lost the evidence, or never collected evidence in the first place. Security tapes that exonerate the cruise line? Feds are welcome to them, but if they happen to show the cruise line at fault? Ooops! Wonder what happened to that tape? Camera must have been broken, or we accidentally recorded over it.'

Pia paused to take a breath. 'When I was on the *Voyager*, before Char went missing, a fifteen-year-old was kidnapped, raped and left for dead in a sex cabin on deck three. Did they secure the cabin? They did not. Housekeeping was instructed to clean it up. So there was absolutely nothing for the F.B.I. to investigate when they finally came on board in Los Angeles.'

I held up a hand. 'Back up a minute. "Sex cabin?" Please tell me you're joking.'

Pia smiled grimly. 'It's an empty cabin – could be anywhere on the ship. The crew knows where they are and they use them for sex, generally with each other.'

'Pia, you're telling me that Security has a vested interest in covering things up, but yesterday I got exactly the opposite impression from Ben Martin. He responded quickly, got his team organized, found Julie fairly quickly, and seemed really concerned about conducting a thorough investigation. I'm sure he wants to get the case off his desk – as he says, he's not a policeman – and he's assured us he's planning to turn everything he's got over to the Feds.'

'That's Ben. He's seems to be a straight arrow. The security guy that came before him? Not so much. He'd actually offer the parents of the victims stateroom upgrades, fifty percent refunds, trip vouchers . . . and if they really made a fuss, he was authorized to pay them off in cash, if only they'd just shut up and go away.'

I couldn't imagine Georgina settling for any amount of money as compensation for what had just happened to Julie. And I wouldn't want to be within shooting range if anybody tried. 'Despicable,' I said.

'But if you felt you had no recourse . . .' Pia shrugged. 'I guess getting some money out of it was better than nothing. Once you get off the ship? Forget about it. Phoenix lawyers up.'

I thought about Ben Martin's call to Boca Raton and got a sudden chill.

'Ouch! Dammit!' Tom was sucking on his finger, scowling at his screwdriver.

'Need help?' Pia asked.

'No, no. It's under control. You girls go ahead, chat, have fun.'

'Fun?' Clearly the man hadn't been listening.

'Back there you asked me if I was frightened,' Pia continued. 'I'm freaking paranoid, Mrs Ives! As you know, Charlotte worked as one of the youth counselors, so she must have seen something. She'd figured it out, I'm pretty sure of that, and she was about to blow the whistle. That's why she was murdered.'

'You were her roommate. Did she tell you who she suspected?'

'We shared a cabin, that's all, Mrs Ives. Our schedules didn't coincide. I'd be finished with the show by around nine, but she'd often be up until one or two in the morning, babysitting the little brats until their shit-faced parents showed up to claim them. By the time she came stumbling in, I'd usually be asleep. So, no, she never said. But she was upset about something; I couldn't help but notice that.'

'And we know from Charlotte's father that she had a problem and needed his advice.'

'Yes.'

'Have you seen David lately, Pia?'

She shook her head. 'Not since he tracked me down at the beginning of the voyage – you came over to speak to me just after that, remember? – and asked me some questions about Charlotte.'

'Like?'

'Like the questions you've just been asking me.'

'You know what I think, Pia?'

Pia's eyes narrowed cautiously.

'With Charlotte out of the picture, there are three people who can solve this puzzle – you, me and David Warren. I think we should get together, lay all the pieces out on the table and see what we come up with. Are you willing to do that?'

Pia shifted uncomfortably on the crate, slid her hands under her thighs and rocked back and forth on them, considering. 'OK, but we need to be careful. I don't want to end up like Char.'

'We'll be very careful. And we may have an ally that Charlotte didn't have. The security officer on this ship *seems* to be an honest man, but I really trust his assistant, Molly Fortune.'

I had a sudden thought. 'They tell me Julie was found down near I-95 in the crew-only area. Do you know where that is?'

Pia nodded.

'I'd like to see it. Can you take me there?'

'You're serious? No, wait a minute. I can see from the expression on your face that you are.' She hopped off the crate. 'Stand up, let me look at you.'

I did as I was told.

'I think that outfit will do.' She turned to the magician. 'Tom, what did you do with that clipboard?'

Tom gestured vaguely with his screwdriver. 'Over there, under the drape.'

Pia retreated into a dark backstage recess and returned holding a clipboard with a pen and several pieces of paper attached to it. She handed it to me. 'As long as you have a clipboard, you can be in any place at any time.'

Patting myself on the back for being clever enough to dress in a uniform-like polo shirt, Bermuda shorts and running shoes that morning, I followed Pia out of the Orpheus Theater and around the corner to a crew-only elevator, tucked away in a corner. I'd passed it almost every day without noticing.

Pia flourished her staff ID. 'Magic powers!' She swiped it over the magnetic card reader next to the elevator and, when the doors slid open, we climbed aboard.

When we emerged from the elevator on one of the lower levels of the ship, Pia led me through narrow hallways that were marked off into zones; the stairways were also numbered. 'This way,' Pia said as she preceded me down a steeply pitched, uncarpeted stairway. Clutching the clipboard to my chest, I grabbed the iron railing with my free hand to steady myself as I practically stumbled down the steps after her. We passed a white wall phone and a water fountain in a crew assembly area where framed citations and extensive deck plans hung on the bulkheads. I didn't see any security cameras, and there were no windows.

'Here we are,' Pia said at last.

Ahead of me, green and white linoleum stretched on forever down a wide corridor that must have run the entire length of the ship. To one side of the door hung an oversized, shield-shaped, red, white and blue Interstate road sign. 'I thought Martin was kidding about I-95,' I told Pia. 'But there it is.'

'All Phoenix ships have signs like that,' she explained. 'And don't ask me why I-95 and not, say, Route 66.'

As we were talking, a man passed by wearing a white cook's uniform and a red bandana tied loosely around his neck. He considered us curiously, but I simply waved my clipboard. 'Have a great day,' I said, smiling toothily. He touched fingers to his forehead in a casual salute and hurried on.

The recycling center was unbearably hot and reeked of wet, rotting vegetables. Ranging off to one side was a double row of large plastic garbage cans, exactly like the ones Paul and I put out on the curb at home. A couple of yellow handcarts sat to one side, next to a cube of folded cardboard boxes about four feet high that was stacked on a pallet.

'This is horrible,' I said, trying not to breathe as I gawped at another row of trash cans brimming with glass bottles – white, green, brown – all sorted by color. 'This is where he brought her?'

Pia sighed. 'I think this is where he dumped her.'

'But Officer Martin told me that he'd roped off the place where Julie was found with crime scene tape or something. I don't see that.'

'Let's explore.' Pia skirted a small forklift, led me past an enormous steam pipe – about eight feet in diameter, wrapped with insulation – and around one of the pallets. There, in a corner, stretched between a pair of smaller steam pipes and wrapped around an electrical conduit, was a length of barrier tape. I expected it to be yellow, imprinted with the words 'Crime Scene Do Not Cross.' Instead, the tape was red and warned, 'Danger Do Not Enter.' For some reason I was disappointed, as if Officer Martin had let me down. But perhaps they didn't have the right tape to hand, or had just run out of the yellow kind.

I crouched, stared at the scarred linoleum and thought of Julie lying alone and unconscious in that hot, dirty corner of the ship, so close to the throbbing engines that it was difficult to carry on a conversation without raising your voice. Whether it was that image, or the heat, or the stench of the garbage, I'll never know, but it made my stomach churn. 'Thanks for bringing me here, Pia.'

Pia didn't answer. Perhaps she, too, was thinking about Julie, and about other girls who had suffered in the same way.

I pulled my iPhone out of my pocket and, as Pia watched silently, I took pictures of the area. When I'd finished, Pia squared her shoulders, faced me and said, 'Tell you what: let's go find David Warren.'

'Can you get away?' I said to Pia's back as we climbed up the stairs and made our way back to the crew elevator.

It had been my observation that cruise ship crew works practically 24/7. The guy who serves you drinks in the piano bar at 11.30 p.m. might be the same guy who brought you your cheese omelet at 7.00 a.m. the following morning.

'I think so,' Pia said, punching the button for deck four. 'This is my time to rehearse with Tom, but he's pretty flexible, especially this late in the run. I'll just check with him . . .' She paused as the elevator glided to a halt and the doors slid open. 'When you find David, will you let me know?'

'Where shall I find you?'

'Backstage,' she said as the elevator doors slid closed.

SIXTEEN

'Over the last five years, sexual assault and physical assaults on cruise vessels were the leading crimes investigated by the Federal Bureau of Investigation with regard to cruise vessel incidents. These crimes at sea can involve attacks both by passengers and crew members on other passengers and crew members.'

Cruise Vessel Security and Safety Act of 2010

(H.R. 3360)

When I went to check in with my sisters, I found Georgina napping in her cabin, an open book propped up on her chest. She'd been keeping Julie company while she slept. Ruth was there, too, paging through an issue of *People* magazine. When I came in, she looked up. 'Did you know that Katie Holmes was voted by *Fitness* magazine as having the best revenge body of the year?'

'Revenge body? What the hell does that mean?' I asked.

Ruth shrugged. 'Eat your heart out, Tom Cruise?'

I crooked my finger and pointed to the communicating door. 'We need to talk,' I whispered.

In the privacy of our cabin, I said, 'I know Georgina asked us not to call Scott, but I'm sorry, that's nuts. What is the point of keeping the bad news from him? He's going to find out when she gets home anyway and, if I were Scott, even though I know there's nothing he could do until the *Islander* returns to port – unless he flew in on a helicopter – I'd be pissed off that she didn't call me right away. When she wakes up, I'm counting on you to talk some sense into her.'

I took a deep breath. 'And, we need to take Fortune's advice and call a lawyer. We can't wait for Georgina to do it. Julie was kidnapped, and that's a federal crime. Ben Martin seems to be cooperating now, but there's absolutely no guarantee he's going to follow through once we reach dry land and Phoenix's lawyers get involved.' I touched her arm. 'What I'm getting at is I think you should call Hutch, let him know what's happened, and ask what steps we should take *before* leaving the ship.'

'I already have,' Ruth whispered, pointing to the cabin phone. 'Per minute cost was simply outrageous. Seven freaking dollars, but what can you do? Hutch said that as soon as we hung up he'd contact the F.B.I.'s Baltimore field office to make certain that they've been notified.'

'That's good,' I said, patting her arm. Then I told her about my plan to meet with David Warren.

As it turned out, tracking David down was ridiculously easy. I picked up the cabin phone, asked the operator to ring his state-room and when it rang, the man actually answered.

My voice still a little shaky, I told him about the attack on Julie.

'God damn,' he said. 'Not another one. We need to talk.'

We decided to meet in the library, which was such a hotbed of drunk and disorderly activity – as if – that Phoenix hadn't even bothered to install surveillance cameras there. Pia wasn't backstage, so I left a message for her at the Oracle bar, then headed for the library where I made myself comfortable at one of the game tables, sipping a latte I'd picked up on the way. Pia arrived, still wearing her server's uniform, followed shortly by David, who was dressed in shorts and a T-shirt and was toting an oversized briefcase.

'I'm sorry about your niece.' David pulled out a chair and sat down. 'Maybe I should have posted warning signs all over the ship: Danger: Sexual Predator On Board.'

He plunked his briefcase on the tabletop and got right down to business. 'I'm convinced that Charlotte had stumbled on the identity of that sexual predator. He learned of it somehow and killed her to shut her up. I have a list of the people that were aboard the *Voyager* on the day that my daughter died, Miss Fanucci. By keeping my eyes open and asking discreet questions, I've confirmed that a number of them are aboard the *Islander* today. I've started a list. I'm wondering if you could look it over.'

David extracted a thick folder from his briefcase and slid the folder across the table. Pia tilted her head and opened it cautiously, as if expecting a Jack-in-the-Box to spring out at her.

'Holy cow, Mr Warren! Where did you lay your hands on *this*?

I can't believe that Phoenix Cruise Lines gave up a passenger manifest voluntarily.'

Inside the folder was a sheaf of papers held together with a black binder clip, the print so tiny I thought Pia'd need a magnifying glass to read it.

David's grin was humorless. 'The Miami detective I hired had someone on the inside and called in an I.O.U, but you didn't hear that from me.'

David had given Pia an impossible task. 'There are *hundreds* of names on that list, Mr Warren,' I said. 'How can Pia *possibly* know everyone on this list who is also aboard today? My head hurts just thinking about it. I attended the captain's cocktail party for the Neptune Club – same as you, David. Half the people in the room that night were frequent cruisers and could be suspects – you, me, the lady in the wheelchair, even Cliff and Liz Rowe.'

'Not you, Hannah. You weren't on the *Voyager*,' David pointed out reasonably.

'True,' I said.

'But, Cliff and Liz?' Pia hooted. 'You've *got* to be kidding! They're as nice as they come.'

I flapped a hand. 'Just saying.'

'Isn't that what the neighbors always say when a pedophile is arrested?' David said. '"He was such a nice man! Dressed up like a clown and passed out candy to all the kids on Halloween. Shoveled snow off my sidewalk. Jump-started my car when the battery died." Being personable is the pedophile's stock in trade, Miss Fanucci. It's part of the job description. Charisma. Think Ted Bundy.'

'I'd really rather not,' Pia said, shivering. 'But Cliff and Liz? Surely . . .'

David's gaze didn't waver. 'Why else do you think I arranged to be seated at their table?'

I sat back, speechless. The man was as relentless as Inspector Javert.

'I think I have a way to narrow it down,' Pia said after a moment as she leafed quickly through the reams of paper David had set in front of her.

'I don't think we're looking for a passenger at all. As far as I know, Charlotte wasn't fraternizing with any of the passengers – she didn't have time for it – and I'm sure she wasn't being stalked, or she would have said something. So, it's got to be a member of the officers, staff or crew, or maybe even one of the concessioners.'

'What do you mean, concessioners? I thought everybody on board works for the cruise line?'

Pia shook her head. 'Absolutely not. Tom and I don't work directly for the cruise line, for example. We get our gigs through a booking agency. Tom's immediate boss is the ship's cast performance manager who reports to the entertainment director, that lounge lizard who introduces all the programs, acting as if he wrote, produced and directed them all himself. Our agency provides acts to a lot of the major cruise lines. We're just one of them.'

'And all the shops are concessions, as you probably guessed,' David cut in.

'I figured that,' I said. 'Like duty frees everywhere, stamped out with a cookie cutter. Frankly,' I added, 'I don't get it. I can buy my Courvoisier just as cheaply at the liquor store back home in Annapolis.'

'Not in the market for diamonds?' Pia teased. 'Or Chanel No. 5?'

'I'm not the Chanel type. With my husband, it's splash a smidge of Eau de Bifteck behind my ear and he'll follow me anywhere. But, seriously,' I said, 'if you don't actually work for the cruise line, why are you tending the bar at the Oracle?'

Pia blushed. 'They were short-handed – the regular girl is confined to her cabin with a stomach virus. They asked for volunteers, I was available, and . . .' She winked. 'They pay me extra.'

I noticed that David was drumming his fingers lightly on the table. Taking the hint, I got back on message. I rested my forearms on the table and leaned forward, giving him my full attention. 'So, to summarize. Charlotte was a youth counselor on *Voyager* and spent almost all of her time while on board in Tidal Wave, right?'

Pia was quick to confirm this fact. 'Except for the early morning hours – and sometimes even those were taken up with staff meetings – Char had practically no time on her own.'

'Therefore, it's reasonable to assume that whatever information she'd stumbled on had to do with the teen center. Do you agree?'

David nodded and laid his hand on the sheaf of papers that still lay on the table in front of Pia and pulled it back. 'As I said, this is a printout where I've marked everyone on *Islander* who I know was also on *Voyager*. In the teen center, that narrows it down to Wesley Bray, who now manages the Tidal Wave – although he was just a youth counselor back then – one of the other youth counselors, and the overall supervisor, the Activities Director, Ethan Hines.'

That was a new name to me. 'Pia, do you know Ethan Hines?'

She shrugged. 'Just to say "hi" to.'

I wondered if I'd seen him hanging around the Tidal Wave. 'What does he look like?'

'Medium height, five-eight or five-nine, brown hair in a buzz cut to cover up the fact that he's going bald. Looks like a Mormon missionary, if you want to know the truth.'

I didn't remember seeing the guy, but wanted to learn everything I could about the folks in charge of the place where Julie went missing. 'What does an activities director do, exactly? My only frame of reference is Julie McCoy on *The Love Boat.*'

Pia looked puzzled, and then I remembered that she probably hadn't even been born when *The Love Boat* was popular on television. 'Basically, they are in charge of making sure everybody has a good time,' she said with a shrug.

That covered a lot of territory, I thought.

I turned to David. 'Earlier, Pia was telling me that during one of Charlotte's voyages, a girl, a fifteen-year-old, was drugged, abducted from the teen center and raped. Did Charlotte ever mention that incident to you?'

'Yes, she did. When the ship docked in Montego Bay, she called me. At the time the girl, Noelle Bursky went missing, Charlotte was on a white-water rafting expedition in the rainforest with a bunch of kids, but it upset her all the same.' David bent over, fumbled in his briefcase and pulled out a manila folder. 'This incident was reported in the Florida *Sun Sentinel*,' he told us while thumbing through its contents. 'Damn it, I have it here somewhere. Well, never mind. The gist of it is that the girl was drugged, raped and then stashed in one of the lifeboats. The parents were party-hearty types – didn't even notice their daughter was missing until hours after the rape – so by the time they reported it, she'd already come to and climbed out of the lifeboat. The girl had the good sense to flag down somebody and report the incident, but when she got to Security, she couldn't remember anything about the attack – it was all a blank between the time she drank a Coca Cola in the bar and the time she woke up in the lifeboat early the following morning. Nobody was ever accused. The girl had something of a reputation for being a cock tease – I beg your pardon, Miss Fanucci – so her interrogation was emotionally brutal. The family disembarked in Jamaica, hired an attorney, but eventually they declined to pursue the matter, saying they wanted to save their daughter the embarrassment of a court trial. Char was pretty steamed about that.'

As David told the story, I was staring at the etched glass doorway, thinking it was possible that the same person abducted both that poor fifteen-year-old girl and my niece, Julie. Both girls had been drinking sodas in the ship's teen bar, and both had no memory of the attack. Julie wasn't a cock tease, as David had so crudely put it, but what if the attacker had been scouting for victims, had observed Julie getting drunk on Sex on the Beaches with the Crawford boys in the bar and figured she'd be a vulnerable target?

If so, Julie had been extremely lucky. Somehow, she had managed to escape. Why had the rapist not followed through? Had he lost his nerve? Or had the crime been interrupted?

I turned to David. 'You have reams of paper in that briefcase, David. You know there have been previous assaults. Do you have any statistics on how many girls have been sexually assaulted while hanging out in the Tidal Wave area on Phoenix Cruise Lines?'

'I was more interested in the statistics on persons overboard, of course, but all those numbers are hard to come by.' He adjusted his reading glasses, flipped over a couple of pages and ran his finger down a multi-columned table. 'Between October 1, 2007 and September 30, 2008, there were one hundred and fifty-four sex-related incidents on board cruise ships, twenty-eight of them against a minor, and of those, four – or about fourteen percent – were on Phoenix ships.'

Fourteen percent of an industry total seemed like a lot to me. 'What about since 2008?' I asked.

David considered me over the top of his eyeglasses. 'Ah, that's where it gets difficult. Because of last-minute changes to the wording of the Cruise Vessel Security and Safety Act of 2010, comparable data simply isn't available.'

'That's crazy,' I said. 'Doesn't the public have a right to know? If I were taking a kid on a cruise, I'd certainly want to be able to check out the safety record of the cruise line I was considering.' I shuddered. 'We never *dreamed* that Julie would be in any danger.'

'I filed a Freedom of Information request in 2011, but when I finally got the reports, all helpful information had been redacted.' David leaned forward, resting his elbows on the table. 'The act requires that cruise lines operating in and out of U.S. ports report all alleged crimes to the F.B.I., and that the Coast Guard maintain that information in a public database.'

'That's good, isn't it?' Pia said.

'Yes, but . . .' David smiled crookedly and raised an eyebrow. 'There's always a "yes, but," isn't there? Anyway, just before passage, the bill was amended so that the F.B.I. is only required to tell the public about their *closed* cases. Until the law is changed back to its original language, all we have to rely on now is media reports, or when lawsuits are filed in U.S. courts.'

Holy cow, I thought. If the public only got to see information about *closed* cases, nobody would ever have heard of Jon-Benet Ramsay, the Black Dalhia, Andrew and Abbie Borden, D.B. Cooper or Jack the Ripper. I was mentally scratching my head. 'Surely that can't have been the intent of the act?'

'No, and as the father of a murdered daughter, I feel let down by the Congress. This absence of data serves no one's interest except that of the cruise lines. When you get home, write your senator,' David ordered, wagging his index finger for emphasis. 'We need to get this law changed.'

'What's in it for the F.B.I. to keep cruise-ship crimes so hush-hush?' Pia wondered. She raised a hand. 'Never mind, I just answered my own question. Maybe they're embarrassed because shipboard crimes have such a low solve rate.'

'Well, not reporting crimes doesn't make crime go away,' David grumped. 'It simply lulls the public into a false sense of security. And if this kind of thing happened in a junior high school in the United States, you'd better believe the cops and the media would be all over it. According to these *recent* statistics,' he continued, ruffling the pages on the table in front of him, 'serious shipboard crimes have dropped from more than four hundred a year to only a few dozen.' He snorted. 'Defies belief.'

'So, what we know for sure is that in 2008 there were four sexual assaults against minors on ships owned by Phoenix.'

'Yes.'

'And since then?'

David shrugged. 'Only two that I know of. The one on *Voyager* on the cruise when Charlotte was murdered and the attack yesterday on your niece.'

I turned to Pia. 'Didn't you tell me that you knew of four, maybe five, Pia?'

Pia nodded. 'Unofficially.'

'Somebody with easy access to the Tidal Wave had to be responsible for drugging those girls,' I said. 'What if Charlotte discovered who it was?'

Pia frowned. 'Wesley Bray is a common denominator.'

I shook my head. 'Yes, but he couldn't have attacked Julie because he was on desk duty in Tidal Wave at the time. I saw him there myself.'

'But, he would have had time to slip the drug into your niece's drink,' Pia observed.

'What would his motive be?' I asked.

She shrugged. 'Maybe he's in cahoots with the rapist. Maybe they work as a team.'

I tried to imagine what would motivate a personable, clean-cut guy like Wesley to enter into an infernal partnership with a serial rapist. Money? Blackmail? Or maybe . . . my heart did a somersault . . . maybe they took turns?

'What about that photographer, Buck Carney?' I asked after a moment. 'I'm sure I saw him taking pictures at the disco while Phreakin' Phil was performing. And he's practically stalking my sister, Georgina.' I paused, as a thought struck me like a clap of thunder. 'He's got a fetish for red hair. My niece, Julie, has red hair. He's tried to take her picture, too.'

'I know the guy you're talking about, Hannah. He's a bit of

a creep, but aren't all paparazzi creeps? It kind of goes with the territory.'

'Was Carney taking pictures on *Voyager*, too?' David asked.

Pia nodded. 'He goes freaking everywhere with that camera, but, honestly, I think he's harmless.'

'Buck Carney has just shot to the top of *my* list, David.' I sat back in my chair. 'So, we've narrowed it down to the bartenders, Wesley Bray, Ethan Hines and Buck Carney,' I said, counting the suspects off on my fingers. Then I had a sudden thought: 'Pia, who did you mean when you mentioned the "usual suspects"? Am I missing anyone obvious?'

'Only myself and Tom to add to the three you mentioned that I know of, staff-wise.' Pia paused. 'What do we do now?' she wanted to know. 'Do we have a plan?'

'David?' I asked.

David shuffled his papers, tapped them on the table to even up the edges, then stuck the papers back into his briefcase. 'Up until now, I've been keeping a low profile, but I think I'm going to come out of the woodwork. Start playing hardball. Officer Martin doesn't know who I am, but I think he's about to find out. He wasn't involved in the investigation into my daughter's disappearance, so he probably can't see the connection. But I can't imagine any *honest* officer would want to tolerate the presence of a pedophile and murderer on his ship. If we put our heads together . . .' David let the sentence die.

Pia squirmed uncomfortably in her chair.

David noticed. 'Don't worry, I won't involve you, Miss Fanucci.'

'So, what's your plan?' I asked him.

'I'm going to talk to Martin, of course. Lay it all out. I'd appreciate it if you'd come along, Mrs Ives. If there's one thing I've learned about dealing with cruise ship corporations, it's never go in alone. Always take a witness.'

'I think it goes both ways, David,' I said with a smile. 'Ben Martin always has Molly Fortune and her trusty little notebook along.'

I agreed to accompany David to the security office, but I felt a twinge of guilt about blindsiding Ben Martin like that. And then I thought, no, that's why they pay him the big bucks, to

deal with people like me. Martin was between a rock and a hard
place. To keep his job he had to keep the owners happy, but that
meant keeping customers happy, too. If so, we might find him
more willing to cooperate.

'When shall we beard the lion in his den?' I asked.

'What's wrong with now?'

SEVENTEEN

'The owner of a vessel to which this section applies (or the owner's designee) shall contact the nearest Federal Bureau of Investigation Field Office or Legal Attache by telephone as soon as possible after the occurrence on board the vessel of an incident involving homicide, suspicious death, a missing United States national, kidnapping, [or] assault with serious bodily injury.'

Cruise Vessel Security and Safety Act of 2010
(H.R. 3360)

'**B**en isn't here right now,' Molly Fortune told us. 'He's checking on an issue with one of the security checkpoints. Why don't you come back in about half an hour?'

'That's OK, we'll wait,' David said, claiming the seat nearest the door.

The frown lines between Fortune's eyes deepened. 'Is Julie OK?'

I was quick to reassure her. 'Julie's fine under the circumstances, Officer Fortune, but we're here on a related issue.'

'Is there anything I can do to help?'

Figuring it would do no harm, I introduced her to David Warren. 'David and I met quite by accident,' I said, 'but we recently discovered we have something in common. We think the information might help Officer Martin solve the mystery of who attacked my niece.'

Fortune's eyes widened with interest. 'Can you tell me about it?'

'We could,' David said, 'but it's rather complicated. Rather than have to explain it several times, I'd rather wait for your boss.'

'Completely understandable,' Fortune agreed. 'I'll page him, then. In the meantime, can I get you anything to drink?'

It was almost lunchtime, and the only thing I'd eaten all morning was the latte I'd brought with me to the meeting in the library. 'Coffee would be great,' I told her. 'If it's not too much trouble.'

'Coffee's fine for me, too,' David said.

The Firebird café was only one deck above our heads, so the steward who responded to Fortune's call arrived within minutes carrying a carafe, four cups, assorted packets of sugar, and miniature tubs of cream. I was stirring cream into my coffee and wondering what to do with my bits of trash when Martin returned.

'Mrs Ives, I understand you have some information for me.'

I stuck the plastic stirrer into the empty sugar packet and tucked them away in my pocket. 'Not me, exactly, but Mr Warren here.'

David stood and offered his hand to be shook. 'Officer Martin, I'm David Warren. My daughter was Charlotte Warren, a youth counselor on board *Phoenix Voyager* some eighteen months ago.'

Martin inhaled sharply, replied carefully, 'Ah, yes. Quite naturally, I've heard about the case.'

'Whatever they told you, Officer Martin, I need you to understand that my daughter did *not* commit suicide. When you hear what I have to say, I think you'll agree with me.'

Martin nodded and released David's hand. 'Why don't we all sit down?'

After everyone was settled, I said, 'David and I believe there's a connection between the fifteen-year-old girl who was drugged and raped on that *Voyager* cruise and what happened to my niece, Julie, here on the *Islander*. We believe that there is a serial predator on board the *Islander* who was also aboard the *Voyager*, that he attacked these two girls – and perhaps others we don't know about as well – and that, given the opportunity, he will do it again.'

'Charlotte knew the victim, you see,' David continued. 'When she heard about the attack, it upset her very much, so much so that she called us about it. I believe that Charlotte subsequently discovered the person who was responsible. Whether she confronted him or not we don't know, but somehow he must have gotten wind of it and murdered my daughter to keep her quiet.'

Martin considered us in silence for a moment. 'Two attacks separated by eighteen months on two different vessels. As deeply invested in this theory as you appear to be, even you have to admit that it's a bit of a long-shot.'

David reached for his briefcase and set it on his lap. 'There were some peculiarities about the Noelle Bursky case,' he said, as he began to leaf through the documents. 'It's clear that the attack was planned, because two of the security cameras had been put out of commission. The one covering the Tidal Wave club on the *Voyager* had been vandalized, and the other camera was neutralized by the simple expedient of draping a pool towel over the lens. When my daughter disappeared, a similar trick was used. A towel was draped over the camera that covered the area where she presumably went overboard, the area on deck five where her red heel was later found.'

Martin and Fortune exchanged a quick glance, but David was too engaged in his narrative to notice. 'Because of this person's familiarity with the ship's security cameras, I think it's reasonable to conclude that he was *Voyager* staff or crew. Now! We know that there are a number of individuals on board *Islander* who were also aboard *Voyager* when my daughter fell to her death. Fast forward. Julie Cardinale was attacked under very similar circumstances to the attack on Noelle Bursky. This leads me to believe that whoever attacked Julie Cardinale is the same person who attacked Noelle Bursky and the same person who murdered my daughter, Charlotte.' He took a deep breath, exhaled. 'One. And. The. Same.'

Martin reached out. 'May I see that report?'

'Certainly.'

Martin scanned the report, flipped to the second page, scanned it, too, then looked up. 'Where did you get this information?'

'I hired a private investigator.'

Martin handed the report to Molly Fortune. 'Take a look at that, Molly.'

While Molly was going over it, I said, 'Because of the drugs, Julie's memory of her abduction is patchy, but as you know, she was able to describe an individual wearing a black polo shirt and a ball cap. Would you be agreeable to letting Julie watch the security tapes to see if she can spot that person? Perhaps if she sees his face, it will jog her memory.'

'I'm sorry, Mrs Ives, but that's simply not possible. It would be against company policy. We've made copies, as I promised. Our legal department has authorized me to turn the copies over to the F.B.I., along with all the other evidence we've collected, as soon as we reach Baltimore. They're the ones to do a proper investigation.'

David turned to look at me, his upper lip curled. 'I warned you that Phoenix Cruise Lines would circle the wagons.'

Ben Martin stiffened. 'Mrs Ives . . .' he began.

'It's all right, Officer Martin. You're just doing your job. I appreciate that you're following federal guidelines, and that you've been so cooperative.'

David muttered something under his breath that might have been 'balls.'

'But since you've reviewed the video tapes and I haven't,' I continued, 'there's something that's been bothering me.'

'Yes? How can I help?'

'There are two cameras in the Breakers! bar area, correct? One near the entrance that also covers the Tidal Wave Club, and the other in the bar area itself?'

'Correct.'

'Earlier, when you described what was on the tapes to me, you said that one camera captured Julie and her friends sitting at a table in the corner, and that other than the waiter who delivered their drinks, nobody else approached them while she was sitting there.'

'I believe that's what I said. Something like that, anyway.'

'I know that Julie's glass had a secure-fitting lid, with only a small hole to accommodate the straw, so it's reasonable to assume that none of the young people sitting at the table with Julie had the opportunity to introduce Ketamine into her drink.'

'That would seem to be the case.'

'I'm not familiar with Ketamine and my old standby, Google, doesn't work all that well out here – doesn't work at all, in fact – but, I've been wondering. Does Ketamine come as a liquid or powder?'

'Both,' David answered without hesitation. 'Ketamine was used on Noelle Bursky, too.'

I gave him a 500-watt smile. 'Thank you, David,' I said, then turned back to Officer Martin. 'OK, so help me out here. Julie ordered her drink at the bar. The bartender on duty at the time – I think she said her name was Kira – mixes the drink in the blender and while it's whirring around, she fixes soft drinks for the others at the table. All the drinks go on a tray, get capped and stuck with straws, and the waiter carries the tray to the table. Correct?'

'Yes, I believe so.'

'Well, frankly I can't see how it's possible that Julie's drink was drugged anywhere except at the bar, either by the bartender who was actually making the drink, or by the second bartender on duty that day, or by somebody else entirely, perhaps when the bartender's back was turned.' I paused to let that sink in. 'It was a very busy time of day, remember? The pizza party was over, the movie was about to begin. Wesley was frazzled. I saw for myself that the tables were crowded. There *had* to have been other people to-in and fro-ing around that bar. Those people must have been captured on the security tape, so tell me, who else did you see?'

Officer Martin cleared his throat. 'Uh, this is embarrassing. I'm afraid that particular camera was not in operation.' To his credit, he actually flushed. 'The men minding the monitors picked up on it, of course. When the technician they sent up to check on it got there, he discovered that someone had draped a towel over the lens.'

I recoiled as if I'd slapped in the face. 'You knew about this and didn't tell us?'

'What was the point? We've interviewed the staff, and we have a pretty good idea which adults were in the Tidal Wave area at the relevant time, but as I pointed out to you earlier, Mrs Ives, we are not the police. We cannot make arrests.'

'Oh, for the love of God, we're talking about a *kidnapping* here!'

At least he had the decency to look embarrassed.

David shot to his feet, snatched his report off Molly Fortune's desk, crammed it in his briefcase and said, 'Come on, Hannah, let's let Officer Martin and Officer Fortune get on with their work. I'm sure they have many important things to do.'

He seized me by the elbow and hustled me out into the corridor so fast that I barely had time to say goodbye.

'What was *that* all about?' I asked when we were out of earshot of Security.

'The towel!' he crowed. 'That proves it! It's definitely the same M.O.'

I shook my arm free. 'I realize that, David, but why are you in such an all-fired hurry?'

'While it certainly would have been helpful to see the security tapes, Hannah, that's not our only option. What did people do *before* there were security tapes?'

I stopped so quickly that my shoes squeaked on the marble floor. I had been so focused on state-of-the-art, hi-tech options, on what the security tapes might tell us, that I had overlooked the obvious. 'We talk to people. We schmooze. That's what we do!'

We'd reached the elevators. Without consulting me, David pushed UP. He glanced at his watch. 'And if we hurry, the same young people who were there yesterday will just be coming on duty.'

EIGHTEEN

'Unless you have the rotating eye skills of a chameleon, it's hard to watch out for your drink at the same time you watch out for that cute guy on the dance floor. No matter how self-aware you are, there's always a chance of getting an unexpected pharmaceutical present in your beverage on a night out. Any drink, even an innocent tonic water, can turn into a cocktail that takes you to the Twilight Zone if it's unattended.'

http://howto.wired.com/wiki/

U p at the Tidal Wave, Wesley Bray, as usual, had his hands full. Teens and parents, signing in, signing out, wave upon wave. The rock wall was open, we learned from one of the parents standing in line, as well as the bungee trampoline, and don't we wish *we* could do that. Other events included a blindfold obstacle course, a silly dives contest in the pool area, and another showing of *Hunger Games*.

David and I waited impatiently until Wesley had finished gathering the rock-climbing contingent and had sent them off to the stern of the ship with one of the youth counselors.

'Wesley,' I said.

He looked up from his clipboard, his curious look changed to recognition, then back to serious again. 'We are so glad to hear that your niece has been found, Mrs Ives. How is she doing?'

I gave what was becoming my stock answer. 'Fine, under the circumstances.'

I was surprised that he knew my name. Then it occurred to me: the staff had been briefed.

'We've just been meeting with the security officer, Wesley, and he tells us that the surveillance camera that covers the bar in there . . .' I pointed to Breakers!, where two bartenders were already busy fixing drinks. '. . . well, it was out of commission.'

The line between Wesley's eyebrows deepened as he seemed

to be considering what to say, then relaxed as he came to the right decision. 'That's true, I'm afraid.'

'I'd like you to meet someone, Wesley.' I turned to David Warren. 'You knew David's daughter, I believe. Charlotte Warren.'

Wesley's eyes widened as recognition dawned. 'Char. I did. I'm so sorry for your loss, Mr Warren.'

David nodded in acknowledgement, his mouth set in a grim line. I wondered how many times he had heard those empty words coming out of the mouths of Phoenix Cruise Lines' personnel.

'Do you also remember a passenger on that cruise, a young girl named Noelle Bursky?' I asked.

'Oh, Lord, how could I forget? She disappeared from Breakers! on . . .' He blinked. 'Oh, shit. I don't think I better say any more.'

'I'm going to be perfectly frank with you, Wesley,' David said as he eased closer to the counter. 'We think, and by "we" I mean Mrs Ives here as well as the security professionals aboard the *Islander*; we believe that the same person who abducted Mrs Ives's niece also abducted Noelle Bursky and pushed my daughter overboard to her death. If that's true, then the list of suspects is narrowed down to individuals who are here on *Islander* who were also on *Voyager* that day. We know you fall into that category, but we also know that you were right here on duty at the time Julie Cardinale was assaulted. What I'd like to ask you now is, do you remember anybody who was hanging around Breakers! that day, anyone who either worked or was also a passenger on *Voyager*?'

During this long speech, Wesley eyes had been riveted on David's face. Once the speech was over, Wesley took a deep breath, then gazed over David's shoulder, as if his answer lay somewhere out at sea.

'Wesley?' I said.

Wesley started, and turned his dark hazel eyes on me. 'I wish I could help, honestly, but I simply can't remember anyone hanging around that day, other than the parents who were coming to drop off or pick up their kids, you know?'

'You sign them all in on that clipboard?' I asked.

Wesley nodded.

'Do you still have the sign in sheets from yesterday?'

'Of course. We have to keep them until the cruise is over, then they get filed away.'

'Do you mind if we look at them?'

Wesley stood silently for a while, gnawing on his lower lip. Then he reached under the counter and pulled out a plastic file folder, flipped up the flap and withdrew several sheets of paper, stapled together in the corner. 'I can't let you take them, you understand, but you can look at them here.' He leaned forward. 'Please don't tell anyone I did this.'

I favored him with a huge smile. 'Promise.'

David and I moved to the end of the counter so as to be out of Wesley's way, and also, not coincidentally, out of range of the security camera, which was probably functioning perfectly now.

I leafed through three pages of names, neatly printed in boxes, with Time-In and Time-Out and the parent's signature in other boxes ranging out to the edge of the paper on the right.

'Jesus,' David said. 'There are a lot of Crawfords.'

'Yeah. So I noticed. But I don't think any of these Crawfords were cruising on the *Voyager*, do you?'

I ran my finger down the sign-in sheet until I got to the rows covering the time when Julie arrived. There was Georgina's signature, and in the next row down, the signature of Katie's dad, Steven Krozak. As David hung over my shoulder, I called up the Notes app on my iPhone and tapped in the names of everyone who'd signed in between the time when Julie arrived and the time she supposedly headed for the restroom. 'No name pops out at me,' I said, tucking my iPhone back into my pocket.

When Wesley was free again, I handed the sign-up sheets back to him with thanks. He hastily refilled them in the plastic folder. 'That help?'

'Afraid not. But thanks anyway.'

'No problem. That kind of thing . . . drugs . . . just shouldn't happen – not here, not anywhere. Makes me sick. I hope they find the bastard, lock him up and throw away the key.' He paused. 'But don't quote me on that, please.'

'Wesley, one other thing,' I said. 'Do you remember if there was anything in particular about the day that Noelle was abducted and yesterday, when Julie went missing? Did they have anything in common at all?'

Wesley laughed out loud. 'Mrs Ives, *everything* is in common on Phoenix Cruise Lines. The titles of the movies change, of course, and some of the games, but management keeps the schedule more or less the same for every cruise. Movies, pizza afterwards. Talent shows, scavenger hunts, trivia contests. Same old, same old. Events that are weather dependent, like the bungee trampoline and the rock climbing wall? That's harder to predict. They're both open today, for example, but I remember that the rock wall was closed on *Voyager* that day because of high winds, so we were a bit more crowded in Breakers! than usual, and much more crowded than we were in here yesterday.' He shrugged. 'Sorry I can't be of more help.'

'It's OK, Wesley. We appreciate your cooperation.'

'Come on,' I said to David. 'I can see that Kira's on duty in the bar.'

David and I eased our way past a clot of boisterous teens heading out of Breakers! and approached the bar. Rohan wasn't on duty, but Kira was there. Her back was turned as she added ice to a rank of four blenders, dropped fresh fruit into three of them, and set them whirring. She snagged several glasses, made a U-turn, then stopped short when she saw us, pressing a hand flat against her chest. 'Whew! You startled me.'

I flashed my brightest smile. 'Sorry! We just wanted to speak to you for a minute.'

She swung her arm in a wide arc, taking in the chaos on the bar in front of her – trays holding drinks, French fries, slices of pizza, hamburgers – then swiped sweat off her forehead with the back of her hand. 'Don't have anything else to do. Hah! As if.' She raised a hand to summon one of the servers, and pointed to the drinks tray. 'Look,' she said after he'd taken the tray away, 'I'm really happy to hear that your daughter turned up.'

'My niece, actually, but thank you. We are, too.'

'You and your husband want something to drink?' she asked.

I decided not to correct her. 'No, thanks. We'll be picking up a sandwich at Surf's Up shortly. We just wanted to ask you a couple of questions about yesterday.'

Kira dried her hands on a towel she had tucked into her waistband. 'Sure. Shoot.'

'You heard that my niece's drink was drugged, didn't you?'

'Yeah, man, shook me up, I can tell you.' She considered me

with serious eyes then said, 'God! You don't think *I* had anything to do with that, do you? No way!'

I smiled in what I hoped was a reassuring way, not wanting to alarm her, afraid she'd clam up. 'Relax, Kira. I don't know how the drug got into Julie's drink, but I'm fairly certain you didn't do it. If you had, there would have been no reason for the security camera to have been covered up, would there?'

'Well, that's a relief.'

'The only reason to do that would be if it was someone who wasn't normally in Breakers! Someone who couldn't afford to be seen.'

'That makes sense.'

'So, can you think back to yesterday? Did you notice anyone come in who didn't belong?'

'Two sours and a muddy moo!' a waiter called out.

''Cuse me,' Kira said. We watched while she filled two plastic glasses with lemonade and a third with chocolate milk, fitted plastic lids on the glasses then slid them down the bar, tossing three paper-wrapped straws in their wake.

When that was done, she turned back to us. 'So, you asked if anybody came into Breakers! yesterday who didn't belong. Gosh, it was so busy!' She stared hard at the ceiling as if the answer was written on one of the crabs, lobsters, seashells or miniature surfboards that decorated the rafters. 'A parent or two, couple of big brothers and sisters, but they never stay very long. Everyone else was staff. Wes, of course. He popped in from time to time looking for a particular kid when their parents showed up to collect them. Channing was here for a bit while waiting for Pia to finish her shift at the Oracle, sitting with a couple of boys at the end of the bar, teaching them card tricks.' She grinned. 'He's *so* amazing. He wrote one boy's name on an ace with a marker pen, then . . .' She paused, blushed. 'But you don't want to know about that. That photographer from CLIA came through, taking pictures. He might have noticed something. Then, let's see . . . ah, Ethan Hines, and . . .'

'Hines? The activities director?'

'Yeah. He's, like, the big boss. He had this new guy with him called Liam – don't know his last name – who's been shadowing him this cruise. Liam's going to be activities director on, let me think . . . yeah, on the *Odyssey* when it comes out of dry dock next month. Then Jack Westfall stopped by to shoot the breeze, like I have the time!' She spread her hands, palms up, empty. 'That's about it!'

'Jack Westfall is staff?' I asked. 'I saw him at the Neptune Club reception, so I assumed he was a passenger.'

'Well, *technically*, he's a passenger, but his wife runs the art auction concession, so he's always around. We think of him as staff. I do, at least. He's one of those "little acts of kindness" types, like yesterday when he saw I was so slammed he stuck the straws in the glasses for me.' She leaned forward across the bar, spoke softly. 'The stewards say he's an awesome tipper!'

'What was he wearing?' David asked.

'Wearing? Like I can remember!' Kira whipped the towel out of her waistband and wiped away the wet rings on the bar. 'Wait. He had a black shirt on. I remember thinking he should always wear black, makes you look thinner, especially if you've got that little paunch thing goin' on.'

My heart raced and blood roared into my ears. I reached out blindly and grabbed David's arm, then held on tightly. Perhaps I was gasping like a beached fish, perhaps not, but when I could breathe again, I thanked Kira and dragged David out of Breakers! and hustled him down the staircase to a table in a quiet corner of the pool deck.

I thought I knew the answer to this question, but I asked it anyway. 'David, who ran the art auction on the *Voyager*?'

'I don't even have to consult my files, Hannah. Eastaugh Galleries. The company belongs to Nicole Westfall. She inherited it from her father, an old-school art dealer out of London named Cyril Eastaugh. Moved the business to West Palm in the eighties. Jack sits on the board, but otherwise he just tags along for the ride.'

'Do you realize what was going on yesterday when Julie was abducted? The art auction! As auctioneer, Nicole would have been busy, wouldn't she? She would have been nowhere near their stateroom. What do you want to bet they have one of those suites that might look like "somebody's living room" to a teenager totally spaced out on drugs? Jesus, I think I'm going to be sick!'

I didn't realize that I had been gripping the table with both hands until I felt David's hand on mine, squeezing gently. He kept his hand there while I continued to vent, running through a litany of medieval amusements that included thumbscrews, the rack, the wheel, and a device that could be heated in red-hot coals and applied to . . . well, never mind.

'The auctions are always on the same day, you know,' David said quietly. 'The last day of the voyage but one. That's the day Noelle Bursky disappeared, too.'

'He put it in the straw,' I said with conviction. 'The sonofabitch put powdered Ketamine in a straw and stuck it into their drinks.' I looked up and caught David's eye. 'What do we do?'

David took a deep breath. 'What if we could get a positive I.D.?'

'That means Julie.'

'Yes.'

'How the hell do we engineer that?'

'They'll be having a fire sale in the gallery today. Everything must go and all that crap. Jack Westfall is likely to be there. If not, you can try to catch him at dinner. The Westfalls are usually at the last seating, unless it's lobster night at the Garuda Grill.'

'How do you know all this, David?'

'I've been watching these people for a long, long time.'

'So, let's say Julie identifies the creep. Then what?'

David's gaze was steady. 'Why don't we cross that bridge when we come to it?'

NINETEEN

*'A few great magicians . . . have always realized that these
ephemeral, temporary miracles could be restorative for their
audiences. They listened for the brief pause between the
end of the trick and the start of the applause – the split
second when the entire audience shares a gasp of genuine
amazement. At that moment there's always been an honor-
able quality in illusion.'*

Jim Steinmeyer, *Hiding the Elephant*,
Da Capo, 2004, p. 331

After I left David, I took the stairway down to deck six,
waited in line for a cappuccino at Café Cino then carried
it, casually sipping, as I wandered through the boutiques.
I was heading for the art gallery.

Although a surprisingly large number of paintings had sold at
the auction the previous day, the empty easels had been refilled,
as if by magic, with equally unappealing offerings. I wondered
if Nicole had artists chained in the bilges, churning them out.

She wasn't there, but a young man who identified himself as
Nicole's assistant assured me that if I came back at two o'clock
I could talk to Nicole directly.

'I really, really like that Dutko over there,' I gushed, pointing
to a hideous oil of a dark-haired woman posing cheek-to-cheek
with a horse to whom she bore an uncanny resemblance. 'But
Buddy would just *murder* me if I paid six hundred dollars for it.'

'I'll speak to Nicole about it. I'm sure she can do better than
that.' The man actually winked.

'Thank you so much. It's absolutely *perfect* for our family
room.'

Back in our stateroom, I found Ruth sitting on her bed reading
a book. When she saw me, she tossed the book to the floor.
'There you are! It's almost one o'clock! We were about to

give up on you. I'm starving. Where do you want to go for lunch?'

I'd hustled and bustled so much that morning that the thought of fighting my way through the buffet lines at the Firebird, or trying to talk over the din, gave me instant indigestion. 'Let's be civilized and go up to the dining room,' I said. 'I'll go collect the others.'

I stuck my head around the door. 'Georgina?'

Breep-breep. Breep-breep. I nearly jumped out of my sandals. 'What the heck is that?'

Georgina was rummaging through her cosmetic bag. 'Get that for me, will you, Hannah?'

Ah, the phone. That white, ultra-mod moebius that sat on the desk in our cabins. I'd never heard it ring before.

I crossed to the desk and picked up. 'Hello?'

'I just wanted you to know I'm really glad you found your daughter,' someone said.

'I'm . . .' I started to say, then thought better of it.

'Look,' the voice hurried on, low and urgent. 'There's something you need to . . . oh, shit!'

'Who is this?' I demanded, but the caller had already hung up.

'Who was that?' Georgina wanted to know.

I stared at the silent receiver, thinking that the voice sounded familiar. Male, for certain. Young, but not too young. Nervous. Connor Crawford? What was that all about?

Not wanting to send Georgina off on a killing spree, I shrugged and said, 'Wrong number. Are you ready for lunch?'

'Give us ten minutes,' Georgina replied as she attacked her unruly mane with a hairbrush.

'I'll go ahead and get us a table, then,' I told her. 'Tell Ruth I'll meet her there.'

Once I reached the dining room, I used the extra time to cruise among the tables, looking for David. I found him sitting alone at a table for two near a window, studying a menu. 'May I?' I pulled out the chair opposite him and sat down.

'I'm expecting Oprah Winfrey to join me,' he quipped, looking up at me over the top of the menu.

'I won't stay long, then,' I said with a smile.

David Warren, cracking a joke. Would wonders ever cease? 'A burden shared is a burden halved,' someone a lot wiser than I had once said. Perhaps I had lightened his. I hoped so.

I leaned across the table and told David about the mysterious phone call I'd just received.

'Who do you think it was?' he asked after I'd finished.

'Not sure. It could have been that young Crawford boy, the one who got Julie drunk.'

David tented his fingers and tapped his chin thoughtfully. 'If the lad is interested in your niece, perhaps he's been keeping tabs on her. It sounds like he may have seen something.'

'My thoughts exactly.'

'Only one way to find out,' David said.

'I know. Track him down and ask him.'

'*There* you are!' It was Ruth.

'Gotta go, David,' I said, rising. 'If you see him first . . .' I didn't need to finish the sentence.

'I know what to do.'

Two minutes later, at my request, our waiter escorted Ruth and me to a table for four tucked away in a private corner near the sweeping staircase that led up to the balcony.

When Georgina and Julie finally joined us, I was happy to see that Julie's appetite had returned. 'I want one of everything,' she told the waiter brightly, 'but I guess I'll settle for the moussaka. And the lamb!'

Between the *avgolemono* soup and the *loukoumades*, I updated my family on the information David and I had learned that morning. Up to a point, that is.

'Julie,' I said. 'I think we have identified the man who attacked you. We're not one hundred percent sure, but I was hoping that if you saw him again, you might be able to recognize him.'

Julie lowered her fork. 'I don't know, Aunt Hannah. It still seems all fuzzy, like a really bad dream.'

Georgina reached out and seized her daughter's hand. 'I don't know, either, Hannah. I'm not so sure I want to put Julie through another ordeal. Hasn't she suffered enough?'

Ruth stared at Georgina as if she'd just sprouted horns. 'If Julie can positively identify the man, we can put the bastard away. You want him wandering the streets, Georgina? Preying on other unsuspecting young victims?'

'Well, no. But . . .'

'It's OK, Mom.' Julie turned to me. 'Just tell me what to do.'

After lunch, we returned to our staterooms. At my instruction, Julie changed out of her shorts and tank top into a conservative pair of jeans and a 'C is for Cure' pink ribbon T-shirt borrowed from her mother. With her hair tucked into a ball cap, and a pair of dark glasses, I didn't think Westfall would recognize her unless he got a close look, and I didn't intend for that to happen.

When we arrived at the art gallery around a quarter after two, the close-out sale was in full swing. Nicole's assistant sat in a chair behind the desk, writing up sales slips and wearing out his smile. Nicole herself was loudly explaining the investment value of a Thomas Kinkade signed and numbered limited-edition print and hand-embellished canvas called 'Gingerbread Cottage' to a woman leaning on a walker. I'd seen similar prints in a gallery in Annapolis for around two hundred and fifty dollars, so I hoped this woman wouldn't shell out the five hundred dollars Nicole was asking for it.

Of Nicole's husband, there was no sign.

'Spooky,' Ruth declared, indicating the Kinkade. 'If you were Hansel and Gretel, would *you* go into that cottage? There's a hellish glow behind every window. Something diabolical is going on in there, you just know it.'

We wandered on. Ruth kept us entertained by making up imaginary captions for the paintings as we browsed. 'Randy later regretted mating his Rottweiler with an ostrich,' she observed. Or, 'And they said radiation from the H-bomb wouldn't affect us at all,' helping to keep the mood light, even though we knew it could be deadly serious the moment Jack Westfall decided to make an appearance.

'What's the orange dot mean?' Julie asked as we pretended to admire one of the many renderings of seascapes in the Eastaugh Collection.

'I think it means it's already been sold,' Georgina said. 'Honest to God, can you believe some of this crap?' We'd reached 'Wild Girls,' the painting of the woman with her horse, and I noticed

with amusement that it carried an orange dot and would be going
to a good home. Ruth contemplated it for a moment, then said,
'Although she put on a brave face, Miranda was not happy with
her mail order dentures.'

It was too perfect. I had to laugh.

'Oh, that's so cute!' Julie pointed to a painting of a cat dressed
as a ballerina. She flounced over, leaned closer, moved her
sunglasses to her forehead and squinted at the price tag. 'It's two
hundred dollars! No way!'

'Way,' I said.

Julie favored me with a grin. 'If I had a hundred dollars . . .'
In mid-sentence, she froze. With one quick motion she flipped
the sunglasses down over her eyes, did an about-face and sidled
up to her mother. 'That's *him*,' she croaked. 'Don't look now,
but oh my God, I think that's the guy!'

Georgina tucked her chin down, kept her voice low. 'I need
to get Julie out of here.'

'Mom, mom, I can't breathe!'

'Hannah!' Georgina whispered urgently.

'Just wait until we can confirm exactly who Julie's looking
at,' I whispered back. I swung around slowly, casually.

Jack Westfall had made a poor wardrobe choice that morning.
Had he shown up at the gallery in a tux, or even a bathing suit,
it's possible Julie wouldn't have recognized him. But there he
stood, schmoozing with a potential buyer, wearing a black polo
shirt with a little squiggle on the pocket. Not an alligator, nor a
polo pony; not a penguin, nor Pegasus. Not a brand name owned
by millions. Oh, no. It was an image I'd seen before – on posters,
on signs, in the catalog, on bid sheets. Westfall wore a company
shirt, with an Eastaugh Galleries logo.

And if I had anything to say about it, his goose was about to
be cooked.

'Take Julie out the back way, through the photo gallery,' I
ordered. 'You won't run into him there.'

For once, Georgina didn't give me her famous well-aren't-
you-the-bossy-boots glare. She wrapped her arm around Julie's
shoulder and the two of them strolled off into the photo gallery.
Not until I'd lost sight of Georgina's red and white shirt disap-
pearing into the crowds that were mobbing the boutiques just

beyond, taking advantage of the half-price sales, did I dare to
turn around and look at Westfall again.

'Ruth, I think I need to kill him.'

'I will not stop you, Hannah.'

Jack Westfall moved with ease among the passengers, smiling
at one here, shaking another hand there. My sister and I watched
as he paused to point out a gouache of an owl camouflaged in
a tree to a well-coifed blonde, resting his hand lightly on her
back as he did so.

'We are looking at a man who raped at least one girl, kidnapped
another, and almost certainly murdered David Warren's daughter.
That's what a murderer looks like, Ruth, should you ever need
to paint a picture of one.'

'What are we going to do?' she whispered as Westfall and the
blonde moved on to the next painting.

I reached into my pocket for my iPhone. 'Stand over there,
next to that horrible owl thing.'

Ruth looked puzzled, but did as I asked.

'Now smile!' I instructed.

Ruth posed in front of the painting, her best 'say cheese' face
obediently in place.

'Turn around, dammit,' I muttered under my breath. After fewer
than ten seconds, my wish was granted. Jack Westfall turned,
abandoned the blonde, and smiled at someone new just behind
me. I moved the iPhone subtly to the right, gave it time to refocus
and snapped the bastard's picture. 'Got it, Ruth!' I waved gaily.

Ruth hastily rejoined me. 'What next, Hannah?'

'We're going to tell Officer Martin, that's step number one.
Now that Julie's identified Westfall as her attacker, hopefully
they'll take him into custody.'

'Well,' Ruth said. 'At least Westfall's not going anywhere.'

'True, but I'd feel better if he didn't have the run of the ship.
If he knew that Julie recognized him . . .' I shivered at the thought.
'Come with me to the security office?'

'Of course,' my sister said, and linked her arm with mine
as we walked out of the gallery.

We stood like statues in the lobby, waiting for the elevator that
would take us to the security office on deck eight. When the

elevator doors opened and Officer Ben Martin stepped out, I nearly fell over. He didn't see us, but veered to the right, striding purposefully toward the piano bar.

'Officer Martin!' I called.

Martin performed a neat, military about face. 'Mrs Ives. How's your niece this afternoon?'

'She's out and about,' I told him. 'In fact, that's what we were coming to talk to you about.' I touched Ruth on the shoulder. 'You remember my sister, Ruth.'

Martin stood at parade rest, his hands clasped behind his back. He bobbed his head. 'I do. Sorry it was under less than ideal circumstances.'

Pleasantries over, I got right to the point. 'My sisters and I wanted to take advantage of the fifty-percent-off sales, and we just happened to wander into the art gallery. Julie was looking at a painting when Jack Westfall came into the gallery. Do you know Westfall?'

Martin nodded. 'Very well. Married to the gallery owner, Nicole Westfall.'

I glanced around the elevator lobby to make sure nobody was in earshot, lowered my voice. 'Julie recognized Westfall as the man who abducted her from Breakers!'

Martin couldn't have looked more surprised if I had pulled a baseball bat out of my handbag and bashed him over the head with it. When he spoke again, his voice was low, urgent. 'Mrs Ives, I don't mean to question your niece, but when I last saw her, she was practically unconscious, and she stated – for the record – that she didn't remember what the man looked like.'

'That's true,' I admitted, 'but what else did she say? Do you remember how she described what her attacker was wearing?'

'Black shirt, black cap.'

'And?'

Martin grimaced. 'What is this? Twenty questions?'

Ruth was quick to refresh his memory. 'She said it was a polo shirt, with a squiggle on the pocket.'

Martin's head ping-ponged toward Ruth. 'Don't all polo shirts have some sort of logo on the pocket?'

It ping-ponged back to me when I said, 'Some. But if you go to the art gallery right now, you'll see Jack Westfall wearing a black polo shirt with a unique squiggle on the pocket.' I drew a representation of the logo in the air with my finger. 'It's a stylized E and a G floating on top of a wave. It's the Eastaugh Gallery logo, Officer Martin. When Julie saw Westfall wearing that shirt it scared her so much she started to hyperventilate. Her mother had to take her back to the cabin.'

Officer Martin stroked his chin with a thumb and forefinger. 'You'll want me to arrest this man, I suppose.'

'Of *course* I want you to arrest him!' I sputtered, then lowered my voice a few octaves. 'If for no other reason than he kidnapped and assaulted my niece. But there's also the rape of Noelle Bursky and the murder of Charlotte Warren on *Voyager* to consider. Jack Westfall is the common denominator.

'Officer Martin, I don't have access to your crime reports,' I forged on, 'but I'll bet you a million dollars – that's how sure I am of this – that if you examine cases of rape of teenage girls on Phoenix ships over the course of the past few years, you will discover that the majority of them occurred on ships where Eastaugh Gallery was the art gallery concessioner and further-more, that the rapes happened, without exception, at the same time as the art gallery auction was taking place.'

It was a long speech, and I stopped to take a breath.

'Jesus,' Martin said. 'How did you . . .? Never mind. Warren, right?'

But wait, there's more, I thought. I explained my suspicions about the Ketamine, and how Kira's evidence suggested it would have been possible to introduce the drug into Julie's drink using a straw. Knowing that the straw would had to have been prepared ahead of time, I added, 'I'll bet if you search his room right now, you'll find evidence of that. Ketamine. Straws. Probably hidden in his underwear drawer.'

For the first time since I began talking, Martin hauled out a notebook and jotted something down.

'So, what are you going to do now?' Ruth wanted to know.

Martin tucked the notebook back into his breast pocket, his face immobile, grave. 'As I explained to your sister earlier, I am not a cop. I can't search a passenger's room without good reason, and I have no authority to make arrests. I'm sorry, ladies, but the best I can do is take down what you've told me and pass it on to the F.B.I. I am simply not equipped to carry out a proper investigation. I don't have the trained staff, or the facilities. They do.'

'And by then, the evidence will be gone . . .' Ruth let the thought die.

I'd already been down that path with Officer Martin. I knew it was a dead end. What we needed at that moment simply wasn't in the man's job description. 'I'm disappointed, of course,' I told him, 'but I understand that you're just doing your job, and I appreciate the time you've given us so far.'

To give him credit, Martin looked genuinely sorry when we thanked him and said goodbye.

'Thanks for nothing,' Ruth muttered as we watched Martin disappear into the piano bar. 'What's next, Hannah?'

'I think it's on to Plan B,' I said.

TWENTY

'What's Plan B?' Ruth wondered as we made our way
down the corridor that led to our stateroom.

'Hell if I know,' I said.

'David Warren is going to be royally pissed,' Ruth predicted.
'He's worked so long and so hard. This was a big breakthrough
for him.'

'I'll give him a call. But I don't think he'll be surprised.
He's been dealing with cruise-line politics for a lot longer than
I have. Out here in international waters, it's a whole other
world.'

I slotted my sea pass into the lock.

Once inside, I stuck my head into the cabin next door. Julie
sat on her bed, swaying to music that was leaking – *chicka-
chicka-chicka-chicka* – out of her earbuds, and playing a game
on her iPhone. If the encounter with her abductor that afternoon
had upset her, she was hiding it well.

I drew Georgina aside. As I described our meeting with Officer
Martin, my sister's face grew progressively more concerned. 'What
are we going to do about Julie, then? What if Westfall . . .?' She
couldn't finish the sentence, but I could fill in the blank. I
shivered.

'We'll keep Julie close, of course,' I said. 'It's only one more
day.'

Georgina agreed. What choice did she have? 'No more late
nights at Tidal Wave, that's for sure.'

'Look at it this way,' I said, sitting myself down on the foot of her bed. 'Jack Westfall is a cocky bastard. He's gotten away with rape before, and he thinks he has done it again. He uses drugs on his victims so even if they *do* remember seeing him, their testimony will be unreliable. What a power trip.'

'Westfall has no idea that Julie has identified him,' Georgina rationalized. 'As long as he thinks he's in the clear, I suppose she'll be OK. It'll be my job to keep it that way!' Suddenly, she straightened. 'What about dinner tonight? It's formal. Since we missed it the first time, Julie has her heart set on going so she can wear one of her new dresses.'

'I don't think you need to worry. David Warren told me that the Westfalls almost always eat at the second seating, so I think we're good to go.'

'Julie!' her mother called. 'Ju-lee!'

Julie yanked out her earbuds. 'What?'

'If you ran into Jack Westfall, what would you do?' her mother asked.

Julie puffed air out through her lips. 'Walk right past and pretend like I don't know him, of course. Duh. You think I'm one of those "ooooh ooooh something's making a noise out in the woods so let's go see what it is" kind of bimbos?'

Georgina sighed. 'Fourteen going on twenty.'

'I'm afraid so.'

Back in the cabin I shared with Ruth, I called David's stateroom and left a message that I needed to see him. I asked the operator to connect me to Buck Carney's cabin, too, but he didn't pick up either, so I hung up, figuring he'd be easy enough to track down. With the focus now on Jack, I was hoping Carney had taken some pictures at Breakers! that could help us where the security cameras had failed. I also needed to telephone my husband and bring him up to speed.

Until *Islander* entered the mouth of the Chesapeake Bay at Norfolk later that evening, cell phone reception was simply a fantasy. We could have Skyped from the library, of course, but then everyone within earshot would have overheard the conversation – both sides.

After discussing a plan of action with my sisters, I used the cabin phone to telephone Paul.

'Sweetheart! I was hoping you'd call.' He sounded so cheerful, I hated to burst the bubble.

I twisted the telephone cord around my finger, trying to calm my nerves. 'Not sure you'll be so happy when you hear what I have to say.'

'What's happened? Is everyone OK?'

'Sort of,' I told him. 'Do you have a piece of paper and something to write with?'

While Paul grunted, cursed, ranted and raved, using words of power I didn't even know were in his vocabulary, I filled him in on the previous twenty-four hours. Then I told him what we wanted him to do.

After I hung up, with reassurances from him that everything would be OK, Ruth checked in with Hutch. Hutch agreed to cancel his appointments for the day, swing by to pick up Paul and drive up to Baltimore where they would bring Scott into the picture.

I imagined the pow-wow: a tenured college professor, a prominent attorney and a well-respected C.P.A. The F.B.I. would never know what hit them.

When David Warren returned my call he asked to meet me in Athena, the casino bar. Hoping it wasn't smoking hour at the slot machines, I agreed. When I arrived, he was sitting on one of the banquettes near the window. A glass of white wine sat waiting for me on the coffee table. 'That was thoughtful,' I said as I sat down next to him.

As I predicted, he expressed no surprise over Martin's reluctance to clap Westfall in irons and perform a thorough search of his cabin.

Knowing that his main concern was not Julie or Noelle, who had survived, but to avenge the murder of his daughter, who had not, I said gently, 'But, surely you can turn this information over to the F.B.I. agent working your daughter's case. It has to be relevant.'

'There is no case,' he said sadly. 'Charlotte's death was ruled accidental, possibly suicide. Case closed. And Westfall will never confess to it.'

'But they *can* nab him for kidnapping Julie, and maybe pin

Noelle's rape on him, too. He could go away for a long, long time. That would be better than nothing.'

'I've lost my daughter, Hannah. I've lost my wife. I've spent the last year of my life trying to get justice for Charlotte, and I'm not going to stop now.'

While I considered what David had just said, I twirled the wine glass slowly in my hands, admiring how the multicolored lights of the casino shape-shifted in the condensation. Justice! Justice for Charlotte had been David's all-consuming purpose. Together we'd tracked down her killer – and found Julie and Noelle's attacker, too. It wasn't perfect justice where Charlotte was concerned, for sure, but I prayed David would settle for that and move on with his life.

'The sensible thing is leave it to the F.B.I.,' I said at last. 'My sisters and I have decided we have no choice but to do that.' I explained about the troika of fuming father/uncles that would be descending on the Baltimore field office of the Federal Bureau of Investigation like enraged bulls. 'I figure you know that's the sensible thing to do, too. But, if you have something else in mind, please, tell me how I can help.'

David considered me over the rim of his martini glass. 'Do you know how to get rats out of your drainpipes, Hannah?'

I smiled. 'Call the Orkin man?'

David actually laughed. 'No, you flush them out.'

'"Where the river Weser, deep and wide, washes its walls on the southern side . . ." I quoted.

His dark eyes gleamed with a spark of recognition, but perhaps it was simply a reflection of the casino lights. He leaned back and sipped his drink appreciatively. 'Ah, yes. "The Pied Piper of Hamelin."'

I could have bitten off my tongue. I'd forgotten that when the Pied Piper wasn't paid for getting rid of the town rats, he'd used his magic pipe to lure their children away, never to return. 'I know the poem by heart,' I told him, hastening to change the subject. "The Rime of the Ancient Mariner," too. Shall I recite it for you?'

David chuckled. '"The very deep did rot: O' Christ! That ever this should be! Yea, slimy things did crawl with legs, upon the slimy sea."' He winked, raised his glass. 'Thank you, Sister Mary Carmelina at Sacred Heart Academy, may your soul rest in peace!'

'So, David,' I asked after a bit. 'How do you now plan to lure this particular sea-going rat out into the open?'

He took a deep breath and exhaled. 'I wasn't on the *Voyager* and neither were you, Hannah. We've got to make Westfall believe that somebody has finally put two and two together. That somebody has twigged to what he's been up to.'

I was pretty sure I knew where David was going with this. 'Pia Fanucci.'

'Exactly. Pia holds the key to everything. She's the only person among the crew that I think we can trust.'

I set my glass down, swiveled in my seat to face him. 'Do you think that's wise, David? Things didn't turn out too well for poor Charlotte. Pia could be – no, make that *would* be – putting herself in danger. You'd never forgive yourself if something happened to her, and, frankly, neither would I. I've grown very fond of that girl.'

David nodded. 'I know. It's a dilemma.'

'What do you expect her to do, David? Send Westfall a note like in that old movie, "I Saw What You Did! And I Know Who You Are"?'

'Something like that, except I think it'd be more compelling if Westfall believes that Pia might be amenable to a little financial compensation.'

I sank back against the cushions. 'Oh, what a good idea!' I said, my voice dripping with sarcasm.

David stiffened his back. 'No, no, I think it might work. What if Pia tells him that she has written everything down in a letter, and she's mailed it to her sister with instructions that should anything happen to her . . . blah blah blah.'

You'd have to be a fan of grade B movies to come up with that sort of lame brain plan. Still, I could tell from the expression on his face that he was deadly serious about it. 'Even so,' I said, 'it could be risky.'

'I think Pia should make that decision, don't you, Hannah? Where would we find her right now?'

I knew the answer to that question. 'She's got a show tonight, so she should be backstage with Channing, getting ready.'

David set his empty martini glass down and started to get up. 'Shall we go talk to her, then?'

I laid a restraining hand on his arm. 'Why don't you let me talk to her? Then, if she's willing, we three can put our heads together and come up with a safe and workable plan.'

When we stood up, I asked, 'Do you intend to tell Officer Martin?'

David laughed. 'He'd never sanction such a thing. If this is going to work, we'll need to do it on our own.'

TWENTY-ONE

'The end of all magic is to feed with mystery the human mind, which dearly loves mystery.'
Harry Kellar (1849–1922)

I t was a short hike from the Athena bar to the Orpheus Theater located on the same deck in the bow of the enormous vessel.

Pia was backstage, as I had predicted. She sat on a straight-back chair, surrounded by Channing's illusions, using a needle and thread to sew up the tear in the leg of her yellow harem pants. 'Just now getting around to it,' she said, drawing the thread to her mouth and cutting it with her teeth. She held the pants up for my inspection. 'Do you think anybody will notice?'

'Don't you have costume people to do that?' I asked.

'Oh, sure, they'll make me a whole new costume eventually, but I'm partial to this one.' She stroked the fabric as if it were an old friend, folded it carefully, then placed it in a small bin that had her name on it: Fanucci.

'Channing's working on the new illusion,' she told me. 'Come see.'

Pia picked up her costume bin and tucked it under her arm. She held aside a curtain until I had passed through, then escorted me down a short, narrow corridor to a room full of oddly shaped items covered in plastic sheeting. In the corner stood a beach umbrella, a suit of armor and a life-sized giraffe.

Pia waved vaguely, taking in the whole room. 'Props.'

'Is Channing going to be introducing the new illusion at the magic show tonight?' I asked as we circumnavigated a gaily painted wheelbarrow.

'Sorry, no, it's not quite ready. We should be rolling it out in a couple of weeks, on the next Baltimore-Bermuda trip.' She gave me a lopsided smile. 'I'm sorry you'll miss it.'

I leaned close to her ear. 'Maybe I'll just have to stowaway, then!'

Channing was working on the far side of the room, hunched over his Plexiglas cylinders. From where I stood, I could see that the propeller had already been installed about midway inside the apparatus. It looked high-techedly wicked, like something SPECTRE would design to extract secrets out of James Bond.

When Tom noticed us, he straightened and grinned, wiping his hands clean on his jeans. 'Hannah, good to see you. Did Pia tell you? We've decided to call it The Turbine of Terror.'

'I can't wait,' I said. 'How do you get the water to it? I presume there's water.'

'Yes, there's water. There's this little gizmo . . .' He made a twisting motion, as if turning a doorknob. 'Better yet, come back in a few days and I'll show you.'

'Alas, in a few days I'll be back home, trying to get caught up with my email.'

Channing slapped his forehead. 'Of course. When one's on a ship for so long, you sometimes lose track of what day it is.'

'Tom is exploring the possibility of debuting the illusion outside on the trampoline deck. I think that would be awesome, don't you?'

I had to agree that it would.

'Tom,' I asked after a moment. 'Can I ask you a question?'

He looked up from a screw he was tightening with his fingers. 'Sure.'

'When you were performing those card tricks for the kids in Breakers! the other day, did you notice anyone hanging around, acting suspicious?'

'The afternoon your niece disappeared, you mean?'

I nodded.

'Sorry, Hannah. Even though I've been doing it for years, sleight of hand requires intense concentration. I didn't notice anything much beyond the deck of cards in front of me.'

'Just thought I'd ask.'

'And I don't believe I've ever been introduced to your niece,' he added. 'I don't even know what she looks like, I'm afraid.'

'Oh, right.' I felt pretty stupid. Julie had only been present in the crowd at one of his shows. How on earth would Tom recognize her, not to mention know if any lowlifes had been hanging around her?

Channing fished a screwdriver out of his back pocket and seemed eager to get back to work, so I said, 'Can I borrow Pia for a few minutes? There's something I'd like to talk to her about.'

'Be my guest. We're all set for tonight.'

Pia and I left the theater, walked through the casino and out on deck. A fierce wind lifted my hair and roared hotly across my ears. We strolled aft, with no particular destination in mind, while I told Pia what David and I had discovered about Jack Westfall. She listened carefully, not asking any questions, only asking for repeats when the wind tore my words away.

When we reached the cage-like barrier that led to a crew-only section of the ship, we reversed direction, stopping at one point to lean against the rail and stare out at the water.

'Every time I stand here,' Pia said, her voice breaking, 'I think of Char, floundering all alone in the middle of the Caribbean.' A tear rolled down her cheek, but was dried almost instantly by the wind. 'You'll think I'm a horrible person for saying this, but I have often prayed that she was dead before she went over.'

She closed her eyes, took a deep breath, faced into the wind with her head tipped back. 'I just love the sea. How can such an evil thing happen in such a beautiful place?'

I scooted over, until our forearms were touching where they rested on the rail. 'It's sad, really. David is convinced that because of the passage of time and the lack of evidence, he'll never get justice for his daughter.'

'I like the guy,' Pia said, 'but what a sad case.'

'My sisters and I feel pretty certain that the F.B.I. can nail Westfall for Julie's abduction.' I counted them off on my fingers. 'There's whatever physical evidence Officer Martin was able to collect when Julie was examined, Julie's positive identification, as well as the testimony that Kira will be able to provide.' I told Pia that we hoped the F.B.I. would meet the ship in the morning, armed with a proper search warrant in order to give Jack Westfall's cabin a thorough going-over. 'Julie's father should be talking to the F.B.I. now, in fact, along with my husband and Julie's other uncle.'

Keeping her head bowed, Pia turned it to study me sideways. 'A formidable team.'

'Yes.'

'But David has a team, too,' she said.

'He does?'

'You and me.'

Amazingly, Pia had given me an opening, and I stepped right through it. 'What do you suggest?'

'This morning,' Pia said, 'all I wanted to do was take the guy down a few pegs, scare the crap out of him. I saw him in the Firebird café, strutting around and glad-handing everyone like he's running for president or something. Now? He doesn't deserve to be walking the streets. He should be cooling his heels in a federal prison.'

Pia turned around, leaned her back against the rail. 'So, Hannah, how are we going to fit that SOB up with an orange jumpsuit?'

'I saw David earlier, and he has a plan,' I confessed, 'but I'm not sure I like it.'

'Try me,' she said.

'You worked on the *Voyager* and the *Islander*, you were there when both attacks occurred, you were Charlotte's roommate.' I tilted my head so I could look directly into her eyes. 'How would you feel about a little blackmail? You know, I saw what you did, but I'll keep my mouth shut as long as you . . .' I let the sentence die.

Pia was silent for so long that I thought I'd lost her. 'Pia?'

She raised a hand. 'I'm thinking, I'm thinking.'

After a bit she said more quietly, 'This could be dangerous to my health. Look what he did to Char.'

'You'd have to have an insurance policy. You'd have to convince Westfall that as long as he plays along, everything will be cool. If he doesn't, you have a letter on file with your attorney that lays it all out.'

'Sounds like a bad movie.'

'That's what I thought when David first suggested it.'

'But it could work.'

'Maybe, particularly if you don't hit him up for a *lot* of money.'

'How about a lump sum payment? I'm just so tired of the cruise ship routine, I'll say, and all I need is the down payment for a modest home in Arizona and I'll go away and leave him alone?'

As serious as the discussion was, I had to laugh. 'You remind me a bit of myself. My husband calls me Nancy Drew, girl sleuth, and he's not always being funny.'

Pia grinned. 'When I was growing up, Nancy was a little too homogenized for my taste. I cut my teeth on Harriet the Spy. Know who my heroine is now? Flavia de Luce.'

I, too, had enjoyed Alan Bradley's stories about the irrepressible eleven-year-old in fifties England with a passion for chemistry and murder. Flavia's volatile relationship with her two older sisters had struck some familiar chords, too.

As I thought about it, though, my passion for righting wrongs had gotten me into some very hot water. A sailboat had sunk out from under me, my car had been run off the road into a pond, I'd been kidnapped and locked in a wine cellar, and I was once arrested for murder. And that was all before breakfast on Monday, as my father had been known to say. As much as Pia might want to help bring Westfall to justice, I couldn't let her do it, not this way.

'It's fun to fantasize about being Nancy or Flavia,' I said after a moment. 'But that's fiction and this is real life. It was crazy of David to come up with this blackmail idea, and crazy of me to suggest it to you. You know and I know that Westfall is far too dangerous.'

Pia folded her arms, stared out to sea. 'Yeah, but it sure would be great to watch the worm squirm, up close and personal.'

I tugged on her arm, forced her to look at me. 'Pia, promise me you won't do anything foolish.'

'I promise,' she said. But I had seen that determined look before. In my daughter's eyes when she told me that she wanted to waste the entire year following her college graduation by following the rock band, Phish. In my own eyes in the mirror.

'I *mean* it,' I said. 'There must be a better way.'

'Like what?' she asked.

I didn't have the slightest idea, but I squeezed her hand and said, 'Don't worry. Leave this to David, and to me.'

TWENTY-TWO

'In the queer mess of human destiny the determining factor is luck. For every important place in life there are many men of fairly equal capacities. Among them luck decides who shall accomplish the great work, who shall be crowned with laurel, and who shall fall back into silence and obscurity.'

William E. Woodward (1874–1950)

D avid was not in his room when I called, nor in the Firebird café. I was thinking about having him paged when I found him exactly where I had left him, in the Athena, sitting on a bar stool nursing a martini.

'Fancy meeting you here,' I said, sliding onto the bar stool next to him.

He blinked twice, as if trying to focus. 'Hannah. How did you get on with Pia, then?'

'Club soda with lime,' I told the bartender.

David sipped his drink appreciatively, one eyebrow raised.

'It's far too dangerous,' I told him. 'There has to be another way.'

David's head bobbed, his lips never leaving the rim of the glass.

I touched his hand lightly. 'I'm sorry.'

David set his glass on the coaster, rocking it this way and that until the base was precisely centered in the middle of the Phoenix Cruise Lines logo. 'Don't worry,' he muttered. 'It's not that I didn't expect it.'

The bartender had delivered my drink. I took a sip and set it aside. 'Westfall's going to be put away, David. The F.B.I. is going to see to that.'

Head still bowed, he considered me with a single, watery eye. 'Just let nature take its course, then, is that your recommendation?'

'Not nature, exactly, but the long arm of the law.'

David drained his glass and raised it in the air, signaling for another. 'I want to thank you, Hannah. You've been more than kind. I appreciate that.'

We sat side by side, drinking quietly. There seemed nothing more to say.

I finished my club soda, brushed his cheek with a kiss, and bid him goodbye. I left him sitting alone at the bar, long-faced, looking as if he had lost his last friend which, in a way, he had.

'I have to pack,' Georgina said, 'and I won't let her go up there alone.'

'Go where,' I asked, 'and where's Ruth?'

'I'm hungry,' Julie whined. 'I was going to the Firebird to score some nachos. Mom's being a pain.'

Georgina folded a hoodie and placed it carefully in her suitcase. 'Ruth's at guest services, arguing with them about something on her bill. She may be there for a while. The line was humongous.'

'I'll take Julie up,' I said. 'You get on with your packing.'

Julie tore out her earbuds, hopped off her bunk and presented herself to me, beaming. She wore flip-flops, a pair of skinny denim jeans and a white T-shirt that had 'Friend Me' on it, printed in glitter.

'Come on, you,' I told her. 'Let's go get those nachos.'

The Firebird was crowded so it took us a while to find an empty table. 'Go get your nachos,' I told my niece, 'while I save the table. And bring me a Coke!'

Julie bounced off to the buffet tables while I looked around. Diners passed me with trays heaped high, as if pigging your way from one end of the All-You-Can-Eat buffet tables to the other was a lifetime goal.

I was thinking about snagging some of the chicken tikka kabobs we'd passed on our way in when Julie came streaking back, empty-handed. She grabbed my arm and pulled me down, her mouth nearly touching the tabletop. 'I need to get out of here, Aunt Hannah. I saw him! He's here! And he saw *me*!'

'Jack Westfall is here?' I asked, my head bowed, too, on a level with hers.

Julie buried her face in her arms and began to weep. 'I think I might have made a terrible mistake.'

I laid a hand gently on her arm. A horrible sinking feeling came over me. 'What do you mean, sweetie?'

'I was positive that the man who attacked me was that guy, Jack, from the art gallery, but now I'm not so sure. I just saw . . . oooh! I'm really not sure, now, Aunt Hannah, and it's freaking me out!' She began to sob.

'Let me get this straight. You just saw a guy you think could be your attacker, and that guy is *not* Jack Westfall?'

Without raising her head, Julie nodded miserably.

'Who is it, then. Who did you see, Julie?'

'I don't knoooow!' she wailed. 'I was going to the nachos, and this guy was coming from the other way, and I didn't see him, and I practically ran into him, like, and when I looked up to say sorry, he gave me this creepy look, and I went *eeeek*, and I wanted to barf and I saw in his eyes that he knew that I knew, so what am I going to do now?'

'Breathe slowly, Julie,' I suggested, gently stroking her back. 'In. Out. In. Out.'

I was kicking myself for allowing Julie to go off to the buffet alone, but that ship had already sailed.

'What did the man look like, sweetheart?'

'He's wearing a black shirt with a squiggly logo, and a black hat!'

I raised my head, stretching a bit so I could see over the decorative etched glass panel that divided our section of the café from the others. A man in a yellow T-shirt waiting for a burger; a guy in a festive Hawaiian number loading his brownie with whipped topping; uniformed wait staff bustling about, but nobody in a black polo shirt.

I swiveled in my chair to check out the other side of the café, but my view was blocked by a broad expanse of black cotton knit with 'Waterway Marine' embroidered on the pocket. Then, next to me, a familiar voice said, 'I came over to apologize.'

Buck Carney.

I gasped and pressed a hand to my chest. 'Mr Carney! You startled me.'

'I think I startled this young lady here, too. Zigged when I should have zagged,' he explained. 'Ran right into her.'

'Julie,' I said, trying to breathe normally and give nothing away. 'This is Mr Buck Carney, a photographer who's doing a book for the cruise lines. He took some photographs of your mother the other day.'

'I need a napkin,' Julie sniffed, turning her face toward the wall.

I gave her mine and watched while she pressed it to her eyes, using it as a delaying tactic, I imagined, to gather enough courage to look at Carney.

'I hope *I'm* not the guy responsible for all those tears, little miss,' Carney drawled.

Julie squared her shoulders, gazed up at him dispassionately. 'No, no,' she improvised wildly. 'My boyfriend just broke up with me, is all. It was kind of a shock.'

Carney flashed a disarming, toothy grin. 'Well, begging your pardon, miss, but that boy must be out of his cotton-pickin' mind.' When Julie didn't respond, he focused his attention on me. 'Gave me quite a turn when I ran into Miss Julie here,' he said. 'Never saw a girl who so favored her mother, never. Thought it *was* her mother, in fact, until I got a closer look. I'd love to be able to photograph the two of them together. Do you think that'd be OK?'

I thought of the times Carney'd appeared to be stalking us in the past few days and knew he was lying through his expensively capped teeth. What had Georgina said about Carney earlier? That she was sure he'd been following her and Julie. Considering his disturbing obsession with my sister, the man would have to be blind not to have noticed Julie and try to take her photo, too. Julie, in all likelihood, would have been oblivious. A sudden, sickening through came over me. Had all the attention he had given Georgina simply been a ruse in order to get close to her vulnerable fourteen-year-old daughter? How far would Carney go? I could feel the bile rising in my stomach.

'You'll have to ask her mother,' I practically spat, trying to hold myself back from saying more. 'I'm just the aunt.'

'Will you be at dinner in the dining room tonight, then?' Carney asked.

'Maybe,' I said, and let it go at that.

'Good, good. Perhaps there'll be an opportunity then.' He stepped away from the table, then stopped short. 'Sorry if I upset you, Julie.'

To her credit, Julie dredged up a smile from somewhere and pasted it on her face.

We both watched, waiting until Carney was seriously busy filling up his plate at the buffet – heavy on the fried chicken and mac and cheese – then we fled the café. When we reached the elevator lobby, Julie dragged me into the ladies' restroom, where she stopped to catch her breath, pressing her back against the wall of the handicapped stall.

I closed the door of the stall, flipped the latch, and sat down, fully clothed, on the toilet.

Julie bent at the waist, rested her hands on her knees and took deep breaths. 'What are we going to do, Aunt Hannah?'

What *were* we going to do?

'First thing,' I told her after collecting my thoughts, 'is we tell Officer Martin. If you have any doubts, we mustn't let him go on thinking that you've positively identified Jack Westfall as the man who attacked you.'

But before seeing Martin, I wanted to make sure that Carney was the actual perp, not simply a man who had made an unfortunate wardrobe choice and had the disconcerting, creepy habit of always being there, taking photos. 'Are you *sure* the man who attacked you was Buck Carney and not Jack Westfall?'

'I'm not sure of anything anymore, Aunt Hannah!' Julie whimpered. The child was miserable. I couldn't help thinking to myself that if Julie was going to be traumatized by the sight of any man wearing a black polo shirt with a logo on it, she was going to need extensive therapy.

'Second, I think we should try to behave normally. This man has victimized you once. Don't let him victimize you again. There is nothing anyone can do to hurt you when you're surrounded by family, or in the middle of a crowd. And tomorrow morning, when we get back to Baltimore? The F.B.I. will be in charge, and somebody will be arrested. Your father and your uncles will see to that.'

Julie turned her tear-stained face to me. 'What if he has a gun?'

'No gun,' I said. 'We passed through the X-ray machine,

remember? And they screened the luggage, too. I'm quite sure there are no guns aboard this ship.'

Julie nodded, her breathing still ragged. Women came and went, toilets flushed, hand-dryers roared like jet engines and still we waited, not saying another word until Julie's breathing had returned to normal.

I deposited a still-shaken Julie with her mother, then hurried off to the security office. Ben Martin wasn't there, but Molly Fortune gave me her full attention.

'So, it could be anybody, is what you're saying,' Fortune summed up when I'd finished explaining about Westfall and Carney.

'What I'm saying is that Julie would have a tough time picking the man out of a lineup, especially if they were all wearing black polo shirts and ball caps.'

'This complicates things.'

'I know. I'm sorry, but Julie was drugged, remember?'

Fortune smirked. 'Yes, and because of that, any reasonably competent criminal defense attorney would make mincemeat of Julie's positive identification anyway.' She raised both hands, palms out. 'We certainly can't lock up every passenger fitting your niece's rather vague description, now, can we?'

'You owe us safe passage,' I said, a bit steamed that she seemed to be brushing off my concerns about Julie's safety with a predator still running about loose on board. 'If anything happens to my niece, we will sue Phoenix Cruise Lines up one side and down the other, starting with Gregorius Simonides and going all the way down to *you*!'

Fortune must have earned straight A's in How To Deal With Disgruntled Customers 101 because she nodded and smiled and soothed until I came down from the ceiling. She gave me her word that Security would keep both Westfall and Carney under surveillance, suggesting, but not coming right out and saying, that plain-clothes officers would be involved. She also assured me that she would contact the F.B.I. and make sure they were brought up to speed on the situation.

Slightly mollified, I returned to Georgina's cabin where the four of us gathered for a sisterly pow-wow. After some discussion, my sisters and I decided to dress for dinner and try to act as if nothing had happened. 'We can't let scum like that spoil our last night on board, can we, Julie?' Georgina argued and, surprisingly and bravely, Julie agreed.

Ruth and I watched as Georgina stepped into a mint-colored, one-shouldered silk georgette sheath that was a knockout with her pale complexion and apricot hair.

'You look like a model, Mom,' Julie commented as she removed a silk watercolor print dress from its hanger. It had a narrow belt, with a high-low skirt that floated elegantly just below her knees. This was the dress she had long-planned for the evening. After I zipped it up the back, she spread her arms, twirled. 'Tar-jay,' she told me. 'Can you believe?'

I topped my pants with a teal lace tee, and Ruth hauled another oldie but goodie out of her closet, a red silk jump suit. A fringed shawl gave it an updated look, but she still resembled a refugee from *Charlie's Angels* and I told her so. Julie twisted her hair into a loose knot, holding it in place with a pair of decorative chopsticks. 'There,' she announced. 'I'm ready for anything!'

Thus attired, the Alexander Sisters Plus One proceeded to the Oceanus Dining Room and presented ourselves to the maître d'. Three couples were ahead of us in line.

'I thought it was supposed to be formal night,' Julie complained.

'Shhhh,' cautioned her mother, 'but I see what you mean.'

A woman just ahead wore blue jeans and a tube top. She had managed to teeter to dinner on spike-heeled sandals of eye-stabbing blue. Her companion apparently believed that 'formal' meant Bermuda shorts and a collarless tee.

The maître d' gave the couple a disdainful look up and down, straightened to his full five foot ten and said, 'Perhaps sir and madam would be more comfortable dining in the Firebird café this evening.'

As the man huffed and the woman tottered away, Julie gave an arm pump. 'Yes!' Since we had made an effort to acquire the wherewithal to dress up on formal night, I was happy to see the cruise line maintaining high standards.

On the way to our table, we made a detour to visit the Rowes. Cliff and Liz were seated at their table with Elda, the school-teacher, already enjoying their salads, but David's seat was empty. Elda was all dolled up in a pink Michael St George suit that fit her slender frame like a dream and must have cost her a month's retirement check. Her pretty features were accentuated with just a hint of makeup and her silver hair had been freshly coifed. She was probably in her late fifties, though she looked much younger. Liz had chosen a midnight-blue sequinned top for the occasion. 'Do you think David's coming?' I asked.

Cliff shrugged his tuxedoed shoulders, seemingly disinterested, chewed on a forkful of bib lettuce.

Liz spoke for both of them. 'I doubt we'll see David at dinner again. Poor man. I talked with him about moving on, but that's simply not on his agenda. Sometimes I just wanted to slap his face and scream, "David, get a life!"'

We bid Elda and the Rowes goodbye, saying we hoped to see them later at the magic show. As we crossed the dining room to our table, I wondered if David was still in the Athena bar, curled up at the bottom of a martini glass.

'Surf and turf!' Julie squealed when our server handed her a menu. 'I am so going to have that.'

I ordered a bottle of Vigonier for the table, and a Sprite for my niece.

'Vee-awn-yay,' Ruth repeated after the server left with our order. 'Always wondered how to pronounce that. Helpful to have a French scholar in the family.'

I flushed. I'd majored in French at Oberlin College, but rarely had the opportunity to use it these days, with the exception of translating menus or watching *Cinemoi* on cable TV. The server had brought us some dakos, a kind of Greek bruschetta made with cheese and tomatoes, and as I munched on a rusk of bread decorated with the black pepper- and oregano-laced concoction, I scanned the room hoping to spot some of the plain-clothes guys who were supposed to be keeping an eye on us.

I didn't spot anybody, but if I had, they wouldn't have been very good at their jobs, would they? We didn't see Buck Carney, either, which I took as a good sign.

After dinner, I left Julie in the capable hands of my sisters and nipped off to the ladies' room to wash baklava off my fingers. Their plan was to walk off their steak and lobster on the jogging track encircling deck ten, while I made a detour to the Athena bar to check on David. I would meet them at the theater later.

With my hands smelling deliciously of cherry-almond soap, I hit the bar, but David wasn't there. When I asked, the bartender told me that he'd staggered off about thirty minutes before. 'Good thing, too. If your friend had ordered another one, I was going to have to cut him off.'

It was my experience that cruise ship employees rarely, if ever, cut passengers off. I could count on the fingers of both hands, and at least one foot's-worth of toes, the number of times I'd seen passengers, blind drunk, attempting to negotiate their way back to their cabins. On one forgettable occasion, I'd had to circumnavigate a pool of vomit in order to get to mine.

I thanked the bartender, then headed on a path that would take me forward through the casino, directly to the theater. *Dee-doo, dee-doo, clack-clack-clack, cha-chunk, ra-lurl, ra-lurl* – the sounds and strobe lights were an assault on the senses; it was enough to send anyone into an epileptic seizure.

Do you want to play a game? a disembodied avatar inquired from the screen of an electronic blackjack table; his digital eyes were fixed supernaturally on mine. I quickened my pace, seeking the oasis of the elevator lobby ahead, a bright white light at the end of a kaleidoscopic tunnel.

I stepped on the gas, scooting around the roulette table as if the avatars were hot on my heels chanting: *Would you like to double down?*

I was so focused on getting the hell out of Dodge that when someone tapped me on the shoulder, I actually yelped.

I pressed a hand to my chest and spun around. 'Oh my gawd! Connor, isn't it? You scared me!'

'I'm sorry, but I just wanted to talk for a moment. You're Julie's aunt, right?'

I admitted that I was. 'Please, let's get out of here,' I begged.

Once in the relative sanctuary of the lobby, I stopped and faced the Crawford lad who had been the target of truly inventive invective from my sister, Georgina. I planned to ask if he'd made the phone call to my sister's cabin the other day, but decided to wait and see what he had to say. 'What can I do for you, Connor?'

'Not here,' Connor Crawford said. 'Somebody might overhear.'

He led me out onto the deck, where we paused under one of the lifeboats that was suspended from davots overhead. He looked right and left, as if planning to cross the street, and then crossed it. 'I know who kidnapped Julie.'

I thought I did, too, but coming from Connor Crawford, the news shocked. I gasped, gaped, finally asked, 'Who?'

'Well, not his name exactly, but I know what cabin he's in.'

I was dying to wring the cabin number out of him, but Connor was wound so tight that words erupted in one nearly breathless stream. 'I was up in the Internet room on deck eight, you know, and coming down this hallway when I ran into an old dude with his arm around Julie. She had a hoodie on, you know, but I recognized her from her hair. Oh, shit, I thought, that dude is *not* her dad. And Julie was stumbling all over the place, getting her legs all twisted up, and falling down, he was practically carrying her, like, and I thought This. Is. Not. Good.

'So they stagger past me and I'm thinking, shit, what do I do now, so I turned around and saw this perv practically dragging Julie into a room, and the door shuts and I go Oh. My. God. This is so sick! So, I go to the door and check out the number, and I'm heading off to set off a fire alarm or something, then I think, no, he might have really done something to Julie by then, so I go back to the room and I pound on the door . . .' Connor demonstrated by jack-hammering both fists in the air above his head. 'Then I listen and there's, like, nothing.'

I'm sure I was nodding like a bobble-head doll. 'And then?'

'So I go off to get help, and I find this steward named Leon at the end of the hall, changing one of the rooms, like they do, you know, and he kinda laughs and tells me to chill, that this kind of thing happens all the time on cruises. Girls who dress like sluts are just begging to get laid, I beg your pardon, ma'am. So I think, this asshole is no help at all! So I remember that there's a concierge club across from the Internet place. I run down there and I tell the receptionist, and she calls some guy in Security who meets me at the room. He pounds on the door but nobody answers. I'm yelling, like, break it down, break it down, so he uses his pass key and . . . nothing. Room is empty, nothing looks off.'

'Are you sure you got the right room, Connor?'

'Damn sure!'

My heart raced as I imagined what might have happened to Julie if Connor hadn't been checking his email that day. 'What was the cabin number, Connor? Please tell me you remember.'

'I said it over and over, so I wouldn't forget. 8622.'

8622. 8622. 8622. I didn't want to forget that number, either.

'Whose room is it, do you know?'

'Not a clue, and Security wouldn't say.'

'What did the room look like, Connor? Julie remembered a kind of living room.'

Connor shrugged. 'You could say so, I guess. It was a double made up as a single, so there was more room for the sofa and stuff.'

So, there it was.

I've got your room number now, you sonofabitch! And it won't be long before I have your name, too.

'Wanna know how they found her?' Connor asked.

I must have looked puzzled because he said, 'The steward had a laundry basket, one of those things on wheels. When I came back with the security guy, like almost right away, the laundry basket was gone.' He shrugged, blushing modestly. 'I kinda put two and two together.'

I reached out for Connor's arm, held on and squeezed. 'Thank you, Connor. We owe you big time. But, why didn't you tell us this before?'

Connor rolled his eyes. 'I called Julie's room, but when her mom answered, I kinda freaked. Julie's mom? She hates me, man. She'd think I did it, or was helping the perv out or something. Look, I admit I bought Julie those drinks at the pool the other day, and that was really dumb, I'm sorry. But I'd never *really* do anything to hurt her.'

That explanation made sense to me. Georgina *would* have shot first and asked questions afterwards.

'I made a statement to that head security guy, what's his name, Martin. He said the F.B.I. might want to ask me some questions, and I'm cool with that, too.'

I thanked Connor with a hug. It didn't matter whether Julie could identify the creep or not. We had an eyewitness to her attack. I couldn't wait to find David and tell him the good news.

But first, I walked as quickly as I could up to deck eight. I stood in front of Room 8622, willed the door to open and the pervert to show his face. In spite of Julie's confusion, my money was still on Jack Westfall. He certainly had the means and opportunity and, according to Kira, he'd handled the straw that went into Julie's Virginia Colada.

I took a deep breath and knocked on the door.

Nobody answered.

Connor had been in the Internet room on the same deck, so I visited there next. I snatched a sheet of paper out of the printer, borrowed a pencil from a young Turk checking the status of his stock portfolio on the Internet, folded the paper into quarters and scribbled 'Jack Westfall' on it.

Halfway back to cabin 8622, I ran into a steward. Not Leon, thank goodness, who I hoped was cooling his heels, confined to his cabin for the duration of the voyage.

'Carlos,' I said, after a glance at his name tag. 'I promised to get this information to Mr Jack Westfall, but I can't remember whether he's in 8622 or 8624.'

Carlos from Mexico City smiled helpfully. 'Mr and Mrs Westfall are in 8592. But I'll be happy to deliver the note for you, if you like.' He held out his hand.

'Oh, would you? How kind.' I handed Carlos the note, along with a five-dollar bill. I followed along, slightly behind, as he headed down the hallway. 'I can't imagine how I got so confused about the room number. I was *sure* Jack said 8622 or 8624. Are you sure he's in 8592?'

'Yes, ma'am. This section, it's mostly for staff. Mr LeRoy Carney, he is in 8622.'

'The photographer?' I asked, my heart pounding.

'Yes, ma'am.' Carlos paused, turned, grinned.

'8624, now, that's Miss Pia and Miss Lorelei,' Carlos was saying when I tuned back in.

'Ah,' I said as we neared the Westfall's cabin. 'The magician's assistants. I saw them in Channing's sword basket act the other night, and they were terrific.'

'He pulled a silver dollar out of my ear one time. Let me keep it, too. Very nice guy.'

'You've never seen his show?'

Carlos's shoulders drooped. 'I have to work,' he said simply.

I thanked Carlos profusely, feeling sad that because of his punishing schedule, his only exposure to Channing's amazing talents had been a bit of prestidigitation in the corridor. I also tried to hide my annoyance with Officer Ben Martin, who had obviously been keeping information from us. It wasn't as if we were disinterested bystanders. We actually had a need to know.

But it was all good, I thought, as I strolled along the deck toward the bow. Buck Carney was going nowhere, I thought with perverted pleasure, except to a federal prison where he'd meet new, close friends. *Big, ugly, hairy friends*, I thought, quoting Bette Midler in *Ruthless People*. Not that he'd ever see what they looked like, because he'd be facing the other way.

Just thinking about it made me grin.

TWENTY-THREE

'As the cabinet is turned, or seen from the extreme sides,
some spectators will find they are looking at themselves in
the mirror.'

Jim Steinmeyer, *Hiding the Elephant*, Da Capo,
2004, p. 81

B efore I ran into Connor, it had been my intention to arrive
at the theater first, snag four seats in a row near the front
of the stage, and be well into my second mojito by the
time my sisters showed up.

Not surprisingly, they had gotten there first.

I was boiling over with excitement at the news I was carrying,
but I managed not to erupt until the server had disappeared with
our drinks order. 'So, you see,' I said after the server had gone,
and come back, and I'd finally reached the end of my chronicle,
'if it hadn't been for Connor . . .' I let the sentence die. Everyone
sitting round me could fill in the blank.

Julie blushed and smiled a secret smile. She reminded me of
the Mona Lisa, or maybe the Cheshire Cat. 'So I was right after
all,' she said. 'I just *knew* it!'

'I'll have to apologize to the young man,' Georgina said. 'I'm
just so very, very grateful. If only I had known.'

'You can pin a medal on him later, Georgina,' Ruth
whispered.

I'd skipped the part about Connor confessing to buying Julie
booze; an executive decision, and one I do not regret, I thought,
as I melted into the upholstered seat and began to enjoy my
drink.

'May I join you?'

I turned, straw still caught between my lips, as David slid into
the empty seat on my right.

'We missed you at dinner,' I told him.

'Unavoidably detained,' he said, pointing to his forehead.

'What happened?' I asked, squinting at his face as the house lights began to dim. A square white bandage decorated the area just above his left eyebrow.

'Two stitches,' he explained. 'I'll live.'

'You didn't answer my question, David.'

David flagged down a passing server and ordered a club soda with lime. 'When I came out of the bar, I had a run-in with Jack Westfall. He accused me of ruining his life. Blamed me for Security asking permission to search his room.'

'And?'

'He refused, of course.'

'About the run-in, I mean. The bandage. Explain.'

'I'd had a bit to drink, words were exchanged, and I took a swing at him. He swung back and I forgot to duck. Bastard. I'd like to nail his ass.'

'I'm afraid we were wrong about Jack Westfall, David.' In the few minutes remaining before the show began, I briefed David on the occupant of cabin 8622, what Connor saw and what I had subsequently learned about Mr Leroy 'Buck' Carney.

'God damn,' he said. 'Have you told Pia?'

'No time, but I will, after the show.'

Suddenly the house lights dimmed and the intro music began, something slow and tinkling like sands through an hourglass.

The opening act was Cameron Reyes, a recent semi-finalist on *American Idol*, or maybe it was *The Voice*. Cameron's rendition of 'Hey, Gotta Stay Awake' – a song of his own composing, according to the emcee – alternately soared, then plunged through at least four octaves, producing wails so pitiful that Reyes could have been passing a kidney stone, for all I knew, just like our late Aunt Evelyn. If there was a key, he never managed to find it. Autotune was the only explanation for the popularity of the guy. Millions of fans had already downloaded this very song from iTunes. Go figure.

Me? I just wanted to rip my ears off.

Finally, he went away.

After a moment, the *Star Wars* theme began and Channing strolled out on stage. To keep his act fresh for the audience, he'd replaced the floating ball with the Chinese linking rings, solid circles of steel that linked and unlinked, or passed through one another so seamlessly that you'd think the metal had liquefied.

Pia had told me that the Zig-Zag Box would be replaced by the Vanishing Cabinet, so I wasn't surprised when Pia and Channing rolled the brightly painted cabinet from the wings and centered it on the stage.

Wearing a red brocade cheongsam, Pia stood to the right of the cabinet, smiling brightly. Channing smiled upon the audience from the opposite side of the cabinet. Channing approached the footlights, his teeth dazzling as he said, 'We need a volunteer from the audience! Who would like to volunteer?'

Julie's hand shot up. She bounced in her seat making *ooooh, ooooh* noises like a student with the correct answer to the question, 'What is the capital of Iowa?'

Georgina grabbed her daughter's arm. 'Sit *down*, Julie!'

'I want to do it, Mom! Please!' All during this conversation, she continued to wave at the magician, signaling *look at me, look at me!*

Although Channing first appeared to favor a young blonde girl in the front row, Julie's tactic worked. Channing's arm shot out. 'You! The pretty little redhead in the second row!'

Julie shot to her feet, both hands pressed to her chest. 'Me? You mean me?' She favored her mother with a pitiful, pleading glance.

Georgina nodded once, shooed Julie off with a flick of her hand.

Julie's eyes darted right, then left – *where are the stairs?* – but Channing was already striding stage left, hand extended – *this way, young lady, this way* – and in a few seconds had seized her upraised hand and escorted her to stand in front of the cabinet.

He bent his head to her ear and asked a question.

Julie's smile vanished. Her lips moved.

Channing answered, then straightened and waved an arm dramatically over my niece's head. 'Ladies and gentleman, I give you Miss Julie Cardinale, all the way from Baltimore, Maryland, who has kindly agreed to assist us with this demonstration!'

Channing opened one door of the cabinet, Pia the other. A bouncy ragtime tune began playing as Pia demonstrated that the cabinet was completely empty, then Channing took Julie's hand and helped her step inside.

Julie faced the audience, hands folded demurely in front of her, smiling uncertainly.

One gaily painted door closed over Julie, then the other. Pia and Channing together spun the cabinet around three times – *three's the charm!* – and when they opened the doors again, Julie was gone.

Georgina gasped.

'Amazing,' pronounced Ruth. 'And the girl has absolutely no training.'

'Where did she go?' a woman behind me hissed.

'It's a trap door, silly,' her companion replied.

Although Pia hadn't showed me the inner workings of the cabinet, I was fairly certain that Julie hadn't gone anywhere. After three more turns, the doors were reopened and our precious girl was back, bowing stiffly from the waist, drinking in the applause.

'How did you *do* that, Julie Lynn?' her mother wanted to know when Julie rejoined us, reclaiming her seat.

'Before the magician asked me my name, he made me promise not to tell.'

'Ah, the magicians' code,' I explained. 'Julie has just been initiated into the club.'

Julie folded her arms across her chest. 'Some club,' she muttered.

I leaned closer. 'What did you say, Julie?'

'Shhhh, you two!' Georgina cautioned. 'The next act is starting.'

The Vanishing Cabinet was removed and the Indian Sword Basket appeared. One girl went into the sword basket and two girls came out but, unlike last time, both remained completely unscathed.

The magician and his two beautiful and talented assistants exited stage right, the music soared then faded, and the show was over.

We were gathering up our handbags, preparing to leave when Julie stopped us. 'Pia's gone to the dressing room to change,' Julie said. 'She told me to ask Hannah to wait. I want to see her, too.'

'I thought you wanted to sit in the hot tub, Julie,' Georgina fussed, sending a look of desperation in my direction. 'It's our last chance.' Georgina had been my sister long enough for me to read the hidden message.

'If Julie wants to stay with me for now, that's fine,' I said, reading the please-please-Aunt-Hannah-please message in my niece's eyes. 'Maybe Pia will take her back stage and show her the props.' I winked at my niece. 'Now that you're a junior magician.'

'What are your plans, Ruth?' Georgina wanted to know.

'Hot tub sounds divine!' She raised an eyebrow at me. 'Join us when you finish here?'

'Julie?' I asked.

Tight-lipped, Julie nodded.

'As soon as we finish up here, we'll hop into our bathing suits and come find you. Keep the water hot!' I called after my sisters.

Almost the second her mother and aunt turned their backs and started down the aisle, Julie crumpled.

David stepped in at once. 'What's wrong, Julie?'

'Nobody's going to believe me now! Nobody!' Dry-eyed, bathed in the warm lights of the auditorium, Julie began to shiver. I wrapped an arm around her shoulder and drew her close.

'It's his aftershave,' Julie continued, unprompted. 'Up on the stage when he put his head next to mine, I knew. Right away, I knew. Smells like paint thinner.'

David and I exchanged worried glances. 'Tom Channing?' I blurted. 'You mean you now think Tom Channing was the man who attacked you?'

Julie nodded.

'Why didn't you say something when your mother was here, Julie?'

'Mom is so judgmental! She's pissed off at me for wasting everybody's time.'

'No, she's not.'

'Is, too. Before we came down here tonight I got the mother-daughter talk from hell. "A man's life is at stake, Julie Lynn! You have to be one-hundred-percent sure instead of pointing fingers at every man on the ship wearing a black shirt!" Blah blah blah.' She paused, consulting David. 'Because of the drugs, I may not remember much, Mr Warren, but I *do* remember that smell. When Channing put his head next to mine, I gagged. I felt like I was going to hurl.' Then to me, 'But I held it together up there, didn't I, Aunt Hannah?

Suddenly it all made sense. Julie's sudden stiffness on stage, her tight lips. I'd chalked it up to sudden stage fright. 'You did indeed, sweetie. We had no idea.'

To David, I said, 'What should we do? Julie's right. This is the third man that Julie has fingered as her attacker. I doubt anyone will believe her testimony now.' For Julie's sake, I found what I hoped was a reassuring smile and sent it her way.

'He knows that I know, too,' Julie cut in.

'What?'

'Up there on stage? When he put me in the box, I just said it right out. "*You* did it," I said. His face got all twisty in the lights, and when he shut me in the cabinet he threatened me. "If you tell anybody, Joo-lee" – just like that, Joo-lee – "I'll make you disappear for good, just like those other naughty little girls."'

I grabbed Julie's hand, squeezed it hard. 'Oh my God!' Random thoughts, snatches of past conversations were crashing around in my brain like bumper cars. After a moment I asked, 'Does Pia know?'

Julie's curls bounced as she shook her head. 'Nobody heard but me and him.'

Largely silent until now, David spoke. 'You're right. After two mistaken identifications, Julie's credibility is shot. But I have an idea.' David reached into the inner breast pocket of his jacket and began fishing for the iPhone I knew he kept there.

Just then, Julie sat bolt upright. 'Oh my God, oh my God, I am *so* out of here!'

Channing, still dressed in his performing attire, smiling broadly, was striding down the aisle in our direction. Why, I had no idea. Was he trying to intimidate Julie?

'Brazen bastard,' David snarled. 'It's an issue of control with these sons of bitches. He probably thinks he's got Julie under his spell.'

But Julie didn't wait around to be charmed or intimidated. With the aisle blocked by Channing's advancing figure, she vaulted onto the stage and scurried off into the wings.

The instant Julie fled, Channing's smile vanished and he took off after her. David and I were unimportant, invisible.

'Tom, stop!' I yelled. 'What do you think you're doing?'

If I hurried, I thought I could intersect Channing before he got to the stairs that would take him up onto the stage. No way was I going to let him get to Julie.

Thanks to an Olympic-worthy sprint at my end, we reached the stairs at the same time. I threw myself at his legs, and succeeded in grabbing one ankle. He turned and shook his leg free, as if I were a pesky lap dog.

I'd never played football – my sport was archery – not that either skill would have done me much good at the time as I was flat out on the floor, grimacing in pain.

Channing strode purposefully across the stage. By now I was convinced that the man had become seriously unhinged, although, thinking about it as I lay there trying to catch my breath, he had obviously been twisted for some time. But what could he possibly hope to gain by harming Julie in front of me and all these witnesses?

'Call Security!' I yelled to David Warren. 'Tom's flipped out!'

I got to my knees, scrambled to my feet, and charged after him. Channing had reached the wings and as I ran, gasping, I watched him draw the curtain aside.

'I know you're in here, you little bitch!' he rasped, his voice frosty, cruel. Something fell over with a metallic crash, like cymbals. The Chinese rings, I thought. He'd run into the prop table.

When I erupted through the curtain, Channing had sent the Indian Sword Basket flying off its base and turned his attention to the Vanishing Cabinet. He grasped the handles and threw open the doors, then peered inside.

'God dammit! Where have you got to? You can't hide from me, you little slut!' Channing had totally lost the plot. He extended a long arm into the cabinet just as I caught up with him.

'Security's on the way!' I screamed, pounding with my fists on the man's back. 'Get out of here and leave my niece alone!'

I thought I might have gotten through because Channing did an about-face, shoved me roughly aside and went out the way he had come. But where was Julie?

The doors to the Vanishing Cabinet stood wide open. I peeked inside. Empty. Or was it? I didn't have time to figure out how

the illusion worked. I rapped on the open door. 'Julie, if you're
in there somewhere, knock and let me know.'

Tap-tap-tap. Faint, but clear.

Thank God, I thought.

'Stay there!' I ordered. 'I'll be back for you. And don't come
out until I do!'

I spun on my heel to take up the chase, then stopped short. A
large hand was pulling the curtain aside. Shit! Had Channing
doubled back?

'David!' I cried when I saw the man's face. 'God, you scared
me! Thank heaven's you're here. Did you call Security?'

He ignored my question. 'Where's Channing?' he said darkly.

'He went that way,' I said, flapping my hand rapidly. 'I don't
know how you missed him.'

David gazed past me, to the ruin that had been Channing's
props. He kicked at one of the Chinese rings, sending it rolling
across the floor. With the toe of his shoe, he lifted the Indian Sword
Basket and let it fall. He stooped, picked up one of the sabres,
licked his thumb and used it to test the sharpness of the blade.

'They're not trick swords,' I told him. 'Be careful or you'll
cut yourself.'

Empty-eyed, moving with the rigid determination of a cemetery
ghoul in *Night of the Living Dead*, David turned, almost trance-
like, and pushed aside the curtain.

I doubt he even heard me.

TWENTY-FOUR

'Another issue is the cost borne by U.S. taxpayers when the U.S. Coast Guard is enlisted to search for a missing passenger. This expense is not trivial. In just one case . . . the total cost incurred during the search was estimated by the Coast Guard to be $813,807.'
Testimony of Ross A. Klein, PhD before the Senate
Committee on Commerce, Science, and
Transportation, March 1, 2012

Raising the sabre high over his head, David charged through the curtain, screaming like a Rough Rider at the attack on San Juan Hill.

'What the hell are you doing?' I yelled, running after him.

With energy I didn't suspect he had, David sprinted down the aisle, almost catching up with Channing at the theater doors. Amazingly, the few people left standing in the aisle did nothing to stop them; they simply gave way and moved aside, widening the path. With Channing still in costume, and David waving a sabre, they may well have thought it was an impromptu encore.

David followed Channing out onto the deck, into the cool, breezy air with me pounding along after him. Channing looked right, left, then headed for the stern. A poor choice, as it turned out, as he drew up short at a high, steel mesh-covered fence designed to keep passengers, according to the sign, away from a crew-only area.

Channing tried the door, rattled the lock then looked back, his face deceptively calm, to see David gaining on him, brandishing the sabre. Quick as a wink, Channing produced his staff ID, swiped it through the electronic lock and threw open the door. Channing braced his palm against the mesh, trying to shut the door firmly behind him, but he was too late. David straight-armed the door, slamming it into Channing's startled face.

Blood began to gush, running dark and wet down Channing's

upper lip. He swiped his hand across his mouth, studied it in the semi-darkness, stumbled, and fell to his knees.

The door clanged shut, the lock engaged.

On the other side of the mesh, David had Channing cornered at the end of a long, narrow balcony. Here and there dark shapes, which I took to be nautical equipment, were shrouded in canvas. A few sturdy plastic chairs sat jumbled together in an alcove.

'What the *hell* is going on?' I didn't realize Pia had come up behind me until she spoke.

'We have to stop David, or he's going to kill Tom!' I shouted.

'But why?' Pia cried. 'What did Tom ever do to him?'

I grabbed the handle of the door and jiggled it up and down, but it wouldn't open. 'What's out there?'

'It's the crew's equipment area,' Pia said breathlessly. 'They sit out there sometimes, smoke and stuff.'

'The door's locked! Can you scan your ID and open it up?'

Pia's hands flew to her chest, patted the pockets of her white cotton camp shirt. 'I can't, Hannah,' she cried, 'I must have left it in the dressing room!'

'David!' I yelled, banging on the grill with my fists. 'Put down the sword! He's not worth it!'

With his free hand, David grabbed one of the chairs, shook it free from the others, and tossed it after Channing. It slid into him where he lay sprawled next to the rail. 'Stand up!' he ordered.

Channing's mouth gaped. He didn't move.

David took a step closer, brandishing the sabre. 'You don't listen very well. Stand up, I said!'

Channing worked his way into a crawling position, then slowly rose to his feet. He shook his head as if to clear it, then said, 'You're out of your mind, you know that?' His voice shook. Even in the dim light, I could see sweat glistening on the man's brow.

'Now, stand up on it,' David ordered.

'What?'

'Stand up on the goddamn chair!'

When Channing didn't move, the sabre flashed, connecting with Channing's leg.

'Up!' David yelled.

'I can't!' Channing screamed, clutching the gash in his leg as if trying to hold the wound together. Blood drained slowly from it, pooling on the floor next to his foot.

Pia grabbed my arm and tugged. 'What's wrong with David? Is he drunk?'

'We just found out that Tom is the person who attacked Julie, so he's probably the guy who murdered Charlotte, too.'

'Tom? No way! You're both crazy if you think that.'

I covered Pia's hand where it rested on my arm and squeezed. 'There's a witness,' I told her gently.

'God, no!'

'David!' I yelled, trying to be heard over the howling of the wind. 'Put the sabre down!'

He ignored me. 'You have a decision to make, Channing. You can get up on the chair, or I can take this sabre and run you through. You choose.'

Holding on to the back of the chair for support, Channing slowly, painfully eased his wounded leg up on the chair. A few agonizing seconds later, he was standing unsteadily on the seat. His fine, silver hair whipped wildly around his forehead.

What was keeping Security?

Suddenly it hit me. David had never placed the call. 'Pia!' I whispered. 'Call Security! I'll see if I can talk some sense into David.'

On the other side of the barrier, David stood ramrod straight, legs slightly spread, sword tip pointed down in order arms position. 'So, Channing. How are you enjoying the evening so far?'

'I don't even know who in fucking hell you are!' Channing shouted into the wind.

David said, deadly calm, 'I had a beautiful daughter once, Channing. Her name was Charlotte.'

Channing swayed as if slapped, but recovered quickly. 'I don't know who the hell you're talking about.'

'Let me refresh your memory, then,' David snarled. He raised the sabre, rested the point against Channing's chest. 'Careful, careful,' he warned. 'Don't lean forward or you might get hurt!'

'You are out of your fucking mind!'

'*Phoenix Voyager*,' David continued, ignoring the interruption. 'A young girl named Noelle. Do you even remember her name? Maybe she was your first, maybe not. But my daughter was a

smart girl, Channing. She worked with the kids. She had sharp
eyes, and she noticed something. What was it? Did she see you
slip the drug into Noelle's drink?'

David slid the point of the sabre slowly up Channing's chest
until it was resting slightly above his breastbone. 'You murdered
my daughter, you worthless piece of shit.'

Channing's eyes didn't stray from the hand that held the sabre.
A look of desperation clouded his eyes. 'What do you want
from me?'

'I want a confession, that's what I want.'

Channing raised both hands in a sign of surrender. 'OK, OK.
Whatever you say. I admit it. I killed your daughter. There, I said
it. Is that enough?'

'And? Come on, Channing. You can do better than that.
And?'

'I pushed her overboard, OK? She was going to ruin everything.
She was going to turn me in, ruin my career, and that would . . .'
He paused and winced as the tip of the sabre bit into his neck.

'They say confession is good for the soul, Channing. Tell me,
now. What had Charlotte found out?'

'You know exactly what, you maniac. I know you're working
with *her*,' he snarled, glancing in my direction, 'and I overheard
her talking with Pia.'

'Say it! Say it out loud. You like sex with little girls. With
children, you piece of slime. Children you have to drug until
they're too helpless to resist.'

Channing stammered; in that moment, he looked truly defeated.
'You don't understand . . . nobody does.'

'Oh, boo hoo,' David snapped. 'You're breaking my heart
here.'

'Put down the sword, please,' Channing begged, changing
tactics. 'I'll do whatever you say. Write a confession, sign it.
Whatever. Just put down that sword.'

'No need for that,' David snapped. 'We're not quite finished
here, are we? Tell me about Julie Cardinale.'

Channing's head swiveled in my direction. 'I didn't hurt Julie,
Hannah, I swear. And I didn't know . . .'

'Bullshit!' I couldn't help myself. 'Julie may be scarred for
life, not that you gave that possibility a moment's thought!'

'I didn't . . .' Channing stammered.

'But you *would* have, you worm,' I shouted through the mesh that separated us, 'if somebody hadn't knocked on the door.'

Chandler's chin dropped, and I knew I'd hit the nail on the head.

'So, now that's settled,' David said, 'I think it's time for a good, old-fashioned nautical tradition.'

Chandler's head shot up. 'What are you talking about?'

'I think it's time for you to walk the plank.'

'Plank? What plank?'

'Figuratively speaking, of course. When in doubt, improvise. The chair will do nicely, I think.'

'David!' I shouted, looking desperately around me, wishing that Ben Martin or his officers would hurry up before things got even more out of control. 'Stop it! Stop!' I saw a life ring hanging on a railing nearby, lifted it off its hook and held on, praying that it wouldn't be needed.

'Jump,' David said. 'Jump, you sonofabitch, jump!' David feinted; the sabre flicked again. Channing closed his eyes and sucked in his lips like a stubborn child.

''Course, you don't have to jump. I could just run you through and save both of us a lot of time.' The sabre twitched and Channing flinched. 'But the way *I* look at it, Channing, you'd have a better chance of surviving if you jump. Death by water or by the sword, take your pick.'

Channing's wild eyes caught mine, and he mouthed a silent *Help!*

'Security is on the way!' I shouted, hoping that both men heard me.

David risked a quick glance at me. Was he trying to convey some kind of message? Then, 'Too little, too late,' he said, before focusing his attention back on Channing.

'How'd you do it, then, Channing? Drugging those girls – drugging Julie, I mean. It had to have been in the soda straws, but the bartender told me only she and Jack Westfall touched them.'

Incredibly, a slow, sinister grin spread across Channing's face. Now it was his time to boast. 'Sleight of hand, Warren, my stock in trade. You redirect their attention here . . .' His left arm shot

out, the cuff of his shirt sleeve flashing white in the deck lights.
'. . . when all the action is really over *here*!' Using his right arm,
he swept the sword that David held aside.

The trick might have worked, too, if Channing hadn't been
balanced precariously on the chair.

With a desperate glance over his shoulder, Channing teetered
backwards and tumbled over the railing.

'No!' I screamed, and threw the life ring I had been holding
over the side.

Behind me, I heard pounding footsteps, at last. 'Man overboard! Man overboard!' Pia was back on the deck, running flat
out, waving her arms.

Behind her, also moving at full speed, was Officer Martin, his
phone pressed against his chin. 'Oscar Oscar Oscar Starboard
Side.' His voice was steady, controlled. Clearly he'd practised
the man overboard procedure hundreds of times.

Almost immediately, his call was repeated, blasting from the
loudspeaker mounted on the bulkhead directly over my head,
echoing from other loudspeakers all around the ship. *Oscar Oscar
Oscar Starboard Side!*

Whooo! Whooo! Whooo!

As the deafening sound of the ship's horns died away, the ship
shuddered, slowed, and began to turn.

With icy calm, David lowered the sabre and pulled down on
the handle on his side of the barrier that would open the gate. I
started to step aside, but as he approached me he reached into
the breast pocket of his jacket and pulled out his iPhone. 'Hannah,'
he said. 'Take it. I recorded it all.'

'Oh, David, why . . .?' I managed to croak as he pressed the
phone into my outstretched hand and folded my fingers protectively over it.

Then he altered course, heading directly for Pia. 'This is yours,
I believe,' he said, handing her the sabre. 'I wasn't going to push
him off, Hannah, you have to believe me. I just wanted to scare
him so he'd come clean about Noelle, Charlotte and Julie.'

Despite finally having his questions answered, David didn't look
any better for it. If anything, he looked more broken. I believed
him; he may have forced Channing onto the chair, but it wasn't
David's fault the magician had stumbled over the side. I

remembered the look David had given me; clearly he hadn't fore-
seen the outcome – Channing actually tumbling over the side.

My heart ached for my friend as he staggered to the railing,
sagged and rested his head on his arms. Then, suddenly, more
quickly than I believed possible, he had one leg over the rail.

'No!' I screamed, but it was too late. Without so much as a
backward glance, David launched himself over the railing and
flew overboard, too.

I rushed to the railing and looked down. David's jacket had
caught on something. Instinctively I leaned over and stretched
out my hand, but he was too far below me for it to do any good.
David's jacket held for perhaps a second more, then ripped away.
I watched in horror as my friend plunged into the sea.

Someone had grabbed another life ring. I felt the breeze as it
sailed past my face. I leaned over the rail again, straining my
eyes, trying to pick out David's face in the inky blackness of the
water.

I should have known it would be fruitless. The ship had been
traveling at twenty knots. Thomas Channing and David Warren
would already be floating far behind. Strobe lights attached to
the life rings – there were more than a dozen of them floating
in the water now – blinked in the distance like lighthouse
beacons.

From the bow, flares shot into the air as the huge vessel
continued its slow turn, heading back to the area where the two
men had jumped.

Islander decelerated until she was barely moving. I was now
only one of several hundred people crowding the rails as we
watched a speedboat being launched from several decks below.
I could see the white uniforms of the crew that manned the tiny
vessel as the engines revved and the boat sped off, following
the trail of strobes which were bobbing like breadcrumbs on the
dark, oily water.

'Do you think they'll find him?' Pia sobbed.

I wrapped my arm around her shoulders, unsure who she
meant. 'Who? Thomas Channing or David Warren?'

I felt her shrug. 'Both, I suppose. I just can't *believe* it, Hannah.
I thought I was close to Tom – as close as anyone ever got to
him, anyway. But I guess I really didn't know him at all, did I?'

She swiped tears away with the back of her hand. 'It's partly my fault, too,' she sniffed.

'How can *any* of this be your fault, Pia?'

She turned a tear-stained face to me. 'Remember the night I was injured? Before the show I told Tom about my conversation with David. I thought Tom was out of sorts that night but it never crossed my mind that that could be why . . .' She paused. 'And David . . . I really care about David, Hannah. He seems like such a lost soul. Everything he loved most in the world, taken from him, and now a cruel twist at the end. He deserves better than, than . . .'

I considered the dark surface of the sea and knew what she was thinking. 'I think David died the day his wife died, Pia. His life had only one purpose after that. Find his daughter's killer. And he succeeded. After that . . . well, what more did he have to live for?'

'Suicide is never the answer, Hannah.'

'I know. Back when I had, well, health issues, I learned that life is too precious to be given up willingly.'

The sky lit up like the Fourth of July as more flares were launched from the rescue vessel. Spotlights mounted on its pilot house switched on and began slow sweeps, combing the water.

'I guess I'm out of a job,' Pia said, leaning her forearms on the railing, peering off into the distance where rescue lights were dancing around on the waves.

'There's always the Oracle,' I said.

'Hah! My goal in life. Serving wine to knitters. You know what I want to do right now, Hannah? I want to go home and hug my parents.'

I wanted to do the same, but my mother had passed away more than a decade before and Dad had moved away. 'Where do they live, Pia?' I asked.

'Boston. North End. They own a restaurant.'

'Italian?' I wondered aloud.

In the light from the flares, I saw Pia smile. 'How did you guess?'

We stood in companionable silence for a while, until someone shouted, 'Look! They're coming back!'

Pia and I leaned forward, straining our eyes. Indeed, the launch was returning. As it neared the side of *Islander*, we noticed white-shirted crew members performing CPR on someone lying on the deck at the stern. 'Is that David or Tom?' I asked, straining forward, trying to get a better view. 'Where are my binoculars when I need them?'

'I can't tell.'

Neither could I. David had been wearing a jacket over a blue oxford shirt, but the victim's chest seemed to be bare. The rescue launch drew up to *Islander*, port side kissing our starboard, so close that we couldn't see it anymore. But they must have offloaded the victim, because the launch zipped off almost immediately, heading back into the sea of strobes.

For more than an hour *Islander* idled. In the distance, lights swept the water continually, then suddenly they seemed to multiply, divide. I blinked, refocused, blinked again.

A man standing nearby who had been viewing the rescue effort through binoculars shouted, 'It's the Coast Guard!'

The cavalry had ridden to the rescue! Everyone on deck began to applaud and shout encouragement.

According to the gentleman with the binoculars, *Islander*'s launch would be handing over responsibility for the search to the Coasties, who were 'much better equipped.' I watched with a heavy heart as the launch returned, empty-handed, to the mother ship.

Gradually, *Islander* reversed course and picked up speed. I kept my eyes on the strobes as they grew farther and farther away, watching with deepening sadness as they winked out one by one over the dark horizon.

The spectators began to disperse, heading for their cabins, or the casino, or perhaps to one of the bars where they could argue with alcohol-fueled confidence about the events they had just witnessed. By the following day, I knew, Facebook, YouTube and Twitter would take the news viral.

'When do you think we'll find out?' Pia wondered as we lingered at the rail.

'Tomorrow morning, I imagine, at the captain's daily briefing.'

'Think you can pump Ben Martin for information?'

'No,' I said with certainty. 'Officer By The Book will either be adhering to federal patient confidentiality laws or that good old standby, "pending notification of next of kin." Maybe both.'

'What the *hell* happened here tonight, Hannah?'

I didn't speak for a few minutes. 'Tom and David had a scuffle. Tragically, one of them fell overboard. Then the other one jumped in after him.'

Next to me, Pia stirred. 'Of course,' she said in a quiet voice. 'That's exactly what happened.'

A few minutes later, as we turned to go, Pia asked, 'Where's Julie? She said she wanted to see me after the show.'

My heart did a quick *rat-a-tat-tat*. 'Oh my God, I've forgotten about Julie! Come on!' As we raced back to the theater, I explained briefly about Julie's clever hiding place. 'She's been hiding in there for over an hour! What is *wrong* with me?'

But I needn't have worried. We found Julie sitting on the lip of the stage, feet dangling. On the stage next to her sat Connor Crawford.

'Julie!'

My niece beamed. 'I got tired of waiting, so I peeked out through the little . . .' Her eyebrows shot under her bangs, and she looked straight at Pia. 'What?'

Pia placed a finger to her lips, wagged her head from side to side and said, 'Shhhh. Magicians' code.'

After the drama of the evening, it felt good to laugh.

The atmosphere quickly grew serious again as I told Julie and Connor what had just happened. 'We lost them both overboard,' Pia said. 'But one has been rescued.'

'Oh my God!' Then, 'I'm praying that it's David,' Julie said quietly. 'He always believed in me.'

Connor launched himself onto his feet. 'I just came to say goodbye to Julie. I hope you don't mind.'

'Of course that's OK, Connor. Julie owes you a great deal of thanks. We all do.'

He turned to Julie. 'Well, bye.' He patted his pocket. 'I have your email.'

She looked upward at him through her lashes. ''Bye.'

Connor studied his shoes for a moment, then turned and walked out of the theater.

'Well, Julie,' I said. 'Do you suppose he's planning to wait four years until you turn eighteen?'

Julie flushed. 'Something like that.'

'He'll be twenty-five.'

'Aunt Hannah! You're embarrassing me.'

'I'm just teasing, sweetie. Come on, it's time to find your mother. After all this excitement, do you think she's still in the hot tub?'

'Will I see you in the morning, Hannah?' Pia asked as we prepared to go.

I looped my arm through hers. 'I hope so. But if not, let's keep in touch. Do you Facebook?'

'I do.'

'I'll friend you, then.'

'I'd like that.'

I was too strung out to sleep.

Long after Julie and my sisters had gone to bed, I sat on my bunk in my pajamas, staring into the depths of my suitcase, wondering what the following day would bring. *Had David survived? Maybe he'd be better off. . .* I shook away the thought. Nobody, in my opinion, was better off dead. There should always be a tomorrow, a chance to start a better life.

Ruth coughed, tugged at her duvet and opened an eye. 'Are you all right, Hannah?'

'I'm trying to gin up the energy to pack.'

'Well, the elves aren't going to do it for you, and if it's not out in the hall before two, you'll have to carry it off the boat yourself.' She rolled over, faced the wall. 'A word to the wise,' she murmured.

I dumped the contents of my half of the closet into the suitcase, tucked shoes around the edges, laid a couple of paperback books on top and zipped it shut. After making sure that the luggage labels were secure, I set the bag out in the passageway with hundreds of others, extending for what seemed like miles in both directions.

That done, I snagged a bottle of water and let myself out onto the balcony. I picked my favorite of the two chairs, slouched down in it comfortably, and propped both feet up on the balcony rail.

On moonless nights, the sea is as black and sleek as a raven's back. I stared into the inky darkness, then blinked. Where the blue-black sky met the black of the sea, lights were strung like an amber necklace along the horizon. The Chesapeake Bay Bridge Tunnel. We were approaching the mouth of the Bay.

I nipped inside for my iPhone, powered it on and when a three-bar signal appeared, I took it out on the balcony and telephoned Paul.

The meeting with the F.B.I. had gone well, he thought. Based on what the Baltimore agents had told him, Paul fully expected them to meet the ship in the morning.

'There's a possibility that Channing might not be aboard,' I told him.

Paul snorted. 'No? So what happened? He sprout wings?'

'He jumped overboard tonight, in a manner of speaking.' I explained about David forcing Channing on to the chair, Channing's tumble, and then David jumping over the side himself. 'Maybe it was some sort of crazy rescue attempt,' I added. 'Or maybe not. They picked up one of the men, but we don't know which. They're still out looking for the other – at least, they were a couple of hours ago.'

'I worry about you, Hannah. Is everybody all right?'

'A little beat up, perhaps, but we're all fine, honest. Even Julie's pretty solid.'

'We can't wait to see you, sweetheart. We'll be at the terminal to meet you tomorrow, all three of us.'

'Bring leis,' I said, 'and hula girls.'

Back in our cabin, I considered the selection of games on my iPhone without enthusiasm, still thinking about my conversation with Paul. Who *had* been rescued? I couldn't sleep until I knew.

Moving quietly so as not to disturb Ruth, I pulled a T-shirt on over my red-plaid pajama bottoms and slipped into a pair of flip-flops. I opened the cabin door a crack and eased out into the corridor.

A surprising number of people were abroad in the night. While most of the passengers slept, crew members busily collected luggage from in front of cabin doors, schlepping them in carts down to the bowels of the ship where they would await transfer to the terminal's baggage claim facility in the morning.

Walking slowly so as not to draw too much attention to myself,

I made my way forward along deck four to the stairway that would take me down a level to deck three. As I passed the elevator, a man was explaining to his po-faced wife how he'd lost nearly two hundred dollars on the slots. On the stairs, I passed a young couple, giggling as they ricocheting from one banister to the other, clutching one another for support as they staggered back to their cabin, presumably from one of the late-night bars.

As I emerged on deck three, I had to swerve to avoid running into a guy balancing a tray loaded with beverage cups, chip packets and a small stack of triangular boxes that I knew contained individual slices of pizza. 'Ball game,' he explained as he stepped aside to let me pass. 'Nationals at Philadelphia.'

I took in the stylized 'N' on his cap. 'Go Nats,' I said, without much enthusiasm.

There was no guard posted outside the door to the clinic, which I took as a good sign. Cautiously, I peered inside. The nurse who had cared for Julie earlier sat at a desk in the outer office, filling in the blanks on a form with a black pen.

'Jeannie?'

The nurse started, looking around in confusion before catching sight of me in the doorway.

'Sorry,' I said. 'Didn't mean to startle you.'

Worried lines creased her brow. 'Is Julie . . .?'

'Julie's fine. Now that her attacker has been identified, I think she'll be able to sleep a little easier.'

'I heard,' Jeannie said.

'Is he . . .?' I gestured toward the door that led into the examination room.

'I could get in trouble,' she said, reading my mind.

'Sorry,' I managed, choking up. 'It's just that David Warren and I have grown pretty close. If he's still out there somewhere . . .' I took a deep, steadying breath. 'I really need to know.'

Jeannie rose without speaking and crossed to the door, gesturing for me to follow her. She turned the knob and slowly pushed it open.

Inside the examination room, on a gurney and covered by a lightweight blanket, lay David Warren. He appeared to be sleeping. I grabbed the doorframe, weak-kneed with relief.

'Thank God!' I whispered.

In addition to the bandage on his forehead – courtesy of Jack Westfall – David now sported a neon-blue air splint on his right arm. But the biggest surprise was who sat on a chair next to the gurney: Elda Homer. Her hair a bit disheveled, but still dressed in her evening finery, she held David's good left hand.

My heart flopped in my chest, and I couldn't suppress a smile.

We backed away silently. 'She's been by his side for a couple of hours,' Jeannie whispered back as she closed the door on the quiet domestic scene. 'Like you, she just showed up. David asked her to stay.'

'Good,' I said, feeling slightly choked. Perhaps David had found something – or someone – to live for after all.

'Is he going to be OK?' I asked the nurse.

'I can't comment on a patient's medical condition, you know that,' she said kindly.

'But would you do me a favor? When he wakes up, tell him Hannah Ives was here.'

'I'll do that,' she said, touching my arm.

I couldn't speak for a moment. 'Well, that's it, then,' I eventually croaked, completely undone. I managed to hold it together until I got out into the corridor, where tears of relief began to spill from my eyes and course hotly down my cheeks.

I gave into the tears, until there were none left to cry.

TWENTY-FIVE

'If it's calculated in a notebook, it ends up being geometry.
If it's written or researched, it might be history. When people
are watching, it has the potential of being magic.'
Jim Steinmeyer, *Hiding the Elephant*,
Da Capo, 2004, p. 329

Long before dawn, while most of the passengers slept, the
Islander passed under the Francis Scott Key Bridge, veered
left at Fort McHenry, and ghosted into its berth at the Port
of Baltimore. As the great white ship waited for the first rays of
the sun to light its stacks, its generators thrummed, contented.
Islander was prepared for whatever the day would bring.

Beyond our window, the Baltimore sky burned gold with
reflections from the arc lamps that lined the city's streets, streets
that glistened in the gentle rain like black coal.

Eventually, dawn crept in out of the east, defining a building,
the cars in the parking lot, a highway sign. When it was bright
enough that I could read the sign – Fort McHenry Tunnel
Restrictions – dock workers materialized, rolling the gangplank
up to the ship, where they made it fast.

Everything was ready.

'I thought they said we would disembark at seven,' a bulky
woman complained to me in the Firebird café. She'd nearly run
me down as I made the mistake of walking between her and the
Belgian waffle machine. She would have been better off in the fresh
fruit and Special K line, I thought sourly as I found a tray, filled
four mugs with coffee from a pair of urns, then carried them back
to our cabins to await the announcements I knew would be coming.

At eight o'clock, the intercom clicked, hummed. The voice of
the captain filled our small cabin as he apologized for the delay
and asked for our patience. 'As you have probably heard, last
night we had a tragic overboard situation. I have nothing but
high praise for the passengers on deck who reacted quickly,

tossing life rings to the victims and calling in the alarm. Also, kudos need to be accorded to the crew of *Islander's* launch, whose prompt response resulted in the rescue of one victim who is now being treated in the medical unit for his injuries, and who is expected to make a full recovery.'

'How about the other guy?' I shouted at the intercom.

Ruth scowled a warning. 'Shut up and listen, Hannah.'

'I've been in communication with the United States Coast Guard this morning,' the captain continued, 'and I regret to report that despite heroic efforts on the part of their officers and crew, the second victim, a Phoenix Cruise Lines staff member from San Diego, California, has yet to be found. But, the search continues.'

'Good riddance to bad rubbish,' Ruth muttered.

'Still, I hoped . . .' I started to say, then the tears began again.

Ruth handed me a box of tissues, and took one herself. 'At least they found David,' she sniffed.

'Yes. At least, there's that.'

I watched the wharf from the balcony, drinking coffee by the gallon. Because the gangway was covered, and connected directly to the terminal, I never saw the F.B.I. agents arrive.

That they had was confirmed by a knock on our door. Officer Molly Fortune was there to escort us to a waiting area outside a glassed-in conference center on deck six, not far from the elegant Garuda Grill.

One by one we were called in before a panel of serious-faced F.B.I. agents. Our statements were recorded, and affidavits signed. When I came out of the room, Pia was waiting for her turn. We didn't speak, but she gave me a subtle thumbs up as she passed me to go in.

They kept Julie Lynn the longest, but when she finally came out, Molly Fortune said we were free to go.

Is that all there is? I wondered.

Eight hours later, after a corned beef and cabbage dinner around the corner at our favorite neighborhood restaurant, Galway Bay, where all talk of cruises was put off limits, Paul and I settled in on the living room sofa to watch the news. CNN hadn't picked up the story, but it was the lead on WBAL-TV.

How the press had received the tip-off, I'll never know, but the reporter read the story over a video of David Warren being medevaced from the ship to Johns Hopkins, strapped to a stretcher. 'The victim received multiple fractures, but is expected to survive.

'The body of the second victim,' the reporter continued, 'was found early this morning near the town of Cape Henry on Maryland's eastern shore. Thomas Channing, a well-known magician from San Diego, sources tell us, was sucked into the ship's propellers and died instantly.'

I thought about how pleased Channing had been with his new illusion, the Turbine of Terror, and shuddered.

Nestled in the comfort of my husband's arms, I told Paul the whole sorry tale, from the frantic time when Julie went missing right up to when Tom and David had both plunged into the sea.

'What I don't understand,' Paul said once I'd finished, 'is how Channing managed to access Buck Carney's room. Carney sounds like a weirdo too, by all accounts – are you sure he wasn't involved in some way?'

'No, it was purely a case of mistaken identity by Julie. David didn't manage to force it out of Channing before he fell overboard, but Channing was very clever. Buck was a cruise regular who was constantly out and about around the ship, glued to his camera, preoccupied with shipboard events. He's also the perfect suspect – a creepy photographer with stalking tendencies would go straight to the top of anybody's suspect list. I might have worked it out earlier if I'd asked the steward the right question.'

'What question was that?'

'Who was in cabin 8620.'

Paul was silent for a moment, working it out. 'Ah!'

'Exactly,' I said. 'The lock on Carney's door would have been child's play to a lockmaster like Channing and, once inside, he could easily drag his victims through the communicating door that led into his own cabin.'

Paul kissed the top of my head. 'Clever girl.'

'Thank you,' I said.

Paul gave me a hug. 'So, other than that, Mrs Lincoln, how did you enjoy the cruise?'

'Ha! Don't know about my sisters, but I, for one, am all cruised out.'

'Do you have anything good at all to report?'

I thought for a minute. 'Yup. I made some new friends. The hot tubs were divine. And, I'm now an expert on signal codes. "Adam, Adam, Adam . . ." I hope I *never* have to hear that one again. Sierra means they're sending a stretcher, and Oscar means man overboard.' I snuggled closer. 'One of the bartenders who used to work for Disney told me that Code Winnie means there are feces in the swimming pool.'

Paul was so quiet, that I thought he didn't get it.

I jabbed him in the ribs with my elbow. 'Winnie the Pooh, silly.'

He guffawed. 'Don't suppose there's a Whiskey, Whiskey, Whiskey . . . meaning the bar is now open.'

I rocked my head back and forth against his chest. 'Hung out in a lot of bars this cruise, but never heard that one, I'm afraid. Alpha means fire, and Delta stands for a disaster of some kind.' I swiveled my head around so I could look into his face. 'Tango, Tango, Foxtrot!'

'Huh?'

I giggled liked a teenager. 'Let's dance.'

Paul cradled my head in his hands. 'Code Hannah, Hannah, Hannah.'

'And what does that mean?'

He bent his head and brought his lips to mine. When I came up for air, Paul said, 'It means, "let's go to bed."'

After sharing a room with my sister for more than a week, it would have been crazy to refuse.